I stared at the screen for
reading the words over a

Actual fan mail. People had sent me fan mail. I couldn't believe how quickly it had happened. I had just written the Barbie entry. How had so many people read it already? . . .

It felt like Christmas morning. I wanted a column, a book, a book tour. A body of work that took up a shelf. A house. A dog. I wanted to see my paperbacks with the covers ripped off piled in a used-books store, all beat up and worn with the memory of a thousand different fingers.

I wrote another entry immediately where I introduced myself. . . .

~~~

"With wit and spark, Ribon hopscotches through the high-bandwidth dramas of the modern girl's life."
—Pagan Kennedy

"A sexy, muscular ride through the irresistible thrills of online flirting and the all-too-familiar heartaches of real life romance. [The] writing is as moving as it is funny, with a shock and a delight on every page."
—Claire LaZebnik, author of *Same As It Never Was*

"Reading the irresistible WHY GIRLS ARE WEIRD is like hanging out with your best friend just when you need to most."
—Melissa Senate, author of *See Jane Date*

Why Girls are Weird

Pamela Ribon

doWn
tOwn
press

NEW YORK LONDON TORONTO SYDNEY

An *Original* Publication of POCKET BOOKS

 A Downtown Press Book published by
POCKET BOOKS, a division of Simon & Schuster, Inc.
1230 Avenue of the Americas, New York, NY 10020

ISBN: 0-7434-6980-1

First Downtown Press trade paperback edition July 2003

10 9 8 7 6 5

DOWNTOWN PRESS and colophon are trademarks of
Simon & Schuster, Inc.

Manufactured in the United States of America

For information regarding special discounts for bulk purchases,
please contact Simon & Schuster Special Sales at 1-800-456-6798
or business@simonandschuster.com

My heart beats:
"Mommy. Bosie. Stephen."

"I'm a modern girl, but I fold in half so easily
When I put myself in the picture of success."

—RILO KILEY

000001.

The House of Smut Revealed

24 JUNE

It's been a long time since I've played with dolls. I've never really thought back on my time with plastic humans before, but today, as I was watching a group of giggly young girls browsing Barbies in the Wal-Mart, I remembered that feeling—that strange sexual energy and giddy shame of playing Barbies in my bedroom. It was a spinning, dizzy sensation. My friends and I spoke in hushed tones as we held these dolls in various stages of dress. If our parents had ever found out what we were doing, those dolls certainly would have been taken away from us. It wasn't our fault Barbie and her pals released our initial sexuality. We were young and full of questions and those dolls are shaped like hand-held sexpots.

Barbie has big, incredible breasts with this soft spot between them that your thumb fits into just perfectly. She's not wearing anything underneath her clothing. You can put her in panties and a bra for a quick jog or you can have her make eggs in the Barbie Dream Kitchen wearing only a pair of spiked heels. You can pull her hair up or have it going down all the way to her high and tight ass.

Ken is big and bold and square. He's got a strong chin and jaw. His hair is blond, and sort of wavy. You can run your fingernail along the hard ridges on his head. Or can you? I can't remember if Ken had real hair. I think some of my Kens did. He is very muscular, and the bulge under his pants is impressive enough that you wonder if all boys polish their bulge as often as you'd polish Ken's with Windex. Ken has a nice, defined butt that looks good in a pair of swim trunks.

Barbie and Ken were very different from Donny and Marie. Yes, Donny and Marie *Osmond*. The fact that I loved Donny and Marie at three or four or however old I was might clue you in on the kind of childhood I had. I spent too much time in front of the television and I loved variety shows. What four-year-old loves variety shows? And were there so many four-year-olds in love with Donny and Marie that they had to make dolls of them? And why did I still have these dolls once I turned ten? Why didn't I get new dolls? I can't really start thinking too much about the hows or whys because it's all so fucked up that I end up wanting to go back in time to scoop up tiny little me and hold her and tell her about the Partridge Family. Anyway, I had these Mormon musical star dolls, but I had no idea what a Mormon was, so they ended up being gigantic sinners in my house.

Marie had short brown hair that was like Sally Field's helmet in *Steel Magnolias*. She was completely flat-chested. As bad as Skipper, if I remember correctly. Clothes just sat on her, and there was never a need for a belt. Her hand had a hole in it. You could stick her microphone there, but I knew just enough about Mormons to fit a diamond ring in the spot. I had Donny and Marie married, because I was young and thought anyone could get married as long as they loved each other.

Donny was wearing plastic tighty-whiteys. Seriously. There was an extra ridge of plastic that went around Donny's waist and legs. There was no bulge. His hair was dark and slicked down. A plastic shield—there was no fucking around with Donny Osmond's hair. His smile was so bright and big. I think they painted stars in his eyes. He also had a hole in his hand, but if you did it just right, you could stick one of Barbie's spiked heels in the hole and have him sniff Barbie's shoe. Donny and Marie didn't have enough money for rent, so they lived off their love in a Buster Brown shoebox. Only a ten-year-old can create an incestuous Mormon celebrity relationship and have it be romantic.

Barbie's legs were very difficult to open. You had to jam Ken between them. Donny's arms were already bent at just enough of an angle that you could prop Barbie's legs on each one and they were good to go. Marie's head could turn all the way around. The hole in her hand could also hold a small martini glass. Most of my dolls had marks on their backs from being bound, gagged, and jammed into the bed of my Tonka 4x4.

The Barbie without a left pinkie was the fetishist and she'd often blindfold Strawberry Shortcake and sniff her all over. Custard wore a spiked collar made of toothpicks.

One day the Barbie without a head convinced Donny and Marie to put pink and blue Life pegs through the holes in their hands. The Barbies pretended the pegs were hits of acid and got the Osmonds to think they could fly.

The Barbie Town House had a pulley system for the house elevator. Ken and Skipper enjoyed a quick romp on top of the elevator while it was going up, jumping off on the third floor just before they'd be crushed to death.

I had to give some of my dolls distinguishing marks so I could keep track of all of their fetishes. I didn't want the nudist Barbies to end up bathing with the dolls that liked to sleep with Weebles. Barbie GreenHair liked to take baths in cotton balls. She also enjoyed wrapping herself from head to toe in toilet paper. Skipper MarkerFace enjoyed cutting the hair off other Barbie dolls and taping it to her back. One doll had hair that would grow if you pushed a button on her back or shorten if you twisted her arm. The other Barbies would torture her by pulling on her hair while twisting her arm at the same time. Then they'd eat her hair. Barbie BackwardsLegs enjoyed riding cats. She'd strap herself on and hang on for dear life while they'd buck and toss and eventually eat her head. She was a wild one, Barbie BackwardsLegs. I miss the hell out of her.

Boys loved girls, girls loved girls, boys loved boys, and boys loved girls that loved girls. Anything went in the Barbie Town House.

And, oh, man, they still talk about the day Jem and the Holograms showed up with six bottles of tequila and a roll of paper towels.

Love until later,

Anna K

000002.

So that's how all of this mess got started. I wrote a story about sex kitten Barbies, put it online, and my life changed forever. From the best I can tell, this entry got passed around from co-worker to co-worker, friend to friend. Those strangers and friends of strangers kept coming back to see what I'd write next. What I thought would be a tiny little webpage that just a few people knew about turned into one that thousands of people read every day. I thought the web was supposed to be dead. Wasn't that what everyone had been saying? "The death of the Internet!" That was why I couldn't get a better job than my library admin thing. It was why I was so bored and started all of this. I was trying to find a time killer at work and decided to teach myself a little HTML. I soon realized that the more I was typing, the more it looked like I was working. Anyone passing by my workstation would think I was hard at work improving myself, but in reality I was writing story after story, creating an entire life on the Internet. Slutty Barbies (and the fact that e-mail will never be dead) took me from Anna Koval, a nothing-special-twenty-something, to Anna K: web celebrity.

I don't know what I thought would happen. In hindsight, I don't know how I thought nothing would come of it.

But I'm ending the story of Anna K—right here, right now. I'm closing down this website. I want to explain everything before I take it all away. Some people have been with me from the beginning, and I'd feel bad leaving after a year without so much as a good-bye.

It's been a year of strange choices and often embarrassing decisions on my part. I've made new relationships and lost others. Some people involved with all of this were more innocent than others. Those who weren't know who they are. There are others that will be shocked by what I have to say here. There are some who probably knew what I was doing all along. My only defense is that I never meant to hurt anybody. Looking back now, I know I was searching for something. I exposed myself until there was almost nothing left of me to hide. And now I'm removing the final bits of fabric, standing in front of you completely naked. It'll be our last time together like this, and I don't want to keep anything from you anymore.

It all started the night I watched my best friend, Dale, bathing. He had hurt his hand moving his new couch into his apartment and for the first time in a while he was asking me for help.

"You're very cute," I said as I stood over his bathtub.

He lowered himself and floated a washcloth over his crotch: "Just hurry up and then get the hell out of here." He tried to hide his rubber duck behind him, but I had already seen it.

Dale and I met at our first crappy jobs here in Austin right out of college. We waited tables at this restaurant over a Whole Foods store. Three good things about that job: an in-house masseuse, drinking smoothies between rushes, and meeting each other. Every other facet of that place sucked ass.

Dale's my friend who knows the joke I'm about to say because he was about to say it at that exact moment. Like this one time we were both in my car stopped at a red light and a girl wearing a miniskirt and enormous shoes ate shit right in front of us. We both busted up at the sight of those white platforms smacking up and hitting her in the ass as she made this face like she was on *The Benny Hill Show*. She fell to the ground and flipped back upright in almost one swift motion, her hands pulling the bottom of her skirt down as her purse knocked at her knees. But it was the moment when she walked back to stare down the crack in the street that caused her fall—when she had to go back just to show all of us that it was the pavement's fault and not those gigantic shoes—that we completely lost it. It's that laugh that's deep in your stomach where you're sure you'll never breathe again, and nobody else in the entire world but the two of you know why what just happened is the funniest thing that will ever happen in the history of funny moments ever. That's Dale and me.

"I still don't know why Jason can't do this for you." I wet my hands in the water, careful not to brush against his skin. "This is why we have boyfriends to begin with, Dale."

"He can't come over until at least tomorrow and I'm tired of feeling so dirty. I can't clean my hair with just one hand and I hate feeling like I'm wearing a wig."

I grabbed the shampoo bottle and squeezed the liquid into my palm. "A wig?"

"I have very thick hair. Now close your eyes and wash."

"You're not the boss of me," I mumbled. I didn't close my eyes. I watched Dale lean his head back into my hands. As I lathered up his head, I couldn't stop staring at his body in the water. It wasn't sexual. In fact, I was fascinated by how nonsexual it was.

"And why am I the one that gets to come over here and bathe you?" I asked.

Dale opened his eyes and moved his head from my hands. A stream of lather ran down his forehead, threatening to run into his left eye. "You aren't *bathing* me. You're just washing my hair.

And you're the only one Jason trusts not to try anything funny."
He ran his hand over his forehead and leaned back again, waiting.

I wiped my chin, tasting shampoo on my lower lip. I sat back to
dry my mouth. "'Try anything funny?' When did you join the car-
toon mafia? What if I pounced on you right now? I could do that."

"You wouldn't," Dale said, inching back toward my hands as I
leaned over the tub again. "We both know it'd be gross, and even
Jason knows you haven't touched a man since Ian moved out."

There wasn't much left to say after that. I knew Dale regretted
the words. I could feel him trying to think of a way to lighten the
air between us and get us joking again. When something that honest is said it usually needs a few minutes of silence to dissipate.

I was rinsing his hair when he finally whispered, "I'm sorry."

"It's okay, Dale. I know."

Ian and I had broken up six months ago. I tried to act like it
wasn't a sore subject with me, but all of my friends knew that it was.

Dale changed the subject by talking about his screenplay.
He'd been working on a film based on his ninth-grade science
project. To this day he felt the contest was rigged and he should
have taken first place. His movie will expose the inadequacies of
state science fair judges and finally vindicate his second-place
ribbon. It's going to be brilliant.

Dale was washing his underarms as he explained the love
story between the girl who did her project on earthworm regen-
eration and the boy who determined the best metal for conduct-
ing sound.

"She's going to cheat on her project and he won't know if he
can still love her."

Watching Dale in the water, I saw just how much a bathtub
could emasculate a man. His body looked smaller than usual, even
though it filled the tub. The water made everything look suspended. The washcloth had floated to the foot of the tub, bunched
and soggy like a discarded bandage. Dale's body seemed younger
and weak. I saw how his dick seemed completely powerless. It

bobbed inside the water quietly. Wet like that, it didn't look like a "dick." It was a "penis" in that safe, Health class way. It was almost feminine in there, in the shadows of the bathtub. The water lapped around Dale's shoulders as he soaked, now silent in his thoughts of the lunchroom battle particulars, his wet head making him appear even more innocuous. He was a wet child in a basin. It was hard to see someone I thought of as a "capital M" Man reduced to a bobbing waterbaby. I was just about to look away when Dale popped his eyes open.

"All right, Pervy. I need some 'me' time, okay?"

I went to the living room and watched a rerun of *Friends*.

Except for the bath, this was the usual Thursday night at Dale's: "Must See" TV followed by beers on his balcony. But that week the shows were reruns and his hand was hurting, so we decided it'd be bathing and beers. I watched him enter the room still in his bathrobe. He brought out a bowl of popcorn and almost stepped on his cat. Almost, as he and his cat have an elaborate song and dance. Dale and Trevor move completely in step, and although it looked like one of them should trip over the other, they never did. They danced perfect figure eights around the living room, both of them talking but never to each other. I hate that Dale named his cat after a member of O-Town. Dale hates that I won't bleach my hair again.

"You know if you tell anyone about this bath, I'll kill you." His hair was almost completely dry already. It was so much shorter than he kept it when we first met two years ago. Now he hated it when it grew past his eyebrows. When it was longer, I loved how it would flop in his face when he laughed because he'd look just like Paul McCartney. It only happened when he laughed and it only happened when he had his brown hair in that bowl cut, but it was one of my favorite things in the world.

"Hey, for my birthday will you write me a story?" he asked.

I threw myself down on the couch, a cloud of new-couch smell greeting my face. The fabric felt stiff under my arms, and the cushions weren't welcoming yet. "I'm too depressed to write," I said. This was the elaborate song and dance that Dale and I do. I pout while Dale primps me.

"Where is this big book about falling in love with India?" he asked.

"You never listen when I speak. It's about an Indian woman falling in love with a newscaster."

"It sounds wonderfully retarded."

"That's why I'm naming it after you."

"I like it when we're seven," Dale beamed.

"Me too. Being a grown-up is way dull."

"It's dorky."

"Crappy."

Dale hid his face in his hands and whispered, "Shitty!"

"I'm so telling!"

Dale giggled and then pretended to be quite serious. "Write me a story," he demanded with a stamp of his foot. "And I need some body gel. And an R.E.M. CD. Wait. Let me get some paper. I'll make you a list."

I went home and wrote the Barbie entry.

000003.

Subject: Yay!!!!

Dear Anna K,

I feel silly writing to you, but I wanted you to know that I just found your webpage. I really like it and I hope you keep writing because it's really good. I used to do that stuff with my Barbies, too!

Well, I'm going to go before I feel stupid for writing this fan
letter, but I wanted to tell you that I think you're very cool.
How old are you?

Thanks,
Tess

Subject: questions about you.

Anna K,

Your Barbie entry is hysterical! One of my girlfriends sent it to
me. I love it! We printed it out here at my work and we
pasted it by the copier. You should see the looks of the men
in the office when they read it. We got our intern Ted to
blush!

We keep coming back to read more, but you haven't posted
anything else. Would you mind telling us more about you? Do
you have other places where you've written? More, please!

-Kristen

I stared at the screen for ten minutes, reading the words over and
over again. Actual fan mail. People had sent fan mail. I couldn't
believe how quickly it had happened. I had just written the
Barbie entry. How had so many people read it already? Not only
that, but they loved it. They loved the words I had written. I had
fans. Fans—plural!

When I was eleven I wrote my one and only piece of fan
mail, to one of the actors on *Head of the Class*. I had just moved
to a new school and was lonely. I wanted a classroom like the one

on *Head of the Class,* where the only thing that mattered was fifth-period History and the people in it. I wanted a gifted class where the ten or twelve of us were a family, with a wisecracking teacher as our father. So I wrote to the girl who played Simone, the redheaded poet. My thinking was that of all the actors on the show, she was the one most likely to write me back because she seemed so nice and sensitive.

I told her all about me, and asked if she'd write back to say she got my letter. She didn't. I promised myself back then that if I ever got fan mail I'd write back to everyone. And now here I was. Take that, Simone.

Subject: re: Yay!!!

Dear Tess,

Thanks so much for writing. It's good to know who's reading. Hope you stick around. I'm twenty-four years old, but sometimes I'm really just sixteen.

Anna K

Subject: re: questions about you.

Kristen,

Don't get poor Ted fired. I'd never be able to live with myself. I'm not published anywhere else yet, but I'll let you know as soon as it happens. Thanks for writing!

-AK

It felt like Christmas morning, just after all of the presents had been opened. I wanted more. I wanted a column, a book, a book tour. A body of work that took up a shelf. A house. A dog. A dog to write about in my books. I wanted to see my paperbacks with the covers ripped off piled in a used-books store, all beat up and worn with the memory of a thousand different fingers.

I wrote another entry immediately where I introduced myself. I said I was twenty-four and still trying to figure out what I wanted to be when I grew up. I said I liked roller-blading, but the truth was I'd never even tried it. I guess I wanted to appear sporty, but not athletic.

I thought about the stories I'd tell Dale that would put him in hysterics. This was his birthday present after all, so I wanted to fill the website with stories he loved. Then I remembered the story that never failed to crack Dale up. It was back when I was dating Ian, but I figured a little time fudging wouldn't hurt anyone. There was no reason Anna K couldn't have a boyfriend just because I didn't. Besides, they already thought Anna K had it all. Why not give her my ex-boyfriend, too?

The Book

29 JUNE

At a sex shop in San Francisco my boyfriend and I purchased a book called *101 Nights of Grrreat Sex*. Note the repeated *r*'s, as I assume they are supposed to contribute to the fun. Or is it "funnn"?

The first page warns that if you are satisfied in your love life, then the book wasn't for you. I wish I had known that earlier, but since I purchased it sealed there was no going back.

The book comes with a series of sealed envelopes, half "For Her Eyes Only" and half "For His Eyes Only." You are supposed to sit together and pick an envelope each week to read in private. That way you know at some point during the week you'll be surprised with a romantic act.

My first envelope was called "Fantasies of the Orient" and involved honey and hot tea. Following the directions, I made a pot of Chinese tea, draped a black blanket over our futon, and made my boyfriend take off all his clothes. Acting like I wasn't allowed to speak, I pushed him back onto the blanket, poured honey on his leg, and then licked it off. Then I had to put the tea in my mouth and let it hit his skin through my lips as I kissed him. First I scalded his neck and then I burned the inside of his elbow. Soon my tongue was aching from the near boiling liquid, but since I wasn't allowed to speak I just quietly cried on his stomach as I got sick from too much honey. I couldn't eat anything for the next two days.

We decided that it was just a bad envelope and tried again. My next envelope ("Treasure Trail") instructed me to cut out paper outlines of my feet to make a trail from the door to my "hiding place," where I was supposed to "pounce" on my "mate."

By the way, the only time that you ever hear your boyfriend or girlfriend described as a "mate" is when you're reading a sex-help book. *Mate* is the unsexiest word. Besides *tuna*. And *uvula*. Those are the three unsexiest words. But the last two are hardly found in the pages of *Cosmo*, now are they?

While making the cutouts the little voice in my head muttered, *What the hell are we doing here? How old are you?* I used my glitter crayons to make the feet say funny things. It takes a long time to trace, cut, and color feet to tape from your front door to your hiding spot. Plus the card said I should make them go in and out of several rooms in the house. We have a one-bedroom apartment, so I had the feet go into the bathroom, up the wall, and around the corner on the ceiling. Just a little Lionel Richie in there to get him motivated.

I'm sitting in the closet waiting for my boyfriend to get home from work and I'm thinking, *Gosh, I hope he doesn't go out for a drink after work. I hope he just comes home on time. I wonder what I look like in here. Ow. I'm sitting on a high heel. I'm thirsty. Maybe I'll go get something to drink. No, I can't go out there, what if he comes home and I'm standing in a trail of my own toes? This isn't sexy. This isn't even cute.*

It was solitary confinement.

He did come home—late, of course—and apparently didn't even notice the new foot trail installed on our carpeting. I heard him call out: "Hello? Baby? Where are you?" I didn't know if I was supposed to answer. I heard the refrigerator door open and close. The television snapped on and the sounds of a basketball game filled the apartment. Unbelievable. He wasn't going to notice. What if in three hours he finally decided to do something about it? What would I do if he called the police and they came over, followed the paper trail, and found me asleep in the closet cradling a tin of Altoids, wearing only my panties?

I panicked, making noises that were a combination of whimpers and shrieks until I heard him get off the couch. When he finally found me five minutes later, he looked at me with a face that read: "Hello. Did you get lost? Do I need to call a hospital? Do you still understand English?" Then he laughed, and I knew this book was making a moron out of me.

His assignment that week focused on kissing. That was fun.

I pulled my third assignment. I was to make a sex game creating two sets of cards—one with body parts listed on them and the other with verbs. I tried all week, but I just kept wondering what would happen if he pulled the two cards that said "Thrust!" and "Ear!"

I refused to do my next assignment as well, where I had to "innocently" take him to a miniature golf course (because we putt-putt all the time?). I was supposed to go to the bathroom, take off my panties, wrap them around the golf ball, and hand them to him. Can you imagine? I'm sure he'd say, "What the hell—*Hey!*" And everyone would look up to see my panties on hole nine. Besides, there are children on Putt-Putt courses, mostly due to the fact that Putt-Putt is supposed to be a game for seven-year olds.

The only thing I liked about the book was that while planning those ridiculous things, I thought about my boyfriend. I liked thinking that sometime that week there was going to be a surprise for me. But in general the two of us were much more creative than that book—which still sits in the bedroom, by the way, mocking me. Feeling like a dork is a really bad way to spice up your sex life. And come on, do you really want me showing my naked butt to innocent putt-putting children?

Love until later,

Anna K

Subject: me again!

Anna K,

It's me again. I just wanted to thank you for posting all of the new entries. Now I can forward your webpage to all of my friends. You're my new favorite place. I laugh so hard when you talk about your boyfriend because it's the same stuff I went through during my last relationship. That story you told about fighting over the car stereo? That's just like my old boyfriend. I eventually dumped his Classic-Rock-lovin' ass.

Thanks,
Tess

Subject: the book

Hi, Anna,

My husband and I got that book as a honeymoon present.
Can you believe that? You'd think they'd give us just a bit
more credit in the beginning. Apparently they know the sex is
going to go downhill, huh? It hasn't yet, thankfully. I don't
know why I just told you that. In any event, I wanted to
commiserate on that book. I opened one envelope that told
me to strip for my husband. There's nothing worse than
trying to give your husband a lapdance and getting your high
heel caught in your underwear. I fell, Anna. I fell.

I'm not one to support book burning, but maybe we could
make an exception in this case?

A fan in Syracuse,
Gwen

I felt dizzy with excitement. This was becoming more than just
Dale's birthday present. I suddenly had a body of work that
people were gobbling up as fast as I could write it. It was so easy
to write something and then post it online. The instant feedback
was infectious. People loved Anna K. I was creating a celebrity.

000004.

How to Fake a Football Orgasm

30 JUNE

This is my favorite time of the year because there's absolutely no football. If you ever saw just how much football I have to watch, you might

start crying. I've been dating Ian for over three years now and we've lived together for more than a year. He has no idea that I actually can't stand football. He doesn't know I find it repetitive and boring. How have I done this? How have I tricked this man into thinking I'm the coolest girlfriend ever? Because I am an expert at faking a football orgasm.

That's right. I can wiggle, shout, and cheer with the best of them. I spill beer and throw chips and just about paint my face blue and silver every weekend. It's not just a game for me anymore; it's become an art form. I'm willing to share my secrets because I think we're all friends here now, aren't we? Plus I'd like to contribute to happy, healthy relationships.

If you break any of the following rules, it will be obvious that you are faking it, so be careful. Here we go.

1. Don't walk in front of the television while the ball is in play, while they are doing an instant replay, or while the ball is at something called "the line of scrimmage."

2. Walk (and by "walk," I mean "run") past the television only during the commercials.

2a. If you are watching the Super Bowl stay clear of the television at all times.

3. Offer beers to everyone when you stand up. You'll be the coolest girl there, and it's still a feminist move if you're already on your way to get your own beer.

4. Be familiar with shouting the words "asshole" and "pussy."

5. When the ref throws a flag (it's yellow), start shouting possible reasons why. Try "Foul!" "Pass interference!" or "Face mask!" Don't worry, the boys will yell, too. Continue shouting through the ref explaining why the flag was thrown, at which point you will all stop and ask, "What was the call?" Then you will all argue about what the call must have been.

6. Anytime there is a call against your team, it is time for you to yell, "Oh, that's BULLSHIT!" Just like that. Try it. It's fun. I like to say it at the bank when they say, "It looks like you have five dollars in your account."

7. It is called a "touchdown." That's worth six points.

8. Then they try to kick an extra point. That's worth one. Generally they will get the extra point. If it is a close game, they may try for two points. We don't have enough time, so I'm not going into this here. Just trust me on this: If it is a close game and one team gets a touchdown, say, "Do you think they'll go for two?" This will cause a boy debate about field goals and ranges and red zones and things you don't need to worry yourself about. Just sit back and think, *Oh, yeah.* You look so cool. See, girlie? We're gonna make it through this.

9. If the guys are suddenly really upset, ask them what happened. They will be more than happy to shout the injustice of the last play. Let them vent.

10. Do NOT attempt to kiss your boyfriend at any time during the game. Do NOT go "TOUCHDOWN! KISSES!" You will not get them, and people will hate you.

11. NEVER TOUCH THE REMOTE CONTROL.

12. You don't need to know every athlete, but it helps if you know a few names. Here is the athlete that makes you sound like you know your shit. Ready? Vinnie Testaverde (VIN-ee test-a-VER-dee). Is that a great name or what? He plays for the Jets. I think. Or he used to. It doesn't matter. Just say things like, "Well, he's no Vinnie Testaverde." What I like saying is "Well, I was really comparing him to someone like Vinnie Testaverde." Chances are they'll all tip their heads back and say, "Oh. Well, yeah. If you're doing that." It works like a fucking charm, I'm telling you.

13. Know that being a girl means that if there is an argument about sports, even if you know you are right, they will say that you, the girl, are wrong. They will find a loophole in your logic and there's nothing you can do about it because you were born with ovaries.

14. You are supposed to be happy about overtime. It means more football.

15. Make sure you know which two teams are playing because they're going to switch channels during commercials. They'll watch other games at the same time, so be on your toes. If you're only rooting for "the guys in blue," you could end up cheering for the enemy of a different game. At any moment, there might be three different games on the television within an hour. I know. I'm sorry.

16. If, like me, you're ever in a situation where you are in a public place and your boyfriend is standing in the middle of the bar shouting, "That's what I'm talking about! You cannot fuck with the Cowboys!" it is completely okay to pretend you do not know him at all. Get someone to buy you a drink.

17. I don't care how persuasive they are, it is not tradition to take off your shirt when there's a turnover. You don't have to do it.

18. The Super Bowls are counted off in Roman numerals. Don't say the X's and I's. Hey, I don't know what level of expertise you're on. I'm just checking.

19. If you are watching the Super Bowl, you will probably have to sit through the pregame and the postgame festivities. It's okay to laugh at the pregame stuff (which involves a terrible film of some guy making the Super Bowl ring), but it is not okay to laugh at the postgame footage. The levels of beer consumption are so drastically different before and after the game that it's best not to have any reaction that might affect an emotionally vulnerable, boozy sports fan.

20. The season does end eventually. Then you get to watch hockey, basketball, and baseball! (These are things you're supposed to be excited about.)

Now go out there and fake it like a pro. That swirly feeling you might get at first is only the guilt from completely lying to the people that you love. You just have to break through that. It gets much easier with time. Go team!

Love until later,

Anna K

Subject: ORGASMS

> ANNA K, I WILL GIVE YOU A REAL ORGASM IF YOU WRITE TO
> ME AND SEND PANTIES PLEASE YOU WON'T NEED A BOOK
> WITH ME.
> ED

Was it wrong that I even loved my creepy fan mail?

000005.

Dale's birthday party was in three days and my stories were coming along nicely. I knew he was going to love his present. I printed out some of my fan mail to brag about my "audience."

My sister Shannon called to find out what I was getting Dale. She and Dale have always gotten along since last Easter, when he flew home with me. I couldn't find either of them for two hours. Turned out they were hiding in the garage, smoking dope, and going through my fifth-grade diary.

"Is he still into those stained-glass things?" she asked.

"That was last year," I said as I walked out to my balcony, crooking the phone under my head. I gave a quick look back to see if my cat was planning his great escape, but Taylor was sacked out on the kitchen table.

"I can't keep up with his fads," Shannon said. I heard her light a cigarette.

"You know what to get him," I said.

"I am not buying anyone a theatre mask."

Dale collects theatrical happy/sad masks. Some are paintings, others are statues. His Christmas tree is a terrifying ornamental ordeal. We've all spent several nights outside of Dale's company complaining about how creepy the collection is.

"It's cheesy and wrong and it makes me not want to be his friend," she said.

I laughed. "I'll tell him you said that," I said.

"Shut up. I think for his birthday I'm going to rid his bedroom of all the scary masks and it'll be the best gift ever."

"I just don't go into his bedroom. It works out better for all of us that way."

"It only works out better for Jason." We often joked that Dale's boyfriend, Jason, actually hated all of us, which was why we rarely saw him. Apparently Jason didn't want Dale to feel like his relationship had to be his entire life, but I think the truth was that Jason couldn't stand us.

"Hey," Shannon said, and I could picture her grin. I could see her leaning forward, her brown hair brushing over her forearms as she giggled into the phone. "Don't you think that those masks over their bed leave this deep mark on Jason's psyche that never goes away? They're trying to have sex and it's like, 'Mask in your face! Mask far away. Laughing at you! Crying far away. Laughing!

Crying. Closer! Closer! Closer!' You think Jason ever sleeps? I mean, no wonder he's such a grouch."

"Shannon, you're scaring me. Are you coming to my apartment or are we meeting up at Dale's?"

"Go to Dale's. I don't know exactly what time I'll get in. I've got a test in my three o'clock I can't skip. Traffic's gonna be a bitch."

"Are you staying the night?" I asked. I wondered if I had any clean sheets in the apartment for the futon. I thought about the monster laundry beast that was squeezed up against the closet door, threatening to take over my bedroom. I debated doing laundry for the fifth time that week.

"Nah, probably not. Just in and out. I don't know. If we drink I might crash at your place. Or Dale's. Jason makes yummy omelets."

"So now you're a big Jason fan," I said.

"Love his omelets; don't necessarily love him. Are you going to Hartford for Mom's birthday?"

"Maybe I'm not invited. She hasn't said anything about it to me."

"She will. I gotta go, Stinky."

We hung up and I went back in to feed Taylor.

I found my cat slumped around the pillow on my futon, sleeping with one eye open. He always crawled into the place I just left, hoping to find the warm spot made by my ass.

He jumped down onto the hardwood floor and stretched out his hind legs. His gray and white fur spiked up around his neck as he hunched himself forward. His tail lowered as he pulled himself back. He stopped to sniff at the coffee table but saw that I had already cleaned my sandwich plate.

He jumped to the counter. He brushed up against the coffee maker as I offered him a choice: "Chicken or fish?"

He mewed, brushing his left side along a bottle of wine. I caught the bottle before it tipped into the sink. I opened the can and plopped the solid hockey puck of food into a small bowl. The kitchen filled with the sharp scent of cheap tuna fish as I sang "The Taylor Song." It goes: "Taylor! Taylor! The cat with the fur on his face! Taylor!" I was confident the song didn't make me a crazy cat lady, by the way.

Once back on the futon, I held a pillow to my chest. Taylor had recently been eating the corner of the pillow, so the damp stuffing was pushing though the cheap green fabric on one side. It was quiet in the small room. I glanced at my television, my laptop, and my stereo. Nothing was calling to me. I bounced in place. I thought about doing my nails, but it seemed like too much work. The sound of Taylor's wet chomping filled the room. I was so restless, I was excited to hear the phone suddenly ring.

The Caller ID said it was Becca. I hadn't heard from her in a long time. I searched for the cordless, hoping for a twenty-minute chat that ended with an invite to go out with a group of her friends. Dinner and a movie, maybe, or even just watching television at someone's apartment. Becca's timing couldn't have been better.

"Hello?"

"Anna, it's Becca! I'm getting married!" She said it quickly, like I'd been expecting her to call and say exactly that.

Normally those three words produce shrieks and giggles, sending a room or even an entire house into chaos. But those three words were coming out of Becca's mouth, so they only produced a small, worried mental hum that flatlined underneath my restless jitters. See, Becca wasn't the closest friend of mine, but she was a woman in my social circle. Now she was a woman who'd moved up another rung on the ladder of life, while I was still down below. Someone was getting married. Someone else. Another person that wasn't me. As I sat still listening to her recite the engagement story, the hum in my head turned into a murmur. Then it sizzled into a loud, vibrating buzz. I hated that feeling of dread weighing down my arms, that heaviness making my stomach feel so empty. I hated it because I never expected to feel it. I didn't think I was that kind of girl. I looked down to see that my palms were sweating; there were also tiny half-moons indented from my fingernails. I opened my mouth wide when I realized I'd been clenching my jaw. What was happening to me?

"So anyway, we're finally doing it. Married. Hitched! Can you believe it?" Her voice cracked on the last word, and I could tell this phone call was way up in the double digits on her list. By now she was reciting a well-rehearsed monologue. She might not notice I wasn't picking up my cues.

Becca and Mark had been together for about four years and had been talking about marriage for the past year, waiting until they had enough money saved up. I didn't even have someone I was debating marrying to discuss savings and budgets with. Someone else had done all of that searching and finding, and that girl—she wasn't me.

"Congratulations." I hoped I sounded sincere. "When's the wedding?"

"In nine months."

"Oh!"

"No. No baby," she said quickly, laughing. No, nothing was sordid or imperfect about this impending wedding. Hers was just fine. Everything was great. Becca had been declared "A Keeper." She was getting married. I was not. I was "A Releaser." Or maybe even "A RunLikeHellFromHer."

"We wanted a wedding in the spring, and I'd like some time to get myself in shape," she continued.

Becca was what my mother would call "well put together." Always wearing an "outfit" and not just clothes, she's the only person I know who wears a blazer to a bar.

"How'd you like to be a bridesmaid?" she asked me.

I didn't expect this offer, as I hadn't been one of Becca's closest friends. Ian was the closer one to this circle of people. They were Ian's friends first. I had fully expected to lose them after we split up. I appreciated that they all stayed my friends after the breakup. They really liked Dale and were pretty considerate about not forcing Ian and me to get back together.

"Wow, Becca. Thank you. I can't believe you're asking me."

"Donna's not going to be able to make the wedding because she's got a family reunion that weekend."

Oh.

"Oh."

"Shit. I didn't mean that the way it sounded. I'm just glad that I can ask you. I was worried we wouldn't have enough room to have everyone in our wedding party that we wanted and now we can. Besides, you and Ian were really there for us that one time we almost broke up and it would just mean so much to us if—"

"Becca. It's okay. I'll be in your wedding." I politely cut her off before she had to fabricate a loving history between us. I was flattered enough that she was thinking of me. "I'd be honored," I added, in case she was still feeling guilty.

Now, I'm not the kind of girl who defines her personal status and self-worth by the length and quality of her relationships. Or at least, that's what I thought about myself before I picked up that phone to hear Becca's good news. Then I was flooded with the jealousy of another person getting picked first. I didn't need a husband to prove I was worth something. I just hated being second.

Or last. God, don't let me be last. The Spinster. The Old Maid. Aunt Anna With the Cats. I don't have to be next, but please, please, please, I can't be last.

The guy at the Circle K already had a pack of Marlboro Lights and a 20-ounce Diet Coke sitting on the counter when I walked in. "I saw you walking up! I know what you want!" He beamed. How did everyone else know what I wanted? Why couldn't I have that insight?

I got home, grabbed a bottle of beer, smacked my pack of cigarettes against the inside of my wrist and then opened them. I sat down to my computer. I lit a cigarette, took a breath, and I wrote. I wanted it to be okay to feel like this. It'd be okay if I were Anna K.

000006.

girlie thoughts

LATER, 30 JUNE

I never start this off by saying "Dear Diary." Sometimes I wonder if I should. Tonight, because I want to sound more like a diary than a column, I'm going to.

Dear Diary,

I'm going to pretend that you're quiet, secret pages locked somewhere in a drawer and that you're not the Internet. I'm going to pretend it's just me here tonight because what I'm about to say makes me appear to be weaker than I ever thought myself to be. Dear Diary, I'm sad tonight.

A friend of mine is getting married, and even though that doesn't make me any less of a person, and being single at this age is perfectly normal, I want to say right here and right now that I feel like I'm not on the right path. No, maybe I am. I don't know. It's just not the path that my parents followed, and it's not the path that movies are made out of.

My life so far isn't going to make much of a movie. That's something I've been thinking about lately. If my life were a movie, how would I want it to end? Does someone swoop in and carry me off into the sunset? Is it Ian? Does anyone have to? Can't I be the swooper? Why do I have to wait to be chosen?

I like to think that I'm a completely independent woman capable of running her own life without the help of others. I like to think that. I know it's not true. I depend on others for fun, advice, help, and favors. Right now there's nobody around, and nobody's home, and there's nobody to commiserate with about someone else just getting chosen to get out of the game. I'm alone tonight because my friends are busy and Ian's not here. He's been out of town and will be for a while, so I don't know when things are going to get easier. I hate that I feel this way. I hate breaking down, shutting down, just because there's nobody around to keep me up.

Last night I went to get a glass of water, but I couldn't find a glass. They were in the dishwasher, dirty. As I turned the dishwasher on, I realized that it's quite possible I haven't run a load of dishes in over two weeks.

I never remember to do laundry. If I do, I usually forget to put it in the dryer. The next day, when I do put the clothes in the dryer, I forget to hang them up. I run out of steam right there. I'll pull all of the clean, warm clothes out of the dryer, give them a half-assed fold, and then put the basket on the floor of my bedroom. I honestly can't remember the last time I went to the store to buy groceries.

But that's nothing compared to the hardest part. When it gets this lonely, and I'm feeling this down, I can't sleep. I sit silently on my couch, listening to the wind hitting the building, and I think about things I should be doing or things I want to do. I worry about things I haven't done yet. I worry I'm running out of time.

I can't sleep. I try to clear my head by creating a pillow-and-blanket boyfriend to spoon against. It doesn't help. Pillow Boyfriend is way too mushy, and Blanket Boy makes me sweat.

When will I be good enough to be chosen? What do I get to choose? Why does everyone go away?

Weddings bring out the worst in me. All of this paranoia is due to my friend's announcement. I feel silly for getting this upset. When will I be as strong as I give myself credit for? When will I actually feel as independent as I act? Weddings make me hate myself as I count down the days, working to get "pretty enough" to be seen at the wedding, attractive enough to tolerate dancing in front of old friends and ex-lovers. Once I'm at the reception I get mushy and sad, drink way too much, and convince myself that nobody will ever love me and I'll never be as happy as everyone else. It's not pretty, it's not healthy, but it's all a part of being a woman. It's a cycle I've got down to a science.

Love until later,

Anna K

000007.

Mom called the next night. She was trying to remember which baby-sitter used to borrow our Stephen King books because she was missing her copy of *Cujo*. My mom likes to keep all of her Stephen King books in a place where she can see them in the living room because she thinks they have the power to move at night, cursing her belongings and plotting her ultimate demise.

This is sort of my fault. One day I put a magnet inside the pages of Mom's paperback copy of *Salem's Lot* and I made it move along the kitchen table as I pretended to do my homework. I acted like it was freaking me out. I convinced her that she could control the evil by wishing it away and keeping an eye on it. I did it on and off for about a month. Now she makes sure that the Stephen King books are in her sight at all times. I'm a horrible person.

This *Cujo* situation had the potential to become a very bad thing, so I made a mental note to buy a new copy to slip into her bookcase the next time I went to visit. My parents live in Hartford, Connecticut. Of all the places my parents thought they'd end up living, Hartford was probably last on the list. It's boring, but in a "We're done making a family" sort of way that agrees with them. Dad works and Mom organizes rooms to minimize their evil potential. They must enjoy the monotony of Hartford after all the moving around we did when I was young. Dad sometimes got transferred twice a year, which meant that by the time I reached my senior year of high school, I'd gone to over fifteen different schools. Living in the same house for more than a year must be a pleasure for them.

I live in Austin because I went to college here. I got a degree in acting. I did a few plays once I graduated. I found myself working harder and harder, never feeling like I had accomplished anything. I hated performing for eight people. So I quit. I would be lying if I said I didn't miss it.

I think Mom likes telling people that her daughter is an actress. She still uses the word *actress,* even though most people say "actor" now. She also refers to all of my shows as "little plays." She asks about my shows and I make up plays that don't exist. It's easier than admitting I have no idea what I am doing or where I am going. The actor's struggle is much nobler than the haze of postcollege slack.

After the *Cujo* thing had been settled, we were free to go through the rest of our phone routine.

"Are you doing any little plays right now?" she asked me.

"Yeah, Mom."

"What's this one called?"

"More Jock Than Titty."

I heard my mother suck on her teeth. "That sounds dirty."

"I'm not naked in it. Other people are, though. It's about a boy who tries to become a member of the dance team and the other girls won't let him unless he dresses like a girl."

"I don't think I can make it down to see that play."

Mom asks, I describe a play she'd never want to see, and then she politely turns down an invitation I never extended. That's our routine.

"I miss you."

We said it at the same time.

"You should come and see your father. He's feeling down lately."

To the best of my knowledge, I never really saw my father feel much of anything. My mom would often tell me about these emotions he was going through, so I always imagined he had to break down in their bed at night since he was pretty much a blank page whenever I talked to him. That sounds very 1950s, to say that my dad is strong and silent while my mother discusses emotions, but I think they're very much a 1950s kind of couple.

"Well, I'm coming for your birthday," I said.

"I mean I think he'd like you to come."

Another one of Mom's codes. It meant Dad wasn't feeling well again. He'd been getting sick and the colds were sticking around longer than before. He'd had some heart problems in the past, but he didn't like telling me all of the specifics. It was as if simply discussing why my father was in the hospital would hurt his condition, tempting the illness to return worse than before. Dad hates doctors and always assumed that if he was sick it was because he'd been working too hard. Last month Mom told me she saw blood on his handkerchief. (Right. A handkerchief. I said they were 1950s.) Dad always bounces back from these things, but my mother still quietly talks about him like he's just about to slip into a coma.

"I'll be there soon, Ma."

"You're coming up for my birthday, then."

"That's what I just said. I was wondering if you were going to invite me or if I was going to have to crash your party."

"Oh, you." She made a grunting noise. "Always acting like I've forgotten you. Shannon and Meredith are coming. I figured you were too."

"I will, Ma. I am."

"Good. Your father will like that."

I spent the rest of that evening adding more stories to my webpage. I fell asleep at the computer—something I hadn't done since college. I wrote entries about how Ian and I had found our apartment, the time we got lost in Oklahoma, about our first fight over car maintenance, and what it was like to meet his father. The words came easily, and I was surprised at how much I remembered. Even while I was writing I'd find myself giggling or tearing up at times, nostalgic and proud of this relationship I'd had, the relationship I was giving to Anna K. Letting Anna K have these memories made them sweeter, allowed them to be untainted by our arguments and difficulties. Anna K only had the best times with Ian. She got all the good stuff.

It wasn't until that Saturday night, while printing out the entries for Dale's present as I got ready for the party, that I felt my first pang of panic. If Dale disapproved, what would I do? I knew deep inside that I wanted to keep writing. I didn't want anybody to tell me it was wrong. Nobody knew about my writing project and I wasn't sure if I was ready for the criticism exposing it would bring. The opinions. The judging. The confusion. I hoped everyone would understand why what started out as a birthday present was quickly becoming the most rewarding part of my daily life.

I checked my e-mail right before I went out the door. There were three this time.

Subject: re: re: Yay!!!

Anna K,

I can't believe you wrote back! I'm practically blushing. Your latest stories had me in hysterics again. I hope you and Ian

finally figured out which family you're visiting this summer. I
thought Ian was out of town. Did he miss you like you missed
him? Does he read your webpage?

When did you first start writing? Do you get paid for your
site?

Tess

Subject: Fan Mail

Anna K,

I like your website because you're truly showing me why girls
are weird. I knew it all along, but reading your journal is like
getting to read your sister's diary and all of her friends'
diaries as well. There's something fun, twisted, and slightly
sexy about that.

LDobler
P.S. Change "slightly" to "very."

Subject: football/basketball

Anna K,

My friends and I tried out your football tips, but we modified
them to basketball. Guess what? It still worked! We only had
the one slip where my friend Liz compared one of the players
to Vinnie Testaverde. I quickly covered by saying, "But once
we start mixing sports we'll never agree on anything!" I
couldn't believe they bought it.

I'm starting to think that boys don't know anything about sports at all. They just like having a reason to see each other every weekend. You know what happens when they get together and watch a game that they're not interested in? They talk about other games they saw in their past. That's like talking through an episode of *Sex and the City* about how great the last season was. Amazing.

Anyway, thanks for all your help. I'm enjoying being one of the guys.

-Laura

I walked to Dale's thinking about how I'd have to be more careful with my fake time line. I didn't even realize that I had put Ian out of town and in my bed during the same week. Maybe I was posting too many entries at a time, but every time I wrote, the amount of fan mail would grow. As happy as I was for the attention, I did feel a pinch of guilt that the people writing thought I had a different life than I did. I reminded myself that the attention was for Anna K and not me. I was just a writer creating a character. Every story had a ring of truth to it.

Once at the party, I looked around Dale's apartment wondering how so many people fit into a space that tiny. There were six people on his couch, another two resting on his coffee table, and people leaning against every inch of wall space. Two very drunk, very young girls were dancing in the middle of the kitchen, leaning on each other, craning their necks to see if anyone was watching them.

Shannon wasn't there yet. I checked my cell phone for messages. None. I dialed her dorm room but got her machine.

I went outside for a cigarette. I spent some time catching up with a girl whose name I could never remember. Dale and I had met her at another party and she became a part of the party circle, but I never saw her outside of those social events. I tried to steer the conversation in such a way that she'd say her name again, but it didn't happen. She complimented my shoes. I complimented her hair color. Then we sat quietly for a while. I bet she couldn't remember my name either. Still, it was comforting to sit with a near stranger like that. There was no pressure to perform.

I waited for most of the party to clear out before I handed Dale the box that held his birthday present. I used a Gap garment box left over from a Christmas present. We were in his bedroom, the sounds of the party muffled through the closed door.

"It's not from The Gap," I said quickly.

Dale lifted the box up and let it down with one hand, weighing it with a challenging look on his face. "Well, it doesn't feel like a gift certificate, so you're already beating all of my other friends. And I'm not talking to Jason until he apologizes for giving me that blender."

"He gave you a blender?" I laughed and moved some wrapping paper off a nearby chair so I could sit down.

"It means either he thinks I'm a drunk or he thinks I'm his bitch. Either way, he's completely in the doghouse." Dale flopped back on his bed, the box resting on his chest.

"Until you're drunk and need the garbage taken out."

"I am his drunk bitch," he moaned. "I just don't want him to know it yet."

He had someone else's tie around his neck. An empty Shiner Bock bottle dangled from his healed left hand. I was sad he didn't need me to wash his hair anymore.

"Open your present," I said, leaning forward to shake his feet in both of my hands.

He sat up and placed his feet flat on the floor. He yanked the box open with one clean jerk. He made a noise like he was about to blow out a candle.

"Is this what I think it is?"

Dale held the pages to his chest, the silver ribbon I had wrapped them in curled around his fingertips. Somehow he had dropped the bottle, but I hadn't heard it hit the ground.

I didn't know what to say, so I just smiled.

"You're writing again," he said with what appeared to be tears in his eyes.

"You asked me to write. So I did. I wanted to show you what I wrote."

"I'm going to read this now. All of these pages." He stood up, his feet tangling in discarded wrapping paper and ribbons. He unknowingly kicked an Over the Hill shot glass that was resting by his foot. I watched it roll across the room and into his closet.

I lit a cigarette, laughing at his drunken stumble. "You don't have to do that now, Dale. Enjoy your party first."

"Shit. Not one of these fuckers here is my friend. These people are just drinking all of my beer. You! You're the friend." Dale leaned out his bedroom door and scanned the living room. "Okay, I take that back. About six of the ten people here are actually my friends. They're good people. And the four I don't know are probably their dates." Dale's eyes welled up again. "I hate how I do that. I assume the worst."

"Maybe you should read a few pages."

"Then we can talk about how great they are over another beer, okay? Your hair looks fantastic tonight. It's really a pretty color." He grabbed a fistful in his right hand, careful not to tug. The blond ends swirled around his fingers. Dale started humming to himself.

"Happy birthday, Drunkston," I said, kissing his forehead.

As Dale read, I went out on the porch again. My silent stranger friend was gone, so I leaned forward on the balcony railing and looked over our neighborhood. I could see my apartment. Dale and I often joked about putting up a rope between our houses so we could send each other messages. We had walkie-talkies once—until we became obsessed with the cross-traffic interference we could pick up with them. We were riveted to the sounds of neighborhood police CBs and the goings-on of the security team at a nearby hotel. For two weeks we stayed in our own apartments, talking to each other with a phone pressed to one ear and a walkie-talkie to the other, anxiously wondering what would happen next. It was Jason who finally put a stop to that obsession by threatening to call whatever authorities were necessary—whether they were cops or psychiatrists. He confiscated the radios and we've kept to phones ever since.

My living room light was on. I thought I had turned that off.

I loved my tiny second-floor apartment in the Hyde Park neighborhood, even though the rent was too high, I didn't have central air, and every summer I thought I was going to die from the oppressive heat. I loved the Austin nightlife, the way there was always something new to do and the old things hadn't worn out their fun yet. I'd built up years of memories, and the town fit me like a favorite sweater.

When Ian and I first started dating, I always let him lead our life. He chose our evenings, decided where we went for vacations, and was the one planning how long we were going to live in Austin. I told Ian that if he felt the need to move I'd go with him, but deep down I didn't want to leave. Luckily he liked Austin as much as I did.

I felt a pull inside of me now, a yearning to find something new, and I wondered if it meant my time in Austin was running out now that my life with Ian had ended. As I stared at my apartment window, the shadows of the furniture just visible in the light, I imagined saying good-bye to all of this. I tried to picture what would happen to me next.

I realized Shannon had sat down next to me. She was wearing a shiny mauve dress with thin shoulder straps. Her hair was curled and I could see the hairspray straining against the weight of her pretty brown tendrils. She had glitter on her eyelids.

"Wrong kind of party," she said to me. "I thought there'd be lots of dancing."

"Dale's work friends aren't as fabulous as we are," I told her.

She lit a cigarette and looked around.

"Did you drive here wearing that?" I asked her.

"No, I stopped at your apartment and changed."

"That's why my light was on," I said, turning back toward my place.

"You're the only person I know who watches her own house while at a party. Tomorrow we're having fun. I didn't drive all the way from Houston for nothing."

"We'll have fun."

"I'll stay through the holiday weekend, if that's okay."

"Sure. That's cool."

"I'll mostly be studying, but I thought it'd be nice to go down to Barton Creek and read in the sun."

Dale's high-pitched panic voice doesn't normally startle me since he uses it all the time, but it shook me immediately out of my conversation when he screamed through his bedroom window, "Get in here!"

"I think you're in trouble," Shannon whispered.

I ran into the bedroom to find Dale trembling. He was holding a shuffled bundle of pages, letting them fall from the space between his hands and his chest.

Before I could speak he grabbed me by the arm, pushed me into his bathroom, and shut the door.

"Get in the tub!" he said quickly.

"What?"

"I said, get in the tub!"

This certainly wasn't the reaction I had been expecting. I stood, my mouth opening and closing silently, ridiculously.

"Get in the fucking tub, Anna!"

I did what he said. My shoes slipped on the porcelain. I steadied myself by holding on to the soap dish. I took Dale's beer out of his hand and took a sip.

"I don't believe this," he started.

"Do you want me to explain?" I asked.

"I want you to shut up."

"Don't talk to me like that, Dale." I could feel a fight starting. I only had to hold back and let him rant and I could avoid it completely, but something in me wanted to fight back instead of letting him run me down with his words.

"I don't want you to write about Ian."

"I don't want you to tell me what to write!"

"This is unhealthy."

I stood up, narrowly missing my head on the curtain rod. The shoes I was wearing made me taller than I was used to, and I was happy for the extra inches. "I did it for your birthday present, Dale. I don't need a lecture."

"You did it to write about Ian."

"That's not true," I said indignantly.

"No? Then why do so many stories come back to being about him? You've written a webpage worthy of stalker status here."

"I've written a webpage pretending to be some other girl who has a boyfriend that's based on Ian, but not really Ian." My foot slipped, so I quickly squatted and grabbed the soap dish to steady myself again, this time slapping my right hand down on a damp and sticky bar of soap.

"There's no way you really believe that," Dale said as I gently turned on the faucet and rinsed my hand in the cool water.

"This isn't about Ian," I said.

"Everything is always about Ian, including when you deliberately do something that's supposed to not be about Ian. Don't you see that? You can't move on if you wallow around in him."

"I'm not wallowing!"

"And writing about him isn't going to bring him back."

"I don't want him back."

"I'm sure." He turned away from me and gripped the sides of his bathroom sink. The room seemed strangely quiet as Dale waited for me to come to some sort of realization. But he was wrong. I wasn't trying to win Ian back. Besides, none of it mattered because Ian was never going to find the site. And even if part of me was hoping Ian would somehow read it and it'd make him want to come back to me in some mushy, romantic, music-swelling way, it was only so I'd have a good story to tell my children someday. I didn't want the man; I wanted the vignette.

And the truth was I didn't want those children just as much as I didn't want their father. The father that didn't exist. Those children I didn't have. I'd even named the invisible kids that I didn't really want. Veronica and Clay. Veronica was older and Clay was really good in sports. I went to their make-believe soccer games and their fantasy piano recitals. I hung their nonexistent finger paintings on my unpurchased refrigerator in that house I didn't have with a husband I wasn't looking for. I didn't need a perfect ending; I just wanted to borrow the good moments. I wanted snippets of other people's lives. I didn't need the whole thing.

Dale put his hands over his face. "I can't believe this is on the Internet," he moaned. He looked embarrassed for me, just as I'd been dreading.

I tried to brush it off by sounding casual. "It's just a webpage. There are millions of them. Look, don't tell Shannon, okay?" If Dale was reacting this badly, Shannon's teasing would be much worse.

Dale was still pacing, his arms crossed firmly at his chest. "But what if Ian finds it? What if someone he knows reads it? How are you going to start seeing someone new if you're writing every day about your last boyfriend as if he's your current boyfriend?"

I hadn't heard the words put in that order before.

"They're just stories," I explained calmly. "Some of the stories are about Ian and some aren't. I'm not pining or wallowing. I'm just writing."

My hands were trembling, and somehow I had picked up a washcloth from the edge of the tub. I was wringing it in my hands, watching Dale watch me. Seeing the range of emotions in his eyes. Confusion. Love. Pity. It was that last emotion I wanted to erase.

"I wasn't going to tell you," he started, "but I saw him the other day."

"I don't care, Dale."

"Fine. Then I won't say anything else." His entire body language shifted as he said deliberately, "Oh, man. My mouth tastes like a sock."

Dale grabbed his toothbrush and turned on the cold-water faucet. I was exhausted at the thought of playing this game with him. Instead of being coy, pretending what Dale had to say meant nothing to me, I decided to just come right out and take it.

"Where did you see him?" I asked.

"I don't know what you're talking about." Apparently Dale was still interested in the game.

I sighed. "Ian. You saw him. Where did you see him?"

"I don't want to bore you with things you don't want to hear about. You're right. You're past all of this bullshit." As he brushed his teeth he stared at himself in the mirror. I watched his blue eyes widen as he rotated his head, checking his skin for blemishes. He never had any.

I stood up and stepped out of the tub. Taking a step toward him, I tugged the ends of his hair in my right hand. "You wouldn't be bothering me if what you were going to say was really good, like he was crying in the middle of a field or something."

Dale spit the toothpaste in the sink and rinsed his mouth out with his beer. He stood up straight, inches from me, both of us facing the mirror. "Why would I be walking through a field, exactly?" he asked.

"You know what you just did is the grossest thing you've ever done, right?"

"You only think that because you've never dated me."

And then it was quiet. Dale and I stared at each other through the mirror. I knew he could wait much longer than I could. Besides, it was his birthday.

"Spill it."

"He's still dating Susan, you know." The words came tumbling out of his mouth with a touch of glee.

"I know." Ian began dating my friend Susan pretty soon after we split, and since then it had been too difficult for all of us to hang out. I could see Ian by himself, but I couldn't face Susan anymore. Every time she spoke I saw Ian's dick in her mouth. Crude, but the truth.

"He came up to me at the bookstore, acting like I would want to talk to him. I chose your side and I think I made that pretty clear. Actually, I think he came up to me because he knew I chose you and I wouldn't feed him any bullshit."

"You have told me absolutely nothing. This is not your story, you know. I don't want to know about your trip to the bookstore. What did he want?"

Dale's voice seemed lower as he said calmly, "He wanted to know if you were still around. He said you hadn't been calling."

"Like he can't call me!" My face instantly flushed hot and I found myself marching back into the tub. My fancy shoe slipped on the porcelain. I held on to the tiled wall with both hands, bracing myself against the wave of anger as I hissed, "Asshole!" I knew I was playing into Dale's trap, but my emotions had taken over. "He could call me. Why is it me that always has to call him?"

Dale jumped up and pointed at me. "You see? There! Right there! That's why this is dangerous. Let him go."

"I am letting him go." I slumped down into the tub until my knees were at my chest. I held my stomach, opened my legs, leaned forward, and rested my chin on the edge of the porcelain. It was cool and I could feel the blood receding from my face. I hated how much Ian got to me. I hated how I always wanted to be one step ahead of him and how I never, ever was.

000008.

Independent Woman
(song for a new kid)

04 JULY

I once knew a girl that would huff Scotch Guard in class. In the sixth grade. She was hardcore, yo. I wonder what happened to those girls— the ones who didn't talk to me. The ones who pushed past me. The ones who never saw me but who I studied, wondering how they got there. How did they get so cool? How did they decide one day that heavy black eyeliner was the way to go? I was fascinated with the ones who knew how to fray a denim jacket, who knew how to French-kiss when I hadn't even held a hand yet. I studied them because they knew how to make someone look at them. They knew how to draw attention.

I also studied the Pure Girls. The Pure Girls only looked pure, but actually wanted to lose as much innocence as they could on a Wednesday afternoon between the bus ride home and curfew. They were the ones who looked good smoking cigarettes, who hated doing homework. Was I the freak for liking homework? I didn't tell anyone that on summer vacations I gave myself assignments. My mother would buy me college textbooks in biology and English and I'd teach myself mitosis and molecular structures because I thought the more you knew, the sexier you were. How misled I was. How none of that helped that first terrible year of high school when I had no idea who I was or who these people were and they didn't care who the fuck I was. I was in a small town with people who had known each other for years and I was on the outside looking in.

Hi, new kid. Welcome to loneliness.

You always end up getting invited to sit somewhere at lunch the first day. You sit down and quickly realize that you were asked to sit with the other outsiders. You hear your mother in your head telling you to be nice and make friends with these kids because they're just as lonely and sad as you are and they really want friends and they're probably nice, but you really, really want to be popular this time. You've never been popular and you're starting over for the tenth time in another school and you thought maybe this time you'd get it right, but instead you're sitting with kids who never have plans on the weekend and they know all of the television lineups from Friday to Sunday. They ask you if you need help with your algebra. You watch the popular kids when you look up from your hot-lunch plate and you realize that you have two choices: You can suddenly get all cool and tell these losers that you'll smell them later, storm over to the popular table, declare a place, and say that you're lucky you got out without a pocket protector tattoo. Or you can sit there like your mother would want you to and be good, be a nice girl, and meet these kids but still stay distant enough that you don't *really* like them. It's easier to not make friends. You're going to be leaving soon anyway. You always do. Don't get attached.

You keep feeling like you're going to be sick. You sit in class and wonder if anyone will know it's your birthday. You watch the birthday girl with the balloons tied to the back of her chair and realize you won't have that because you haven't had these friends for years. They've all got history. You'll be the one without valentines again. No one will ask if you're going to the dances. You will only be talked to when you forget to put on one of your socks, or if you accidentally make the chair fart when you lean over to get your pencil. You miss every school you ever went to, even when you hated those schools so much you'd cry yourself to sleep every single night.

The sound of a school bus will forever make your stomach drop. The smell of a pencil brings a lump to your throat. Line leaders. Fire drills. The tardy bell.

Then there's that moment when you stop watching everyone else play Boys Chase Girls and decide to go inside and read instead. That moment when there is someone else inside reading, and you start talking to her about Ramona Quimby and Beezus. You suggest books for each other and at the end of the day you find out she rides your bus. Not only that, but she lives down the street! Suddenly you have a new friend and your mom is happy for you. (She stops asking when you're going to make friends. She stops looking at you like you're a broken child.) Everything is so much fun as you spend the night at each other's houses watching scary movies and eating too much and talking about movies and music and you've finally found someone who understands you. She's got some friends and she lets you in and suddenly you are a part of a group. You belong. You've got friends and you like the school and you can't remember ever hating it, and then you go home one day and it's time to move again.

You're moving again and you have to pack up everything in your bedroom. Quickly. Again. There were things you hadn't even unpacked yet. It's happening again. That feeling again. You say good-bye again to your new friend who won't remember you in three months when you are still wishing desperately to see her every day. You will remember her name long after you've become a faded memory to her.

You can't sleep that last night in your room, when it's all boxed up and dark and you don't know where you're going and you don't know anyone where you're going and you don't know what to expect. You get mad at yourself. You promised you wouldn't get attached to this place, and then you did. You went ahead and got attached, and now you have to go through all of that sad again. More sad again. Being new all over again.

Maybe next time you'll be popular. Maybe people will think you're pretty, or that you have the coolest clothes. Maybe they'll have horses. Your friend Becky loved horses. You miss Becky. She never writes anymore. Maybe they'll have braces. You like braces. You've never had them. Maybe they will love you immediately and take you right in. Or maybe they will hate you and make you sit at the fat-kid table again. Maybe they'll have other boys pretend to like you and ask you out and wait until you say yes and then all start laughing in the cafeteria, and even the lunch lady laughs because there's no way that boy was really asking you out and she has a sad and lonely life and her only entertainment now is watching young children be horrible to each other.

You can pretend to be blind in the new school. Or deaf. Pretend you don't understand English. Or you can be British. Or in a wheelchair. Find some reason that they don't have to talk to you, and even if they want to talk to you, you'll act very noble and say you can't talk to them. You're too busy, or too important, or too British.

Maybe the new school will burn down on your first day and you'll never have to go there again and you can sit at home with your college textbooks, apply to Harvard, get in, and be the youngest kid ever in college. People will throw words at you like "genius" and "charming." You won't have to remember that time everyone in class got a thesaurus and had to write words about you they had never learned before on a paper plate with your name on it. And since they didn't know what they were saying and you did, your heart broke when you got your paper plate back and it said, "precocious," "abnormal," "freak," "pretentious," and "egotistic." You turn to the kid in front of you as he studies his plate and asks you what *corpulent* means. You realize that maybe he's better off not knowing. You hate everyone there and you hate the stupid teacher for giving such a dangerous assignment.

You're going to start over and over and over. It's always the same, but the faces are different. The names are different. The pain and the fear are the same.

Hey, new kid. Don't get too attached.

Love until later,

Anna K

000009.

Subject: Sad.

Anna K,

I hope you don't mind that I write to you so often, but every time you write something I find myself nodding my head excitedly because I've finally found someone who thinks the same things I do. I moved three times when I was in junior high and it was really hard every single time. I lost friends I thought I'd know forever, and I have no idea what happened to them. I'm always hoping I'll find them on the Internet, though!

I hope you have a good Fourth of July tonight.

Later,

Tess

Subject: re: Sad.

Tess,

Thanks for writing again. I always like to hear from you. Hope you have a good time tonight as well.

-Anna K

Subject: ramblings.

Anna K,

Earlier today I was washing my dishes and I started thinking about you. I had a strange feeling that you weren't feeling well. Then I saw your latest entry. Now, the first question, of course, is why would I be thinking about a stranger while I washed my dishes? Why should I even care if you were well or not? But more importantly: How did I know you were feeling down? Maybe the answer to that last question is pure coincidence. But the other two questions are staying with me. Do you find yourself thinking about us, your readers? Your fans? I've written to you a few times, and you only wrote back once (something short and sweet like "Thanks for writing," which is exactly what I assumed I'd receive since I'm both a total stranger and a "Potentially Scary Man." I promise I'm not a scary man, and I don't have to be a stranger unless you want to keep me that way. That last sentence makes me sound like a scary man with creepy overtones. I'm not. This letter isn't turning out the way I wanted it to and my parenthetical aside has now taken on monstrous proportions. I'm going to end the parentheses and then continue, if you don't mind, leaving inside these

two parentheses all of the creepiness that somehow bled
out here).

What I mean to say is that I was thinking about you, and I think
you're an amazing writer. Obviously you have to be for me to
wonder about you like I do. I'm washing dishes thinking about
a woman I don't even know who lives somewhere in Texas with
a man I don't know. It's his job to comfort you, not mine. What
the hell right do I have to write to you, anyway? And by now I'm
sure you're thinking that I've overstepped some sort of
writer/reader boundary, and maybe I have. But I wouldn't have
felt right if I didn't let you know that I was thinking about you. I
think it's important for you to know that what you do reaches
people you might never meet in your entire life. And what you
do is good. So, thanks for that.

You don't have to write back, but if you do, know that I'll
sleep with a printout of your e-mail under my pillow for at
least a week. I mean that in a completely nonstalker way
(even though I'm pretty sure there's no way to take that in a
non-stalker way).

-LDobler

P.S. Maybe it's finally time for me to buy a dishwasher so I
no longer have these problems.

Subject: moving

Anna K,

My dad's in the military, so I know what it's like to move
around all the time, always changing schools, wondering if

the other kids are going to like you in the new place. Look at
it this way: At least it's made you this friendly, funny person.
I'm the life of every party now. They just don't know I'm
scared they secretly hate me. Keep up the journal. I think it's
really great.

-doug

Subject: re: re: Sad.

Anna K,

You wrote back so fast! You must still be on your computer
from earlier. Anyway, I wanted to tell you that I hope you and
Ian have a great time together tonight, and I was wondering if
you could give me some sort of P.O. box or address where I
could send you a card. I collect stationery and I found this
postcard that I think you'd love. It's totally up to you and I
understand if you don't feel right sharing your address with
me. That's why I thought you might have a P.O. box. You
really should get one, since I'm sure you get requests like
this all the time. Anyway, Happy Fourth!

Later, Tess

P.S. I hope you write happy and funny stuff again soon, like
the football stuff. You seem kinda down. Are you okay?

Shannon and I wandered through the hundreds of people gathered at Lake Travis to watch the fireworks. We got there just in
time for the sounds of the city's orchestra to float down the

grassy hill as the sun set and the sky settled into a beautiful deep blue. Dale, Jason, Becca, Mark, and a few people from Jason's work were already on their backs, wiggling with anticipation. I could tell they had been there a while from the empty bags of chips and mostly empty gallons of water strewn about their blanket. I flopped down on a space beside Dale as I felt him watch me. Shannon took off her shoes and stretched her legs. I listened to Becca talk about a caterer she was thinking of hiring.

I felt the clumps of dirt and tiny rocks digging into the back of my hips and shoulders through the blanket, but I didn't care. I welcomed the discomfort. This was the first time in a long time I wasn't watching the fireworks from the cup of Ian's lap. I wasn't sad, but I could feel the absence, like riding a roller coaster without someone in the seat beside me. Who would I turn to with excitement, making sure the beautiful sights weren't all just a dream?

When the fireworks started, I leaned forward to grab my disposable camera and saw a couple standing in front of me. They were holding hands and looking at the sky. He would whisper something in her ear as each pyrotechnic explosion faded and she'd giggle, throwing her body toward his. They'd bump into each other and stay closer with each crack in the sky. He held her around her waist, turned her at the chin, and kissed her.

As I looked down, Dale caught my eye. "Hey," he said gently. "They're probably on a first date and both very drunk. Don't go romanticizing them."

I shook my head. "No. See how her body fits into his?"

"This is a conversation I'm not going to win."

I settled my head on his thigh. He put his hand on my forehead as we watched the fireworks above us. I looked over and saw his other hand was holding Jason's. They looked at me like proud parents and then turned their gazes skyward.

I rolled until I was on my stomach. "I'm sorry we fought," I said into Dale's leg.

"What's that, Muffly?"

I looked up at him. Catching his gaze, I felt tears pressing urgently against my face. "I'm sorry," I said, miserably.

"Now that's the reaction I'd been waiting for. Fights aren't over until someone cries."

"Well, then it's over."

"Your entry today was really good. Broke my heart." I looked up and saw he was crying a little too. "I wish I was around when you were growing up so you didn't feel so lonely."

"Me, too, Dale. I'm glad you're here now, though."

He nodded and stroked my hair. I turned back around and watched the rest of the fireworks. When the last explosion hit the sky, I knew it was over, but I didn't move just in case there was still one more that nobody saw coming.

000010.

Subject: re: ramblings.

LDobler (LDobler like John Cusack in *Say Anything*, Lloyd Dobler?),

Hi. I'm not worried that you're a creepy stalker boy. But I am wondering why you'd write so much to me when you hardly know anything about me. This is all sort of new to me, so I'm flattered. Anyway, I do remember your other letters, and I'm sorry that I didn't write back more often. Sometimes it gets a little busy around here. Hope you had a good holiday weekend.

-Anna K

I doubt LDobler would be as interested in me if he saw the five rough drafts of that letter. I was admittedly more interested in him because he was a man, but I also liked that he sounded older than most of my other fans. He sounded like a peer. My daily amount of e-mail was growing rapidly. I didn't have time to write all of them back, but I did read them. People rarely asked a question or wrote something that begged a response anyway. It was more like they were just letting me know they were there, which was a great comfort. Their excitement was infectious and kept me writing with a near daily frequency.

A few days later, as I drove to the grocery store to pick up kitty litter, I wondered if I came across as myself in my webpage. I didn't know how obvious it was that there was a real person behind the stories, even if some of them were fabricated. Was it engaging enough that it didn't matter? If I were someone else sitting in a cubicle, and I happened across the webpage, would I stay and read?

I was still completely absorbed in myself when I walked into the store. Maybe if I paid attention every once in a while I'd avoid the misery I continually fall into.

000011.

Seeing the Ex
(Or, Why I'm Never Shopping Again)

08 JULY

I had only stopped in the store to pick up kitty litter. I do it all the time. I go into that store all of the time. This wasn't supposed to happen.

I bumped into my ex in aisle seven.

I almost did, anyway. I would have if I had taken three steps more. I heard his voice as I was looking down and I snapped my head up fast enough that I could dodge behind a canned peas display before he saw me. Please never remind me when we're old and gray that I once hid from my ex-boyfriend behind a peas display. Also, who needs a peas display? Are we all still buying peas?

He was standing there talking on his cell phone, just acting like he'd never dated me at all. Didn't we divvy up the neighborhood after we broke up? I thought so. There's a Chinese food restaurant that I still crave in the middle of the night that I won't dare enter because it's where we used to go. I could probably walk in there and order Moo Shu Pork, but my gigantic fear is that I'll see him sitting there with another girl and he'll be feeding her food and she'll be laughing.

There was something about not being prepared to see him that yanked my insides down and pulled me back behind that tower of canned goods.

He was chatting on the phone to someone, laughing every few seconds about some story I wasn't getting to hear. He pushed his hair back behind his ear and leaned forward to improve his reception. It had to have been his new girlfriend on the phone. She was probably telling him about her day, babbling on about the most mundane things in the world, and he was charmed by every single syllable that came out of her mouth. Maybe he craves her like that. When she talks he doesn't float away like he would when I'd talk about some crap that happened at work. He probably calls her while she's at work because he misses her so much.

She's probably absolutely perfect with this kick-ass lifestyle. She's smart and talented, with a car that never breaks down and food that always comes out on time and cooked perfectly. I bet she makes her own bread. She probably always has clean sheets and she recycles. She has the perfect dog that catches Frisbees in the park. She gives the best back rubs and never demands one in return. She doesn't eat much, but when she does it's the sexiest thing he's ever seen. I bet her name is something incredibly perky, like Holly or Tiffany. She comes the second he's inside her and she's always satisfied.

And then it happened. He lost the call. I heard him shout "Hello?" a couple of times. The signal must have faded.

Would he call her immediately back? Would he stop the next shopper he saw, demand to use his or her cell phone to call her back and tell her that he's sorry she was interrupted? Would he run from the store to be by her side as soon as possible? What would he do?

He shrugged and shoved the phone back in his pocket. I guess it wasn't Tiffany. Or maybe Holly doesn't excite him enough that he needs to call her back right away.

Or maybe, just maybe, he still wished the girl on the other line was me.

Love until later,

Anna K

000012.

I did hide behind a stack of peas until Ian's phone call was cut off. And I wondered if he was talking to Susan. But when he lost the call he didn't just shrug and walk on. He stood there trying to get the call back until Susan walked up, tossed a bag of potato chips into their cart, and put her arms around his waist. Ian didn't seem to care about his lost phone call once Susan was in his face. But I couldn't have Anna K stare at her ex-boyfriend and her ex-friend in an embrace. Anna K would have left the room with some semblance of pride. Anna Koval, however, never left the room until all dignity had been lost.

I'd known Susan since college so I knew all of her flaws, all of which I will list here: she's dumb, lazy, a bad tipper, likes to hog any food you share, makes strange noises with her lips when she sips drinks, and has the worst laugh I've ever heard. Like a hyena. Oh, and she's got a gigantic face. All puffy and big and it towers over her body. She doesn't even grow enough hair on her head to balance out her enormous face. Susan and I once spent an evening in the dorm listing all of the reasons why we were perfect girlfriends, but when your friend becomes The Girl After You, you're allowed to think nasty thoughts about her. She is not your friend anymore.

Okay, so she's not exactly dumb, but she used to do this thing where she pretended she was incredibly dumb so boys would talk to her. I hated it, and when I dated Ian he said he hated that quality in a girl as well. He seemed to not mind it on Susan, however, as I watched them practically chew each other's lips off right there next to the Frosted Flakes.

When I was a kid, I had to take placement tests every time I moved to a new school. They were all the same and always included an IQ test. One part of the exam was a series of images where I had to identify the one thing wrong in the picture. I was really good at them. The sun was setting on the wrong side of the beach house. The chair only had three legs. The swing set was missing rope. We do it in relationships, too. We can take one glance at the picture and instantly spot what's wrong. She's wearing the shoes he hates. He's on her side of the bed. He's using a condom. If this image was frozen right now and handed to me, I'd fail the test. There were too many things wrong.

There was the kissing. Ian hated public displays of affection. He'd hold my hand, but if my fingers started wandering up his arm, he'd eventually grab my hand and lower it, or he'd move my arm away entirely. I once tried to kiss his neck and he *backed up*. He said it made him look like he was property to have me press my body all over him in front of strangers. Now he was mugging down with Susan in front of some six-year-old grabbing a box of Cheerios.

Ian was clean shaven. That was why I probably would have walked right past him if I hadn't heard him on the phone. He hated shaving. Back when we first started dating, he had this clean face with great skin that I loved to run my cheek against. Two years later, he was sick with the flu for a couple of weeks and let a beard grow that he never shaved off. "What's the big deal?" he'd ask me with that smirk just poking out from underneath scratchy brown whiskers. So I had to date a man with a beard because I'd already been dating the man under the beard for two years? Unfair. I think a beard changes a man. He thought a beard made him look smart. I thought it made him look like a serial killer.

The third problem with this picture is the outfit Susan's wearing. She had on a little blue skirt that, if I was forced to admit it (because someone would be injured or there was a lot of money to win), I'd call "cute." She also wore a tight-fitting short-sleeve top. If I had attempted this outfit when Ian and I were together, he'd have asked why I was "trying so hard." He liked me in jeans and T-shirts. Whenever I put on a skirt he always felt like I was overdressed. He said it made him look sloppy. I hated how his laziness dictated my wardrobe, but I told myself that he liked me in simple clothes because he loved the person inside of the clothes. These are the things we convince ourselves when the person we love is actually making us sacrifice who we are.

When Susan moved forward to kiss his ear, her shirt rode up her back and I had to look away to take a breath. I had seen her thong. Ian was always trying to get me to wear a thong, but I wouldn't do it because it made me feel dirty and I didn't like having a piece of cloth running up my ass. I knew it disappointed

Ian that I wouldn't wear one, but I never understood what he thought he was missing out on. We usually started having sex once we were already in bed for the night. I don't care how much of a sex kitten someone wants to be—nobody wears a thong to sleep. That's pain.

Ian's hands slipped around Susan's waist and he hooked his fingers into the strap of her thong at her left hip. His hand lowered and I realized why he was changing himself for Susan. No matter how many of her flaws I could recite from memory, I knew the one thing she had over me that I could never beat.

Susan had a perfect ass.

She knew it, I knew it, and clearly Ian knew it, the way he was holding her bottom. He kissed her neck and held her ass in his hands. I bet she let him do all kinds of things to her. He probably didn't even have to ask if he could do them, either. I knew he wanted to try things with me that he was too nervous to ask about, and since I didn't really want to try them, I never brought them up either. I could tell that he wanted to do more, but he never said anything. I bet Susan just raised her perfect ass in the air without saying a word and let him do whatever he wanted.

The biggest thing wrong with the picture was that I was still standing there hiding behind a canned vegetable display. Why hadn't I left? Why was I watching him hold her perfect ass, completely forgetting about the phone call he just lost, while he kissed her enormous puffy face?

Then I saw he had a six-pack of wine coolers in his shopping cart. Perfect ass or no, there's absolutely no reason for Ian to buy anyone a wine cooler. He's not dating a woman; he's dating a sorority girl. I knew right then that he couldn't be happier with her than me. She couldn't replace me if she had seven perfect asses stacked on top of each other, silently waiting for Ian to ravage them. Perfect asses standing in a row, accepting his every fantasy. They could be there glistening with perfect skin, smelling like lollipops, but at the top of that stack was Susan's gigantic shiny face sucking on a "cooler" like a hungry toddler.

That's when I laughed, that's when they looked up, and that's when I hauled ass out of the store.

I only had the one ass to haul, you see. And it might not be perfect, but it's fucking fast.

000013.

Subject: re: re: re: ramblings.

AK,

A series of questions led me to write this e-mail. At first I was actually thinking about your webpage (I think of it as "Anna K," and then think of you as "Anna," like Anna K is an object, but Anna is a woman, but then I guess I also think of you as Anna K. But then also I don't really think of you as a person so much as this idea of a woman. I picture you as impossibly cute with a smile that makes all bad things go away. I've never even used the words "impossibly cute" to describe someone before. I don't think I like it. I've gotten myself trapped in another parenthetical prison here, haven't I? Let's just move on together. . . .)

I'm happy you wrote me back, even though I'm sure it was one of the form letters you send to all of your fans. I'm also assuming you have several fans. Because if you've made this one man sit up late in his Pittsburgh apartment reading over your past entries (more than once, I'm ashamed to admit), trying to piece together this most intriguing woman, then I'm sure there are thousands more like me.

I'm finding myself with plenty of spare time to write to you. I'm sort of between projects. (That sounds like I'm unemployed, but I'm not. But what I actually do for money is so terribly boring that if I even tried to describe it, you'd find yourself in a drooling coma within thirteen seconds. The "projects" I'm referring to are more what I do when I'm at home, away from my mandatory "day job." I paint. I paint things and people, and I guess sometimes I've ventured into the scary realm of painting Meanings and Symbols and Themes. Lately I haven't been able to paint a single stroke without getting a tightening in my throat and a quickness in my chest that's screaming, "You suck, LDobler! You suck!" Did I start this with a parenthesis? Dammit.)

What I was going to say (before this third cup of coffee—the stuff of rambling confidence, and the only thing keeping me from deleting this entirely and going back to an old episode of *Family Ties*—(Alex has joined the ERA because he thinks this feminist girl is hot, but now he's about to announce that he thinks it's all bullshit because it's better to be a Republican than to get laid). . . .)

I've lost my train of thought now. Oh, right. "Series of questions." I was going to say that I know you're busy, but I've been wondering a few things. If you find the time, I'd love to know the following:

A) Am I bothering you?
B) Do you want to know more about me?
C) Are you sure?

-LDobler

Subject: re: re: re: re: ramblings.

LD-

A) No, you're not bothering me.
B) Yes, I'd love to know more about you. I find you intriguing. Contrary to what you believe, I'm not swarmed with fans. There are very few of you. Well, there are more of you than I thought there'd be, but in comparison to the entire world, there are very few of you. And in terms of men who seem interested in me, I'd say there are very, very, very few of you. I mean that in the most undesperate way possible.
C) Yes, I'm sure.

By the way, do you find yourself thinking of me in strange places? I'd like to know where this image of me is getting evoked. I don't want to tell you what to think and all, but I'd appreciate you being gentlemanly about your thoughts of me, at least until we get to know each other a bit better.

Pittsburgh? What's that like? Is that a place you go to or end up?

A) I've asked you this before and you didn't answer. What does LDobler stand for? Because right now it means "Lloyd Dobler," John Cusack's character from *Say Anything*. If that's what you're going for, then you're clearly after my heart. Lloyd Dobler is the perfect man.
B) Are you the perfect man?
C) How did you find my webpage?
D) Do you think about me when you're driving? Have you ever missed your turn because of it?

-AK

000014.

A Texas summer can be so hot that people want to kill and maim and cry bloody tears. It starts in April and doesn't let up until October, sometimes lasting all the way to Halloween. I had made it to August without a slaughter, but my rage was quickly turning inward. It had been 102 degrees for three days straight and when a heat wave like that hits, Texans stay indoors for as long as possible. Hiding from the heat inside of my apartment forced me to take a hard look at myself. I got angry about how lazy the heat made me. I had spent so much time playing storyteller for the Internet that I had neglected myself. I hated the way I lived, I hated the way I looked, and I hated the way I felt about myself. I was lonely and unhappy in my own skin. I felt like everyone could see I was uncomfortable and tacky. I was wearing shame like stirrup pants.

It was a Saturday morning and I was on my futon, flat on my back, trying hard not to move, when my phone rang. I tried to move only two fingers to answer it. As I brought my arm to my head a bead of sweat rolled from my wrist to my elbow. All I wanted was central air conditioning. Why couldn't the city provide that? Wasn't that the only humane thing to do?

"Hello?" I answered as I leaned my head closer to the fan beside me.

"I need your measurements," Becca said without even saying hello.

"I can't move," I moaned, feeling the heat make wavy curves around my body. I looked toward my kitchen and swore I saw a mirage.

"I need to measure you for your dress." I could hear the impatience in her voice. It was the heat, I reminded myself, and had nothing to do with me. I couldn't imagine having a list of errands to run during this nightmare. I wasn't even getting into my car these days for fear of getting my thighs stuck to the seats and needing skin grafts to stay alive. Dale had told me Becca was pretty testy these days, so I was glad to be a peripheral friend of hers and therefore the last person she called for anything.

"What's the dress look like?"

"Open your door."

I obeyed. Becca stood with her cell phone in one hand and a measuring tape in the other. Her long brown hair had been pulled back into an official "Don't Fuck Around With the Bride" clippie, and she was smoking with the same hand that held the phone. She squinted toward me.

"Hey, Anna. Can I smoke in your apartment?"

"Are you kidding? Even my cat smokes."

I stood back to let her in. I couldn't remember the last time we were alone together. Since the breakup, she and I only saw each other when we were with the entire group. I never had much to talk to her about. I knew she worked in a PR firm, but I didn't know what she really did for a living. Like all the other women in my life, she floated on its outskirts as a feminine mystery.

"I'd suck your dick for some air conditioning." She walked past me into the living room.

"Right back atcha." The heat also put an end to pretenses. Everyone spoke succinctly, conserving all energy to minimize body heat.

Becca lumbers when she walks. There isn't a nicer way to say it. She stomps back and forth, as if both legs work independently of each other and never get on the same page. It's like they're playing a game with each other to see if each leg can keep up with the other one. I briefly thought of my downstairs neighbor as I watched Becca stomp over to my futon.

I lifted the bowl of ice cubes toward her. She took one and dropped it down the front of her bra. She gave a brief, chilled wiggle and I saw her face relax slightly.

"Thanks," she said with a sigh. "Lift your arms."

I tried to find a place to rest my gaze as my arms floated over her head.

"Let your stomach out. Stop sucking it in." Becca yanked me by the measuring tape. She should have taken more than one ice cube. I thought about dropping one down the back of her pants.

"I'm not sucking it in," I whined.

"You are too. It's not going to help any of us if you can't fit in the damn dress. Just stand naturally."

I stopped sucking it in. I hadn't measured myself in years. The double-digit numbers she wrote to describe my waist and hips shocked me. When did a 4 get in there? I shouldn't have anything that starts with the number 4.

"You look taller than you are. Must be your personality." There was no compliment in her voice.

I didn't have the energy to invent a comeback.

Becca slowly leaned forward, let her hair down, and then twisted it back up into the same shape, only tighter. Her face showed the strain she was under. Her eyes, normally slightly down-turned in a way that made you wonder if she was stoned, were now smaller and squinty. She looked exhausted and miserable.

I wanted to reach out and hug her. I wanted to hold her and tell her to remember why she was getting married. I knew that she had wanted this for a while. About two years ago, Mark told me that Becca had been having nightmares in which her parents were furious with her for not being married. So they had discussed it then and realized they didn't have the money. She never let it on to any of us how disappointed she was that she had to wait, but you could tell. You could see it in the way she looked at married couples and families. She'd get this look like she was comparing, wondering what piece of happiness they had that was still missing in her life.

I didn't hug her. I didn't even move closer to her. Still, she must have known I was contemplating it, because she said, "That's okay." It came out of nowhere, the air so thick and the words so loud that they just hung there, stuck in the space between us.

"Ian is going to be at the wedding, you know." She said it with that look on her face, that look I hate. I wanted to wipe it off of her, make her apologize for wincing, for lowering the corners of her mouth like she was holding back the world's best advice.

The sudden energy propelled me forward. I lit a cigarette. "Fine. Of course he is. He's supposed to be there."

"I'm just saying."

She was warning me. Telling me to prepare.

Then those stupid words poured out of me: "Is he bringing Susan?"

"Probably. You should bring someone, too."

There was that tone in her voice. That sad voice used when someone's not dealing with life. That pity voice that says "We're only here for so long before you're just wasting our time." The tone that told me to suck it up and move on.

After Becca left I went to my kitchen junk drawer, pulled out a measuring tape, and measured out forty-six inches. If my hips were laid out flat, they would be almost four feet long. Holy shit. My hips were almost as tall as I was. How much ass is that? How much fucking ass is that? That's an assload of ass. My refrigerator, minus the freezer, was the size of my ass. My entertainment center, from VCR to television, was the size of my ass. My bathtub was the size of my ass. I continued measuring things around my apartment, moving from room to room with my arms outstretched, the measuring tape pulled taut between my fingers. I was a measurement zombie—eyes bulging and mind swimming as I walked stiff-legged through the heat from one target to another. You could fit three Taylors on my ass. You could store all of my clothes in my ass. My bed? As wide as my ass.

I grabbed a piece of paper and a pen. I tossed my Diet Coke in the recycling bin and poured a tall glass of water. I sat down and wrote at the top of the page: CHANGE.

Eight months until the wedding, where people could say "She's really doing so much better. You should have seen her last fall. No, she was a mess. Trust me. Should have seen that ass. We're so proud."

LOSE WEIGHT. That belonged right at the top. I added a sub-heading: (NOT BECAUSE OF ANY MAN, BUT BECAUSE IT'S HEALTH-IER TO BE THIN AND YOU'LL FEEL BETTER ABOUT YOURSELF AND SELF-ESTEEM IS GOOD FOR YOU.) Just in case there was any doubt.

Next on the list: QUIT SMOKING.

I crossed it out.

DRINK MORE WATER.

Much easier, that one. Cigarettes were part of the diet plan. I wiped my forehead dry as I gave a glance around my apartment.

BUY NEW FURNITURE.

It was time to make this place presentable. I had stacks of books I'd read mingling with stacks of books I wanted to read dancing with piles of old bills that scattered the floor. All it would take was a trip to Target and I could contain it all. Just some shelves, a few storage units, and a shoe-holder thing. How hard could that be? Organize. Buy some drapes. Curtains. Didn't nice apartments always have curtains?

GET OUT MORE. I was still learning this "alone" thing, but it was time I went out by myself. I didn't always need to go out with a friend. I didn't always have to have plans. I could see a movie all by myself. Or eat in a restaurant at a table for one. I'd never done either of those things in my life.

NEW JOB. I was sick of the librarian gig. I didn't want to work there forever, they didn't pay me as much as I could be making elsewhere, and I didn't know if I could handle the new school year that was quickly approaching without strangling a fresh-man. I should be a writer. I should be out there making a name for myself. But just where exactly was "out there"? Getting a different job would take away from my Anna K time. I updated and sent e-mails during the day since I did most of my daily duties at the school within the first five minutes. I was really paid to be there in case something happened to the network or some kid tried to look at porn in the computer lab. I was the glorified porn police.

NEW HAIRCUT. I'd been tired of my hair, but I was scared to do anything different to it. It hung here, long and boring.

I decided to start Task One immediately.

000015.

Backwards Jumping Jacks
(and Why There's a Bruise on the Back of My Leg)

10 AUGUST

Maybe you're one of those perfect people that pay for a gym member-ship and then always, always go. Every morning you bounce off with your perfect ponytail and your teeth gleam as your perfect little mousy voice goes "I'm off to the gym!"

First of all, if that's you? Be thankful that nobody has stabbed you in the eye. Yet.

I'm not one of those people. I'm not even close. I forget to exercise until someone reminds me. I don't like to run unless my life is being threatened. I certainly only try to break a sweat during sex.

Also, it's hot in Texas. It's particularly hot here in Austin this time of year, and it gets so hot that it's physically impossible to move more than a few inches at a time. You have to remain as still as possible, only shifting to lower the air conditioner. It's the only reason I'm still coming to work, since I don't have A/C in my apartment. It's so ridiculously hot that we air condition *outside* this time of year. Amusement parks like Six Flags don't want a thousand people dropping from heat stroke while waiting in line for the Log Flume, so the outdoor areas have overhead cooling units. Mmm, Lovely Overhead Cooling Unit. Why won't you move into my apartment building?

Still can't understand what kind of hot I'm talking about? You try it. Lock yourself in your bathroom, turn on the shower at its hottest setting, and put on a few sweaters. That's what it feels like to walk outside these days. Go sprint in that, bitch.

There's this wedding coming up that I mentioned before, and I'm pretty sure that as my friend was measuring my hips she was shaking her head and sucking her teeth. I could be horrible here and mention that as she was measuring my hip to foot distance I noticed that the hair on the top of her head was thinning and I could see her scalp. But that would be mean and I'm not a mean person so I didn't say that. I don't know where you heard that.

Since I just about broke down after seeing my measurements on paper yesterday, I decided to grab an old Tae Bo tape and work out. You remember Tae Bo, don't you? With everyone's favorite scary, sweaty black man, Billy Blanks? His name's a registered trademark, don't you know.

Y'all, I got schooled by the world-famous Billy Blanks World Training Center.

I had to do these crazy hop things and then punch and run backwards, like I'm a member of the Dallas Cowboys. I'm pretty sure I saw my downstairs neighbor moving out of the house while I was working out. I guess he was just sitting around until heard me jumping up here for the umpteenth time and said, "Well, that's it. The crazy bitch has broken me." And then he started loading all of his things in his truck and moved to Montana.

In one particularly aerobic set of moves you lift one knee, lift the other, kick, kick, and then do four jumping jacks while moving back into your starting position. So I'm doing the knee, knee, kick, kick, jumping jack, jumping jack, jumping jack, jumping jack, and I'm feeling pretty proud of myself:

BILLY BLANKS (tm)
Knee! Knee! Kick! Kick! Jumping jack! Jumping jack! Jumping jack! Jumping jack!

Knee! Knee! Kick! Kick! Jumping jack! Jumping jack! Jumping jack! Jumping jack!

ANNA K
Oh, yeah!

BILLY BLANKS (tm)
Again! Knee! Knee! Kick! Kick! Jumping jack! Jumping jack! Jumping jack! Jumping jack!

Again! Knee! Knee! Kick! Kick! Jumping jack! Jumping jack! Jumping jack! Jumping jack! Let's go! Let's go!

ANNA K
That's what I'm talkin' about, Billy.

BILLY BLANKS (tm)
Again! Knee! Knee! Kick! Kick! Jumping jack! Jumping jack! Jumping jack! Jumping jack!

Knee! Knee! Kick! Kick! Jumping jack! Jumping jack! Jumping jack! Jumping jack! That's it! That's it!

ANNA K
I know that's it. I know! I rule!

BILLY BLANKS (tm)
Knee! Knee! Kick! Kick! Jumping jack! Jumping jack! Jumping jack! Jumping jack!

TAYLOR
ReeeeeOOOOOOOOWWWWW!

TABLE
Crash!

ASHTRAY
Flip!

BOTTLE OF WATER
Splish!

TAYLOR
Weeooow!

ANNA K
Ow! Damn! Ow!

BILLY BLANKS (tm)
Knee! Knee! Kick! Kick! Jumping jack! Jumping jack! Jumping jack! Jumping jack!

ANNA K
Shut up! I fell over a table, Billy! Give me a second to fucking recover.

BILLY BLANKS (tm)

Jumping jack! Jumping jack! Jumping jack! Jumping jack!

ANNA K

I'm sorry, Taylor, is your tail okay?

TAYLOR

Fuck off. I am so incredibly pissed at you. You know I always stand
right behind you when you work out and you know that jumping
backwards is a stupid idea, but you did it anyway, and now my tail
hurts, and you spilled water all over me, and now you've left me with
no choice but to go into your bedroom, find one of your bras, and
vomit a hairball into it.

ANNA K

I understand.

BILLY BLANKS (tm)

Come on now, I know you're tired. I know you wanna quit. But
DON'T GIVE UP! DON'T QUIT! YOU CAN DO IT, BABY!

ANNA K

Okay, Billy.

BILLY BLANKS (tm)

ARE YOU WITH ME, BAYBEEE?

ANNA K

OKAY, BILLY!

BILLY BLANKS (tm)

Keep that hip out when you kick. And don't scream so loud your
neighbors call the cops, Anna K.

ANNA K
Sorry.

BILLY BLANKS (tm)
Uh-huh. That's good, right there.

ANNA K
Billy, can I ask you a question?

BILLY BLANKS (tm)
Sure. As long as you do some shoulder-to-shoulder punches while you
do it.

ANNA K
No problem.

BILLY BLANKS (tm)
Punch a little higher. Good. Now, what's your question?

ANNA K
Am I officially hallucinating?

BILLY BLANKS (tm)
I'd say that's a pretty safe bet.

ANNA K
That's what I thought.

BILLY BLANKS (tm)
Now, a lot of people want to quit when they start hallucinating.
Anyone can quit when they start seeing shit and their stomachs are all
fucked up and their thighs are trembling and screaming.

ANNA K

It's like you can see into my soul.

BILLY BLANKS (tm)

But don't you think that's a small price to pay for firm thighs? Front kick, back kick. Ready? Go.

GHOST OF CHRISTMAS PAST

You need to concentrate. Here, let me help you with those kicks.

ANNA K

That's it. I'm turning the tape off.

BILLY BLANKS (tm)

Are you sure you wanna do that? Only fifteen minutes left.

GHOST OF CHRISTMAS PAST

You can do it, Anna K. I have faith in you.

ANNA K

Of course you do.

So, I'm sitting very quietly at my desk today, as my butt is throbbing beneath me. I learned my lesson. I can't just become an athletic person in one day. It's not like I stored up all my past workouts until I decided to take my ass off the pause button. And most importantly, I probably shouldn't do peyote right before I work out.

Love until later,

Anna K

000016.

Subject: Vacation?

Anna K,

Hi, it's Tess! I'm writing this to you from my school's computer lab. I'm probably going to be in so much trouble now because I was reading your entry instead of working on my history paper, and some people heard me laughing and now they all think that I am a very strange or crazy girl. I'm not crazy, right? Hee!

You know I live in Dallas, don't you? That's so close to Austin! Anyway, if you ever want to come and visit, don't be afraid to ask! I've got plenty of room at my apartment, and lots of hotels close by if you'd like your own place to crash.

I've got to go back to working on my paper now, but I wanted to check in and see how you were doing. By the way, I met this totally crush-worthy guy at a bar this weekend. He thinks I'm twenty-five! Argh! Starting my new relationship out with lies! I guess it's pretty silly to call it a relationship already, since we just met and all, but I really think he's cute and he seemed to be interested in me. That's all it takes. I'm easy!

Later, Tess

Subject: Tae Bo

Anna,

Thanks for making me feel guilty about ditching my Tae Bo.
My thighs hate you. My arms aren't too thrilled with you,
either. Billy, however, should get a kickback.

-Deb

Subject: re: re: re: re: re: ramblings.

AK-

A) Yes, it stands for Lloyd Dobler. I'd be lying if I didn't tell
you the nickname is a total chick magnet.
B) But sadly, I'm hardly the perfect man.
C) I found this webpage searching for sites about Barbies. My
niece had a birthday coming up and I wanted to find a rare
Barbie for her. I figured Barbie BackwardsLegs might be too
advanced for the six-year-old set. Well, that's what I used to
think, anyway. I guess you proved me wrong on that one.
D) I think about you when I'm brushing my teeth. Once I thought
of you as I unwrapped a piece of gum. Sometimes I think of you
as I'm rewinding a video before I return it. It's the little quiet
moments. Then you flood in and I wonder what you think about
while you go through the quieter moments in your life.
E) More importantly, will you tell me everywhere you are
when you think of me? Also, when you're doing this, what are
you wearing?

Pittsburgh is mostly gray, mostly cold, and mostly dreary.
When I look at it, I think about the history of hardship and
suffering that went on here. It's not a sad place, but it has

that ache of an old wound—the way your scars feel different to the touch. Everything works and everyone's happy, but the buildings in this city still carry the weight of the Depression and the clouds sometimes look like they're dusted in coal. The town remembers everyone that ever died here and is constantly in a quiet mourning.

The people here, however, fall into what I like to call "The Three P's": Pale, Pasty, and Puffy. That's mostly because of the lack of sun and the good Polish cooking. If you're ever in town we're going to the Polish Party House. You have no choice.

Print this e-mail out and save it. If you ever find yourself single someday, consider it a proposal for a date. Gosh, I'm getting feisty in my anonymous safety zone, aren't I?

-LDobler

P.S.: More stories about you being all sweaty, please. Or just stories about your breasts.
P.P.S.: FEISTY!

000017.

By Request
(I Give You a Rack for a Day)

12 AUGUST

Small-chested girls and boys of all sizes: Today I give you a set of tits. You wanted big boobs your entire life and today you get to have them. After you've spent ten minutes in the mirror playing with them, get ready to experience the real world of big-tittydom. Here we go:

Your shoulders hunch inward, just slightly—a result of trying to make your chest look smaller while you were growing up, embarrassed to have people staring at you.

The seat belt never stays across your chest. It slides up and sometimes goes around your neck if you aren't careful. You are terrified that you will one day be decapitated in an auto accident because of your 34Ds.

The cuter the T-shirt, the greater the chances it will not fit you. If it does fit in the arms and length, the logo on the front will be stretched so tight across your chest that you look obscene.

The strappy/backless fad? Forget it. Where are you gonna be seen without a bra? There's no way. While you're at it, you can pretty much forget one-piece swimsuits. They don't make any that fit and hold you in. You're buying separates forever.

When you're cold, everyone else is going to know. They won't tell you that you're high-beaming, but will enjoy the free show. You might notice yourself, however, when you scratch your arm on your nipple. Again, the protective hunch will develop in time.

People will "accidentally" brush into you. They like to do this at bars, in tight hallways, and on buses. They will be all "Excuse me," but will raise or lower their arms so that they brush into your breasts. They may even do the hard shove that presses their chest against yours. They won't thank you for it, either.

Your mother will talk about your chest more than your career.

No running. Ever. Invest in three sports bras and wear two at once, but you're still not going to run a mile. Use the elliptical trainer, treadmill, or Stairmaster.

The sight of speed bumps on the road may bring tears to your eyes.

Never close a hardcover book too quickly. You could get a nipple stuck in there. Yes, it happened, and no, I don't want to talk about it.

Babies grab your breasts. They don't know any better. It's only mortifying when someone jokes loudly, "He's looking for lunch!"

Lovers will try and name them. Don't let them. Keep your dignity. Maybe one great name like "Fantasia." But not "Bert and Ernie." "Pooh and Tigger." "Lefty and Lopsy." Fuck that shit.

You wear bras all the time. Constantly. Underwires only. No frilly-soft-lacy-pretty things. Industrial strength. Straps an inch wide. You look like a 1950s nurse who's into S&M.

They itch. Once a month, they start itching like a motherfucker. You will find yourself leaning over your desk and rubbing your chest against the edge so it looks like you're just sort of grooving. You will figure out how to use your forearms to scratch yourself. The itching is terrible. And when it first starts happening when you are young, your mother will tell you it's because they are growing. When it's still happening at twenty-five, it's okay to panic, just a little.

Women outwardly hate you because of your chest. Even your best friends.

There will be lines you can break, drinks that will be free, things that you can have, and tickets you might get out of.

There will also be friendships never had, clothes never worn, sports never played, and pictures ripped to shreds in agony.

Your back hurts. Just all the time. A constant state of hurt.

You have a terrible fear of catching a football. It is completely under-standable.

New boyfriends won't know what to do with them. They will opt for a mix of lifting and lowering, licking all over the place, hoping to hit a spot you like.

Sometimes you accidentally drop food down there, like popcorn. People think that's hysterical.

Sometimes you'll lean over a table to get the salt and will end up dip-ping your breast in someone's ketchup. Yes, you'll be humiliated. No, you probably couldn't have avoided it.

You may catch yourself leaning on a table, resting only your breasts on it. Stop. You look obnoxious. I know you didn't realize it. It just happens sometimes.

Find yourself a period play and act the shit out of it. May I suggest *Dangerous Liaisons*?

Did I frighten you or just make you want your own pair of big boobs even more? No, boys, I'm not talking to *you*. I know what your answer is. Even you gay boys. I know you want a fancy pair for special evenings. I'm just talking to the Itty Bitty Tittie Committee here. All in favor of keeping your new knockers, say "Aye."

Hello? Hello? Yeah, that's what I thought.

Love until later,

Anna K

Subject: we needed a new subject line

AK,

Thank you. Never let it be said you aren't accommodating to
your friends.

I like how I feel I have absolutely nothing to lose by writing to
you. I've never met you and you know nobody in my life, so I
can say anything to you ("Right, LDobler, *'Say Anything'*,
asshole") and not worry that I'm making an ass out of
myself. I never have to see your reaction. You keep writing
back, so I must be at least slightly interesting to you. And
what's sexy? Women who think I'm interesting.

Having said that, I've decided something. I'd like to apply to
be your stalker. Officially. I won't ride by your house on my
bicycle or anything, but I'll be the one to write to you every
day, several times a day, letting you know what I'm doing,
where I'm going, and when exactly I was thinking of you.
Think of it: You'll never be alone again! Of course, all that
love stuff will have to be taken care of by Ian, but I'll be the
person who makes you famous. I mean, you can't have fame
without creepy fans, right? So here's your first creepy
moment with me:

Tonight I will dream of the two of us together trapped on a
small rowboat. When you figure out the way to get us back to
shore, I'll smother you with chloroform (I hid a bottle in the
cooler with the love sandwiches I made before we set off)
and I'll hold your passed-out body, whispering how much we
belong together into your ear. When you wake up you'll be
with me and you'll have forgotten what land looks like. You'll

only know us; you'll only know our world. And we'll live
happily ever after. WRITE ME BACK OR DIE.

Ha.

-LD

000018.

Every time I visit Hartford I feel like I'm in the past. I rarely
leave the house once I get there, so it's like I'm stuck in a time
loop. It's just me, four rooms, and tall trees outside. I make sure
to always bring three books with me and I usually read two of
them. We don't normally all get together for my mother's birthday, but Mom had called all three of her daughters to request our
attendance, so Shannon and I flew in together.

Just after dinner, as we all gathered around the dining room
table, Mom had her hands to her chest in anticipation. Shannon
carefully carried the cake in from the kitchen, kicking off the
birthday song with a shaky "Haaa-ppy Birrrrthday," holding out
the notes until we all joined in. She wore a Radiohead T-shirt
with a thermal sweater underneath. Her jeans were frayed
around the cuffs. Her shoes had holes in the toes that she'd
wrapped with duct tape.

Meredith was by the light switch, wearing a green cardigan
and a long denim skirt that came down to her feet. Her hair was
pulled back in a braid.

Mom and Dad were at either side of the table and I was sitting between them.

As we sang, I watched my family. Shannon's hair was getting so long, curling around the ends, flowing over her shoulders and down her arms. Meredith had lost weight and was looking too thin. I wondered if she was still working two jobs. My mom looked so happy having her entire family wrapped around her.

I looked over at my Dad. He was crying. His hand rested under his chin, and he was looking at my mom's happy face. He lowered his head and wiped his eyes with the back of his hand. Looking back up, he caught my gaze and gave a weepy smile. It was the first time I'd ever seen my father cry. My body felt a shock, like a steel cold rod slammed through my spine. Something was wrong. My stomach twisted; the taste of the garlic and chicken we had for dinner felt sharp inside my mouth.

I was smoking on the swing set in the backyard an hour later when I heard my father's voice behind me.

"Can I have one?"

Instinctively I put my cigarette out under my shoe. Dad knew I smoked, but I still felt strange doing it in front of him. It seemed like a deliberate action, bragging that I was a grown-up and he couldn't stop me.

As I watched him approach me cautiously, I realized Dad hadn't stepped foot in the backyard of any house we'd had. "Are you lost?" I asked him as I handed him a smoke. He took it from me, laughing nervously. I could see the veins in his thin hands. His skin had brown spots I'd never seen before. His face was grayer and his eyebrows had silver hairs. He looked tired.

He sat down on the swing next to me. "Just wanted to talk. How are you?"

This, too, had never happened before. It felt like a trick. "I'm fine, Dad."

He nodded his head and bit his lower lip. He hadn't shaved since yesterday and a full salt-and-pepper beard was threatening to sprout on his face. He wiped his nose with his palm and exhaled.

"How are *you*, Dad?" I said into the silence.

"I'm not so good, Annie."

I swallowed. I knew this was coming, but I still wasn't ready. I didn't want this to be real. I wanted it to stop before it happened. Staring straight ahead, it felt like I was floating outside of us, staring down at the backyard, at the two of us sitting on a swing set, staring away from each other as we concentrated on our cigarettes. Why was he telling me this here? Why now? I wondered briefly if he was going to reach out and touch me or hold me. He never did anything like that before, but the entire afternoon had become a series of new events, changes, and discoveries. Maybe getting sick made you want affection. Were we going to change our relationship right now? Did he need me to become something more?

"What do you mean?" I heard a tiny version of me say.

"My heart's not doing so well."

I wanted to take the cigarette back from him, but I couldn't say anything. I didn't know any of the words I was supposed to say. Was I supposed to even say anything? It wasn't really a conversation. It was just Dad talking to me. Talking near me, really, since we weren't looking at each other. Dad stared at his cigarette as he continued.

"So I thought I'd ask how you were doing, because your mother says I don't ask you enough. Just making sure you're okay. And I guess you might want to think about coming home for Thanksgiving *and* Christmas this year instead of just one."

And with that he stood and walked back into the house.

I sat still, my hands dangling inside of my jacket pockets. I had that same feeling after I found out there wasn't an Easter Bunny. Like I learned something I should have known all along, something that always made sense but I didn't let myself worry about before. My father had just said more to me than he had in years and I just sat there mute. I had a chance to talk to him and I didn't. Worse than that, I did nothing. I said nothing. I had the chance to let him in. He gave me the opportunity. I could have told him I loved him and how I always wondered what it'd be like if we really knew each other. I could have found out what it sounded like to have him tell me that he loved me. The moment passed, and it was never coming back, just like the moment before he told me he was dying. That would never come back, either. Now he was officially dying and I had officially not said a word about it.

I looked toward the house and saw him through the back window. He sat back in his recliner and turned on the television. All I had to do was walk into the house, put my head in his lap, and ask to start our relationship over again. I could place my hands on his and ask, "If we don't have much time, can we try to make this work now?"

Could I turn my father into my daddy just because the clock was ticking? Would that make it harder to deal with him dying? *Dying?* That word had lost all meaning over the years. It didn't feel possible. Although it was quite probable, with the way he'd been getting sick, it just felt like something that was never going to actually happen. We'd had so many false alarms over the years—frantic trips to see him only to have him recover at the bleakest hour. Too many times I had rushed home thinking it was time to say good-bye and it wasn't. He'd always bounced back before. Maybe he'd do it again this time. Maybe this was another false alarm. I couldn't imagine what it'd be like without him around. I knew he was weaker every time I saw him, but he'd been frail for so long I was used to having a fragile father. He always recovered on his own, opting not to talk about it or ask us for help. He didn't even like us in the hospital room with him when he was being treated. He'd send us away on errands and keep us busy until he was released. He'd never needed me then. Why would he need me now? And why was he the one telling me he was sick this time instead of Mom? What was he doing talking to me? What did he want from me?

I held on to the swing chains, leaned back, and kicked my feet up hard. I held the chains until my palms were aching. I pumped my feet back and forth, pushing the swing into gear, jerking and rocking, higher and higher, feeling the wind in my ears melt the sounds of the house out of my head. I could hear the birds in the trees above me. I felt myself rise out of the chair, my stomach getting lighter, my head getting cloudy, my vision numbing into pure blue. I could feel the weight of gravity on my shins as my body crashed back down onto the swing. Tears streaked my face as the wind strained them.

What was I supposed to do? Give up my life and move to Hartford until he died? Did he expect me to move in with Meredith? Did he want me to move back home? Did he think I could just quit my job and move to the other side of the country? Who did he think I was?

More important, who was he?

000019.

Apologies and Gossip:
Courtesy of Hugh Grant

17 SEPTEMBER

Right.

Um . . . yes, ah . . . hello.

So, Anna K has seen fit to . . . uh, sort of . . . you know, *hire* me to do sort of . . . urm, spot work for her. It seems she finds my ability to apologize my way out of anything short of *murder* to be, well . . . uh, rather charming, actually. So today she asked if I might . . . sort of . . . you know, fill in for her and do one of these cute little . . . talking-to-the-computer sorts of things.

I'm supposed to talk to you about whatever's in my head, make a few . . . you know, *points* that Anna K asked me to say and then . . . well . . . urm . . . flash my baby blues to you and do that side grin thing I'm so . . . you know, rather capable of doing, see.

[Imagine me now posed with my hand sort of, you know, cupping my chin, I suppose you'd say, and I'm grinning, but not actually showing any of my teeth. My face says, quite simply, "Ain't I a cutie?" Insert that picture here.]

Right.

You know, Anna K is a wonderful, wonderful woman. Delightful. Charming. Really . . . just . . . can't say enough about the girl, you know. But that's all neither here nor there, right? Time to get on with the talking and the smiling and the charming the panties off of you. That's . . . not to say that you wear panties or anything. Anna K tells me there are a few lads that read this thing so . . . I'll just . . . try to charm . . . well . . . whatever sort of knickers grace your bum.

[Picture this. I'm sitting in a field, and I'm looking towards you but not quite *at* you, really. Sort of . . . near the vicinity of, I guess you could say, your left eye or, rather, just below it and right . . . possibly towards the tip of your ear, I guess. I'm laughing—not *at* you, mind you, but I'm laughing at something *ludicrously* funny that you just murmured towards me. Got it? Good.]

Right. So.

Yes.

Uh ...

Anna K's been a bit absent lately, hasn't she? Well, she took a few days off here and there for personal and family reasons, you see. She can't just live to entertain you all day long, now can she? Well, I guess technically she *can,* but rather she chooses not to, what with the repetitive business of garnering a paycheck in order to pay for rent and utilities and whatnot. She's become quite accustomed to that sort of thing. And I already mentioned the family thing, which, if you don't mind me saying so, is really none of your bloomin' business, is it? I don't even say "bloomin,'" you've just got me so upset with your arrogant nosiness and gossip munching. Really, you should be ashamed of yourself. Look at you. Disgusting. Horrid. Filthy. It's really ... quite ... sexy, actually, you dirty, dirty, disgusting girl, you. Or boy. Whatever. I'm flexible.

[Another shot of me. I'm wearing a black turtleneck and I'm looking upward. Sly grin. Could that possibly be the sparkle of sunlight in my blue eyes? Yes, it could. Lovely. Lovely. Perfection. Yes. Yes!]

So, there's that.

Okay. Now. Let's see here ... urh, right. What else did she want me to say? Huh. Right forgotten, it seems. Oh, well. Have I mentioned just how charming I look in these pants? They're quite stunning. It's the way they caress my buttocks as I sit in this chair. I can't stop rubbing my hands over my thighs. And, uh, well, it's embarrassing to say that I'm incredibly bloody nice to the touch right here next to my knee. And ... really ... what I'd like to say is that ... well, I feel pretty, that's all.

But back to gossip and apologies. Right. Uh, there's not much to apologize for around here. It's been rather *illuminous,* actually. I just said the word *illuminous* there without really caring exactly what it means. Just listen to the way I say that word. "Illuminous." It's beautiful. I'm not even sure if it's actually a word, now that I stop to ponder it.

[Photo of me leaning back on a J. Crew director's chair with hands behind head. Legs up, crossed at the feet. Hair falling impossibly perfectly over one eye. Smirk, with teeth, on right side. Hot damn on a biscuit, I'm a sexy bitch.]

Right. Moving on, then.

So, in any event, I do believe I'm starting to tire. That happens when I have to lay the charm on rather thick, and since I've spent most of this time sort of rambling on about this and that, I haven't really done anything more than chat and pose, which is the reason Elizabeth and I didn't work out in the first place. Honestly, that woman chats and poses all day long and when the two of us would get started, well, you know ... by the end of the day my jaw was practically on fire. I mean, do you have any idea what it's like to be witty and charming day in and day out? You haven't the foggiest, have you? You can't. You're not me.

But that's all right, see. Because, you know ... if there were more than one of me out there, then the world really couldn't take it. Too many babies would be born from Hugh fantasies. And don't you play the innocent. I know you think of me every time you go for that ... urm ... shower massager thingy you have.

Right.

I've taken up enough of my time, here. See my movies, hug your mum, eat your greens, and be careful on Sunset Boulevard.

[Last one. Full-on smile with wit and charm oozing from pores with a face that makes you say, "And ... off go my pants!"]

Love until later,

Hugh Grant

000020.

I had spent the past four weeks in a daze, calling my parents every night. Dad was always already asleep and Mom had no news. They seemed to be constantly waiting on test results, doctors' opinions, referrals, or something to be delivered from a lab. Dad was on medication that made him tired, and he would only be awake for a few hours a day. I rarely caught him during those times, and when I did, he'd tire easily after a few minutes of light conversation. I felt so far away from my family and completely helpless.

Meanwhile, I was trying to live past the summer heat, to make it through September. I found myself spending longer hours at work, writing longer letters to LDobler about the need for Texas to create seasons, to participate in the passing months of the year. He did his best to keep my mind off of my problems at home. He didn't know all of the particulars, but he knew I was troubled; he didn't pry for details.

I was closing up the library one Friday afternoon in late September when a girl rushed up to the desk.

"Hey, can you do me a favor?" she asked. "It won't take all that long, okay?"

She looked at me with serious dark eyes. I recognized her from an earlier class that day. Her black hair was pulled back in a ponytail and her bangs were bright red. Her skin was a pretty brown shade. Her ears were pierced several times. She had a hoop through her right eyebrow. She was chewing gum and leaning forward on the desk, full of that attitude so many kids had when they came into the library, as if I were the one making their lives inconvenient.

"I'm about to leave. Sorry," I said, and started to back away. I didn't feel like dealing with some punk kid asking me to write a paper for her.

"I need you to do this thing really quickly, okay, Miss?"

"Anna. Call me Anna."

"Look, I need a grown-up to sit here with me for a few seconds. You're, like, old enough, kinda, right?"

She explained that she needed me for a group she had organized. Right before they were to have their first meeting today, her adviser had dropped out. She had to have a staff member or faculty person present in the room to hold a meeting.

"There has to be somebody else you can ask," I said to her.

"If I ask anyone else, they'll make me fill out all of those papers and shit again. Please, Miss. We'll be so quiet we won't even bug you." She put her hand on her forehead and pushed back her bangs until they formed tiny red spikes over the top of her fingers.

I checked my watch. I didn't have anything waiting for me at home and I could use the time to write an entry, but I didn't want to be stuck at the school for another hour.

"Fifteen minutes," she promised.

I waved my hand. She turned around and called for the group of four girls standing in the doorway. They rushed forward and spoke in quiet voices.

"Thanks, Miss," she said back to me, her ponytail whipping around. She still wasn't smiling. "We'll be, like, twelve feet away."

Twelve feet. That was three of my asses.

She sat at the end of the table and let the group of girls do most of the talking. Five girls chatted in a mixture of English and Spanish as they played with their cell phones and two-way pagers. Two of them didn't sit, but just dangled over the table. They were the two that talked the most. The other three nodded and shook their heads at the appropriate times.

I coughed when twenty minutes had passed. Red Bangs looked up at me and said to her group, "Okay, you guys? We have to go, but we'll meet again next week, okay? And next time come up with a name for the group, okay?"

The four girls never stopped talking as they left the library. Red Bangs walked up to my desk. "That was cool of you," she said to me.

"Doesn't sound like much of a group," I said.

"Yeah, well, we're new." She had her hands jammed into her jacket pockets, and she was rocking on her heels.

"What kind of a group are you, exactly?" I asked her.

"I don't know yet," she mumbled, popping her gum in the back of her mouth. "I want to go to a good college, and I was reading in this book that lots of colleges want you to, like, have been in groups and stuff, but all the groups here in this school are shitty. And I thought it'd look better if I had my own group that I was the leader of. You know, to show, like, leadership and stuff?"

I laughed.

"Shut up. You know what I mean," she said. That's when I saw her smile for the first time. She had clear braces with red rubber bands.

"So, the group's just your friends, then?" I asked.

"Yeah, kinda. I mean, I guess I could invite others, and I'd like to, but I don't want to do it until I know what kind of a group we are. I want to be a group that, like, has power or can change something."

She was following me as I shut down the library. "I want, like, a group that makes controversy, where, like, we can all talk and have rallies and people can say that we did something, you know? I mean, I want to, like, do something."

"I think Toastmasters is out," I said.

"Okay, so I'm pretty sure that was a dis, but I'm gonna ignore it instead of kicking your ass because you helped me out today. I fucking hate Miss Carlisle for ditching me at the last minute."

Theresa Carlisle was a sophomore English teacher. Word around the teacher's lounge was that she was an amazing drunk.

"Oh, hey, you have to sign this," she said to me. "To prove you observed."

I signed the paper. "Next week you could ask your group to come up with things they're interested in. You don't have to do it all on your own. Maybe they already have something they want to change. Besides killing that girl in your gym class, which is all I heard you talking about today."

"Good idea," she said to me. She held out her hand. "Smith."

I shook her hand. She was strong. She wore rings on the upper parts of her fingers. Her nails were long and painted green. She had written phone numbers in purple pen on the back of her hand. "Smith?" I asked.

"It's a name," she said as she rolled her eyes. "Next week, you tell the group what you just said, okay?"

I turned around from locking the library door. She was already walking down the hallway as I shouted, "I'm not your adviser."

She turned around and kept walking as she held up the piece of paper I had signed. "You are now, Miss!"

000021.

Subject: Begging For Your Help

Dear Hugh Grant,

I waited a little while before writing because I know you're a busy man (what with the chatting and posing and whatnot),

but I thought I'd ask you for a favor. Our friend Anna K's a bit
down in the dumps these days. She's going through a pretty
rough time. She hasn't told me everything, and she certainly
doesn't have to, but from what I've been told she needs
something to boost her spirits. I can write to her all day long,
but my words can't do anything that looks or feels like a hug.
So the next time you see her, would you mind holding her for
a while? Do all that charming crap you do so well. Make her
forget things are sad for a little while. Thanks.

Actually, she probably can get a hug anywhere, so you might
want to hike it up a notch or two. Thrill her, you know? Give
her something memorable. I guess I'm just flat-out asking
you to sleep with her. Please have sex with my friend. Will
you fuck Anna K for me? Come on—it's not that big of a
deal. I'm sure you've slept with worse. Actually, I know you've
done worse (and yes, I guess Elizabeth Hurley might be
considered "better" and therefore it's all evened out. I hear
you, Hugh, I'm just trying to make a point here. Stay with
me). Anyway, from what I hear, Anna's not too bad-looking.
Don't tell her I said this, but I'm dying to know what she
looks like. Will you write me and tell me how it went? I'm
going to need all the dirty details. Just do the deed and spill
the goods. Don't be a pussy, Hugh. Just do it. Come on! Help
a Pittsburgh brother out, my British friend.

If you do this for me, Hugh, I promise to rent *Notting Hill*. I
will additionally promise to watch it. But if you make me cry
again like I did at the end of the last movie of yours I saw, I
will never support your films again. Quit making me look like
a sap.

Give her a kiss for me, Hugh. A nice, deep tongue kiss until
she can't see or breathe. Then please, please, please e-mail

me. Or take pictures and mail them to me. Or you could call
me while it's going on. Come on, Hugh. Don't let me down.

-LDobler

Subject: re: Begging For Your Help

LDobler,

She was fantastic. Really, just . . . I can't even . . . She made
me weep, LD. Weep. Could anything ever be that beautiful? I
now believe in God, in higher powers. We were put on this
gorgeous earth for a reason, and that reason is to bow at
the . . . sort of . . . *altar* of Anna K's secret garden. I'll never
be able to repay you, to thank you enough. What an
incredible creature she is. Fantastic. Brilliant. You totally
missed out.

Orgasmic-ly spent (six times!),
Hugh Grant

Subject: re: re: Begging For Your Help

HG,

"Secret garden"? Gross, man. Get off her before you turn her
into something perverse. Go film something. I changed my
mind. I'll kick your ass, I swear. You aren't so tough. And how

old are you, anyway? Let her go. You're going to ruin her for
everybody else.

-LD

P.S. But send naked pictures of her first, okay?

We went on like that, flirting and writing. LDobler sometimes
made me laugh until I was bent over cramping. It was like he was
inside of my head, whispering little jokes and sharing stories that
nobody else could hear. We were passing notes in class, trying to
write as much as possible before the last bell rang. It felt incredibly intimate. We never seemed to tire of each other, and I found
myself spending hours out of my day telling him childhood stories and hopes for the future. Amazingly, wonderfully, he did the
same.

We talked about his past relationships, about how his last
girlfriend was the heartbreak of his life. They had been together
for five years when she decided to spend a year in Europe. She
said she wanted some space, to decide what she wanted to do
with her life. LDobler said he understood and she left with both
of them assuming they'd be back together when the year was up.
But she hasn't called him once. Her parents tried to reassure him,
telling him to be patient, but he knew he'd been dumped.

I got the feeling that he was older. His discussions of college
seemed farther away than my stories were. He had a group of
guy friends he'd known for a long time, but they were all in the
process of getting married and starting families. He found himself alone in the evenings often. He said that he used to use that
time to paint, but lately he'd been spending that time with me. I
was happy to have his company. Just about every other hour

there'd be something new from him in my inbox. In the morning I would devour his words while I sipped a cup of coffee—both substances were just as addictive, satisfying. At night his were the words I'd read like a bedtime story, making him the last person I talked to before I fell asleep. On the best nights, our conversations would carry on in my dreams.

We once spent an entire day e-mailing song lyrics to each other. I don't even remember how it got started, but by the end we had an entire conversation in song. He sent the words to "Do You Want To Know a Secret?" and I sent back "I Do." He later sent Monty Python's "Henry Kissinger" and I answered with "Here Comes Your Man."

Over the past few weeks I had started writing Post-It notes to keep all of my stories straight. Between the online stories, the stories I shared with LDobler and Tess, some of the fiction, and some of the truth I had told as well, I needed to make sure I didn't contradict myself. The notes became so numerous I had to start color-coding them. Family stories were on blue Post-Its. I had fake names for my parents and sisters, and in a horrible moment of ego I told Tess that I had a younger brother who died at summer camp.

I had yellow Post-It notes for lies about Ian. I told LDobler that Ian and I often went to the batting cages, since Ian loved baseball. I told Tess that Ian and I were thinking of getting married because we both wanted to start a family soon. In reality, I think the entire time Ian and I were together we had only discussed marriage once in a drunken fit of sloppy love. Whenever we had spoken of children, it was with our lips curled, warning each other not to get any ideas.

Green Post-It notes were about my fake acting gigs. Readers of my website were told about a play I was in that was loosely based on Dale's actual screenplay. I used it to see if Dale was still reading. He was, and sent an e-mail threatening to sue for copyright infringement, adding that he'd like me to forward any e-mail I got praising his story. I did get an e-mail from someone asking when the production was going up so she and her friends could come and see it. I didn't answer the e-mail. I hoped that if I ignored it long enough she'd forget she ever asked.

They weren't lies, anyway. They were the life of Anna K. The Post-It notes just reminded me of the differences between Anna Koval and Anna K. Okay, Tess and LDobler didn't think they were talking to a fictional character. And I felt guilty about those lies. But at this point LDobler knew more truth than fiction, and I knew I wasn't ever going to meet either of them, anyway. Did they still count as lies if most of them *wanted* to be true?

Then suddenly September was over. The heat was starting to break and the promise of cooler weather was just around the corner. I woke up one morning to find that I had fallen asleep on the futon with my laptop resting on my legs. I was seated cross-legged, my head dropped back against a cushion, my mouth slack, a line of drool dribbling to my chin. It felt shameful. A pathetic image: a girl having a romance with her laptop. Sleeping with an iBook. Carrying on day in and day out with a machine.

As I rubbed the aching muscles in my neck, I looked over my empty apartment and felt the cold wave of acceptance. Everything that had happened over the summer, every emotion I felt or story I shared, was all in my head. Silent. There was no talking, no touching, and no human contact. My apartment didn't echo with the sounds of new love. It was just me, a quiet cat, and an intricate web of Post-It notes sprawled across one wall. It looked so complicated, so deliberate. Fake. I had been spending my days absorbed in fake relationships. I'd been filling my head with fans. They were just fans, after all. They were people who loved Anna K, not me—people who lived far away who had no idea what I really looked like. I'd spent weeks writing to people who didn't know the sound of my voice.

I'd made it through the summer only to find I was physically in the exact same place I'd been months ago. And now it was

October first, the day that would have been my four-year anniversary with Ian. Where was he now, I wondered? It seemed that he had moved forward, or was Susan just his way of submerging himself in distractions? No, he probably wasted no time getting over me. I was the only one lingering in the past, making it the present in someone else's life.

000022.

happy me
the anniversary girl
01 October

It started very innocently four years ago today. There was a boy. There was a girl. They were both at a very lame party. There were beers. There were cigarettes. There was a way he leaned back against a railing to smoke. There was a way she'd pull her hair back when she laughed. They found each other fascinating. They listened to a conversation that didn't involve either of them as they stole glances at each other. She liked his hands. He liked her chin.

She stood up for no reason. He took a step closer. Finally the room filled with laughter at a joke neither the boy nor the girl heard. They moved toward each other like it had been an order, like they had no choice. They stood face-to-face. She spoke first: "I'm going for more beer. Do you need some?"

Were more romantic words ever spoken? Wasn't it obvious from that moment right there that the two of them were destined to be in love forever? That he was going to fall so hard for her that he never wanted to come up for air again? Couldn't you feel it? Couldn't you smell it?

And that boy and that girl started with that keg, and the pumping motions continued from the refill to his bedroom late that night. The smell of dried Bud Light and Marlboro Lights lingered on their skin until the morning. They woke up and nursed their hangovers with some instant coffee he found in a drawer. It was stolen from a roommate and it tasted like new love.

The romance continued through the years. Their bodies changed shape. They fit together perfectly in bed, their own territories clearly marked out. He had his own blanket; she had four pillows. He grew to love her cat. She grew to understand the importance of leaving a hallway light on for bogeymen.

That boy and that girl found their own home together in a small place that held all of their things. They twined their belongings together— their books, their music, their lives—ignoring logic or reason, allowing *The Miseducation of Lauryn Hill* to sit beside *Hootie and the Blowfish* with total reckless abandon. Their love knew no boundaries.

Sure, there were problems and fights. She liked to cuddle and he liked space. She was sloppy, but he liked a clean kitchen. She stayed up late while he wanted to sleep for nine hours a night. They made compromises, as all great lovers do, and still found time for sex at least once every week or so.

He once gave her a rare J. D. Salinger and told her he hoped one day a girl would feverishly desire an Anna K limited edition. She once blindfolded him and drove out to a racetrack where he raced go-carts with five of his best friends from back home. He told her that she was the nicest person he'd ever met. He was her best friend.

He once told her that he can't stand the smell of her when she's on her period. She once said that the feeling of his dick dragging on her thigh during foreplay sometimes made her nauseous. He once got very drunk at a party and kissed another girl. So did she. They made up once they found out they had both kissed the same girl. He once told her to fuck herself. She once said he'd never really made her come. They both took everything back, but they were all still said. They still made marks, leaving both of them a little sore.

He talked about her as if they'd been together since they were children. She couldn't stay mad at him for longer than a day. They made other people want what they had. They continued to grow together, learning more and more about each other every day. They found each other fascinating. They sometimes found each other revolting.

Four years. Four years ago today that boy found that girl and their lives changed permanently. They stopped being one person and became a team, a couple, and a relationship. For this girl, at least, it's been the best thing that's ever happened to her.

Happy Anniversary, Ian.

Love until later,

Anna K

000023.

"Is that from your boyfriend?"

Smith was standing over my shoulder. I didn't hear her come up behind me.

I was reading the latest from LDobler and was so far away from the library that Smith could have stolen my wallet while I was reading. "Not exactly," I said to her.

"Long-distance boyfriend?" she asked. She had gotten friend-lier with me since I'd been monitoring her weekly meetings. She was three weeks in now and her group was starting to get restless. They knew they wanted to have a rally by the end of the year. Now they had to figure out which of their causes was worthy of all their energies.

"He's just a friend," I said. "Smith, you aren't supposed to be back here behind my desk."

"Yeah, they sure do make lots of rules here, don't they, Miss?" She smiled at me and popped her gum. She sat on my desk and opened up a magazine. "I'm bored with my class so I told my teacher you were helping me with Action Grrlz."

They had come up with a name, at least.

"You know how Sandra wanted us to do something about animal rights? Well, it's hard because we don't have cars, so we can't go and, like, protest the circus."

"There's Rodeo Day here at school."

"Yeah, but I won't be here then. We get the day off."

I looked over at her. "Because you're supposed to be at the rodeo."

"Ugh, it's not even about the rodeo. Nancy's all pissed off because she wants the group to focus on something environmen-tal and she says her dad works in oil and she can swipe some stuff from his office for our rally, but I don't really want to do any-thing illegal. They all want to be renegades and shit. I want to get out of Austin. I want to go to a good college."

"There is a good college in Austin, Smith."

Smith rolled her eyes and pulled up her belt. "I'm so sick of Austin," she whined.

She sat down on the floor and leaned back against a file cabi-net. "Why are you talking to me like a teacher today?" she asked. "You haven't even told me how kick-ass my new shoes are."

They were kick-ass. Black platform boots with a nice chunky buckle in the front. Red flames surrounded the toe.

"They're very cool," I said. I didn't know how she had picked up on my mood.

"What's your problem, Miss?"

"Nothing," I said. "I was just thinking. You ever been in love, Smith?"

She wiggled up her nose and pulled her head back. "Yeah. I'm not a nun or anything."

"I'm not trying to insult you," I said.

"Yeah, I've been in love. Is that why you're upset? You're in love with the boy that's just a friend?"

"No. Today would have been my four-year anniversary with my last boyfriend."

"When did y'all break up?" she asked.

"Almost a year ago."

Smith huffed and stood up. "You are the boy-craziest girl I know. A year ago? Man, I'm sorry you're so sad. It's sad that you're sad, but a year's a long time. I broke up with Dustin after we'd been going out for almost my entire sophomore year and he was devastated. He still calls my house and he sometimes, like, rides my bus just to walk me home and I'm all, 'Give up, Dustin! It's over!' You know?"

The bell rang. Smith hitched her backpack over her shoulder. "I think you should go out and celebrate. You and me should go do some tequila shots or something."

She put her hand on my shoulder and looked me in the eye. "You're too pretty to be like this," she said. "Go out and buy some new clothes or something. Get laid."

Sympathy from high school juniors. How very sad.

000024.

"Hello?"

Damn, he sounded exactly the same.

"Hi."

Damn.

"Hi. Anna?"

"Yeah." I heard my voice crack. I squeezed my free hand into a fist. I cracked my knuckles by clenching my fingers. I felt the blood rush through my joints, into my wrist.

"Oh. Could you hold on? I've got someone on the other line."

He clicked over and I was left with silence. The forced pause gave me the first moment to think about what I was doing. I was calling my ex-boyfriend because I missed him on our anniversary. The anniversary we weren't having. His anniversary with Anna K that he wasn't even aware of because he didn't know he was dating an Internet entity.

The truth was I missed him. Maybe it was because there was no one else in my life to miss and I refused to yearn for an invisible pen pal. I wasn't going to be an Internet freak. It was wrong to pine over someone unattainable, someone who lived very far away and hadn't even met me. At least Ian was real. Tangible. He was made of flesh within my grasp. And just like the pain inside of me, he was vividly palpable.

I heard him click back over.

"Hey, Anna." He sounded like he'd been having a great day in a great week in a string of great weeks in this spectacular month, all part of a gigantically phenomenal year that had just been on the up and up ever since he walked out of our home and out of my life.

"Hi." I went out to the balcony and sat on a milk crate. I lit a cigarette and heard him do the same. I didn't know what his new place looked like, so I imagined him as a mirror image of me, though I doubted his knees were trembling.

"I was just thinking about you," he said. His face just had to have matched mine. Smiling and warm, looking like he'd found something he'd lost. He remembered everything. He knew what we meant to each other.

"Really?" I thought that sounded casual enough.

"Yeah, I was listening to the Beastie Boys, and I think this CD is actually yours. You want it back?"

Ow.

Clearly his face looked nothing like mine. He just always looked that happy. New and Improved Ian didn't need to call on our fake anniversary. He didn't need a damn thing at all. In fact, he didn't even need my Beastie Boys CD anymore.

I cleared my throat, pushing away the emotions fighting inside of me. I let it all go with a breath, telling myself it was good to hear how stable he is now. If Ian was fine with things, I could be fine with things. Maybe we were moving into that territory old lovers sometimes go where they stay close friends, having shared so many experiences that they become like siblings. I could make Ian into a brother. It could be healthy.

"That's okay," I said. "Just tell it I miss it."

I heard him laugh through his exhale of smoke. "I will."

We talked for a while. He went on about how things were for him, including his relationship with Susan, which he said was going well. He asked if I was seeing anyone. I avoided a direct answer by changing the subject entirely.

"We should go out," new Sister Anna said casually. "Dinner or something. Susan could come, too, I guess." Adding the girlfriend seemed like the sisterly thing to do. Sisters didn't mind girlfriends at dinner, right?

"Yeah, let's do that. Susan's busy Saturday night, so I've got nothing to do. Want to meet at Chuy's?"

That was our old Mexican food restaurant. Sister Anna was quickly morphing into Misty Ex.

"Sure," I said. "My treat." I guess for our anniversary present. The words were almost an autopilot response to making plans, as I often paid his way for things when we were together. I had a higher-paying job for a little while, and the guilt over having more money than my boyfriend resulted in me often splurging on the two of us so he never had to discuss his lack of money. I ended up spending way too much on the two of us, and he got used to me being the one to pay for things.

"Thanks!"

"Yeah," was the only thing I could think to say.

"You know today would have been our four-year anniversary."

And just like that, Misty Ex turned into Wishful, Wistful Anna Koval. He remembered. He hadn't changed too much. He was still Ian. Maybe he could still be *my* Ian.

I got off the phone and found my CHANGE list. I had taped it to the inside of my bathroom cabinet, where I was sure Dale wouldn't find it and tease me.

NEW HAIRCUT.

I'd get a new haircut for the imaginary anniversary dinner date and make him yearn for me. I'd show up collected, positive, and loaded with self-esteem. I'd pay for the dinner not because I accidentally offered, but because I *could*. I'd show up gorgeous because I *was*. I'd shove away my feelings because they were *pathetic*.

Saturday afternoon I handed the stylist a picture of Jennifer Aniston on the cover of *People,* assuming hundreds of girls asked for Jennifer Aniston's hair every day, ensuring the stylist would be skilled at that particular haircut. I wanted something different, but I didn't want a challenge. I wanted trendy, but not something that only looked good in certain clothes. Something that I could pull up and get out of my face if I needed to, but still made old boyfriends yearn to be back in that place between your legs where it's soft and smooth and smells like honey.

As the hair fell away, I couldn't stop shaking my head back and forth. My entire head felt lighter. The stylist must have cut off about five inches. He gave me Betty Page bangs that I wasn't too sure about but he promised I'd look great in. When he had finished and swirled me around in the chair to face the mirror, I lost my breath.

I looked horrible. My stomach sank as I felt the hot sting of tears behind my eyes. I started blinking, as it was very important to me that I not cry inside the salon. I knew the stylist had seriously fucked up my head because other stylists came by to coo over how great my head looked. They only get the other stylists to do that when someone's head looks like it fell on a buzz saw.

It wasn't until after I left the salon that I started to calm down. I saw a few people watch me walk to my car, and my gait became more and more confident as I counted off the number of glances in my direction. I caught a reflection of myself in a shop window, and when I couldn't see my face my hair didn't look so bad. Wait. Had I just decided the problem was my face?

Once in my car, I was convinced that all of the staring was because I had, in fact, become a hottie. I'd never been a hottie before, so I wasn't used to all of the attention. I calmed down, settling into my new role as a "Did You See That Girl?" girlie. At a red light, a man took off his sunglasses to look at me. I thought we had canceled that maneuver back in the '80s.

When I was seven, I had a friend named Wanda, who was the sweetest girl in the world. She had short brown hair that curled under her big ears and these huge green eyes that looked so innocent. She laughed very quietly and was the nicest girl I'd ever met. We were in Brownies together. Wanda had a tiny happy-face stamp that I coveted. She never knew. I stole it. She never knew that either. I leaned over one day during Art and swiped it out of her pencil box. Wanda assumed that Jesus needed to borrow her smiley-face stamp. She thought Jesus wanted to make a few stamps on his sticker book. I heard her say a prayer right before recess, asking Jesus to return her stamp when he was done with it. I was so guilt-ridden that I snuck back into the classroom during recess and tossed the stamp on the floor. She thanked Jesus for returning her stamp.

I've never forgiven myself for stealing from my best friend. I've never forgiven myself for letting her think the Lord takes things from little girls when he wants to play with art supplies. Because I'll never be able to build enough Karma points to fix what I did with Wanda and her stamp, the Lord has punished me by sending me Dale. Dale is the best person in the entire world, and he's replaced Wanda effortlessly. The problem is Jesus put honesty inside Dale. Lots of it. More than I need, ever. There are times when I forget how honest Dale can be. Then I go and get a haircut, convince myself that I've turned into a *Maxim* cover girl, and show up on his doorstep.

"Holy shit," he said as he answered the door in shorts and a T-shirt that read I DON'T THINK I LIKE YOU ANYMORE.

"Or you could say hello."

"Someone owes you a lot of money. You look like a Muppet."

"It's bad?" I touched the top of my scalp and smoothed down my bangs.

"You're staying here until it grows out."

I walked into his house and plopped on the couch. "I'm supposed to look like Jennifer Aniston."

Dale stared at me, motionless, still holding the door. "That's the saddest thing I've ever heard," he said quietly.

"No, I've got something sadder." I took a pillow and covered my face so only my mouth stuck out. "I have a non-date with Ian."

As Dale listed the many reasons why he should be in charge of all of my decisions from now on, he tried to salvage what was left of my hair. We tried bandanas, but I looked like I was about to clean my apartment. Despite insisting how horrible I look in hats, he made me put one on. Dale's never looked at me the same since. "I mean, you don't normally look like Dianne Wiest," he mumbled. He plopped the hat back on my head. "Now you're Dianne Wiest again. Strangest thing."

I named my haircut Betty, because Betty is the kind of name that you can hate without needing a reason. I hated Betty for making me think for even a second I was a Jennifer.

That night Betty was ready for my non-date long before I was. I was standing naked in my closet when Ian called to say he'd be an hour later than he originally expected. He called again forty-five minutes later to say he'd be another half hour. On any other evening I'd be fuming, but tonight I was grateful. I used the extra minutes to wet my hair completely and dry it again. I pinned the bangs back with a barrette, but they spiked up like baby hair. I released the bangs and slicked them down on either side. Then I sat on my bathroom floor and cried for a little while.

I decided to act like Betty was on purpose, that I'd invited her into my life. If I felt that I looked good, then I'd look good, right? I also wore bright red lipstick. Draw attention to the mouth, away from the head. Please, gentlemen, don't look at Betty. She doesn't like all the attention.

Chuy's is a rather silly Mexican food restaurant. One room is covered in plastic fish ornaments. There's a giant shrine to Elvis. Another room has hubcaps cluttering the ceiling. But they make a mean margarita and the place is always rocking with loud music and tipsy college kids, so Ian and I spent many, many hours there over our years together. I hadn't been back because the taste of their tomatillo sauce made me too nostalgic.

I was leaning against the front door holding one of those vibrating pagers when I saw him pull up. The warm, comforting smell of fresh tortilla chips wafted over me and I tried to keep calm. I saw him get out of his car. The pager jolted to life in my hands, and my heartbeat kicked up a notch. It probably would have happened anyway, because I saw he was wearing a shirt I'd bought him for Christmas a few years ago—a blue button-down that brought out his eyes and made him look like a movie star. He must have worn it for me. He walked closer, smoking a cigarette, his head down as if it was raining. He looked up and saw me. He smiled.

I forgave him for being late. For being my non-date. For everything he did and didn't do. Something in the way that boy smiled just made everything fine. My body had that same breathless, dizzying reaction it always got around him. It felt like falling forward, my feet weightless, my head high above my body as an awed voice whispered deep inside me, "Ain't he something?"

I hated it and I loved it equally.

000025.

Subject: sad drunk boy.

AK,

Forgive me if I skip the happy-happy in my e-mail tonight. While I usually flirt with ferocity and reckless abandon, this evening I'm feeling like a total loser.

My ex-girlfriend. The one I thought I was going to marry? The girl I love more than anyone else in the entire world? The one who loves Europe more than she loves me? Well, she also loves some French guy more than she loves me. Apparently. I just heard she's getting married.

I heard this from a friend of mine who has a girlfriend who's friends with her, so it's practically fifth-hand information, but I can't help but feel like it's probably true. She's probably getting married. She's probably totally in love and so happy that she's out of my clutches forever.

France. I know nothing about France. I know nothing about French men. Are they better? Is his name Jacques? Is he a better kisser, just by his nationality?

I'm drunk, by the way. Totally drunk. Very drunk. I even went so far as to pull out old letters she wrote and I even watched a videotape that we made. To quote something I often hear you say, "I'm disgusting." You aren't allowed to tell anyone.

(Hey, don't tell anyone this either: I still have some naked pictures of her. What am I supposed to do with them?)

I found the last letter she ever wrote to me. It says right here: "I love you. I love you forever. I will love you forever. I can't believe how strong and secure that feeling is. Love forever. It's the one thing that feels safe in my life. It will always be there. Just like you will always be there and I'm here for you."

Can I sue her over this? Because here it is in writing, and now she's marrying some guy from France. I like calling him that because he sounds made up. Some guy from France. (Don't worry that I'm so overcome with grief by this letter that I'm clutching it to my heart, soaking it in tears, because the next sentence says, "I feel like I'm finally loosing all of my inhibitions." She never could spell for shit. I'm gonna go find me a good speller. One who knows how to use an apostrophe, you know what I'm saying?)

Hey. I bet you're hot. I bet there are all sorts of places on your body that drive men wild. Oh, man. I'm drunk. Ignore this.

But also: Are you hot?

-LD (the booze hound)

Subject: re: sad drunk boy.

LDobler,

Poor thing. By the time you read this you'll surely be nursing a hangover. So grab some aspirin, a cup of coffee, wrap yourself in a blankie, and let Anna K soothe your pretty head.

That sucks about the ex. I'm sorry. I don't even know what else to say about that, really. Do you want to talk to her? Do you want to find out if it's true? Do you miss her or do you miss what you might have had? I'm asking lots of questions because last night I went out with an ex-boyfriend. I don't really want to go into any specifics, but I feel like he thinks his life is better now that we're not together, and I want to see him in pain. I want him to wince when I brush my hair back and smile. I want to see him need me.

I guess we never want to see them move on, do we? We want them on pause where we left them, always wishing they were still with us. We want to be the strong ones, don't we? But here's my secret: I'm not always that strong. I have so many flaws. And when I looked across the table at this guy last night, there were times when I would get so mad at him. And then, LD, I swear to you, I couldn't say anything (ha-ha) because I wasn't sure what was real. So much time has passed that it's quite possible I've exaggerated or created entire arguments in my head that never actually happened between us. Isn't that ridiculous? I think I've been creating fights and problems in my head to push the two of us away from each other so I don't dwell on him anymore. . . .

So I go to dinner with this ex and I'm thinking about how cute he is and I'm wondering if we were better people when we were together and the truth is maybe I'm not good enough for anyone. All of my relationships are doomed to be failures. Because I have patterns. Because I date a certain type of man. Because I'm not strong enough to make it work. Because I'm too trusting too soon. For whatever reason. Eventually he's going to move on and marry that invisible perfect person that drives us crazy just like your ex did with the Frenchie.

In my case, I know the person my ex is seeing. That makes it even worse, because I know she's not perfect. I know where I'm better and where I'm worse. I keep comparing myself to everyone, so I can't seem to find a calm happiness about myself.

And you're now probably wondering about Ian, and why I'm out with some other guy who isn't my boyfriend, wishing that he still had the hots for me. Well that is another complicated story that's difficult to explain to you here. Let me put it this way: Ian is the reason I was out tonight. Can I just leave it at that? Great. Another plus of e-mail: You can't get me to say any more than I want to say. So there.

Oh, and I got the Haircut from Hell. I look horrible and now I'm going to stay inside of my house and write to you full-time. So no, I'm not crazy-sexy with a body that stops men cold. Currently I look like I'm auditioning for a role in *Oliver!*

And here's the last thing I'm telling you before I hit "Send" and you read this and judge me: I've made another date to see my ex. This is dumb. I know I'm going to get myself into trouble. I don't seem to know how to stop myself from doing things that make my heart ache.

Don't tell anyone.

-AK

P.S. Wait. Are you hot? Please describe.
P.P.S. Check out these apostrophes: ' ' ' ' (mmm).

000026.

There's nothing that turns Ian on more than emotionally unavailable women. He wants to dig in, break them open, look at their insides, and then move on. He's a relationship spelunker. That night at the Mexican food restaurant I quietly ate nacho chips and politely drank margaritas while listening to him talk about how he's thinking of asking for a raise at his job. I watched him tug his earlobes and scratch the backs of his hands and go through all of his physical tics that I knew so well. I could tell he was comfortable around me. And I knew that the quieter I was, the more intriguing he'd find me. My silence meant I was fine without him. He didn't know I was wondering what he'd think if he ever found out about the webpage. He didn't know that I was dying to tell him about LDobler and Tess. He had no idea that I'd been living in a world where we still slept together every single night. He didn't know what was going on with me and that was his sweetest ambrosia.

So Ian asked me to his house the next Saturday to watch a movie. I followed the directions to his place, convincing myself we were going to have a casual evening—one where we'd talk like adults. Maybe we'd sit and share a bottle of wine, watch the night sky, and laugh at how much we'd matured. We'd take some blame on our past faults. We'd share stories of our love like it was an old friend that had moved away. We'd respect each other and remind each other of our hopes and dreams. We'd have that wistful look old lovers have at the possibilities that never came to fruition. We'd suffer those tiny heartbreaks of what-never-was that made us stronger lovers for our future relationships. As I parked my car on his street, I congratulated myself for being such a mature, independent, modern girl.

Ian answered the door wearing a T-shirt and boxers. He pulled a pair of jeans over his thighs as he informed me we were having popcorn and watching a movie. So much for waxing nostalgic over Merlot.

Continuing the strange John Cusack thing going on in my life, Ian had rented *High Fidelity*, which I'd seen before but he hadn't. I knew what it did to me emotionally. I probably should have warned him what would happen. I watched the movie in silence, a good distance from Ian's side of the couch. I watched Rob, John Cusack's character, mope and wander from one woman to the next, wailing and whining, begging to find out what was wrong with him. I watched him ruin his long-term relationship with a girl named Laura, only to practically stalk her until she came back to him, when he finally decided to just be with her because she loved him in a way he liked being loved.

As soon as the movie ended, I started to leave. But I stopped at the door, holding my jacket in my hands, wondering if I should say something to Ian. Would he know why I was upset?

"Do you want to go get a drink?" he asked.

I didn't know what I wanted. I looked at Ian, wondering what he wanted. What did he really want from me all of those years? Why couldn't he just say it?

"Why are you looking at me like that?" He was standing by his couch, and I was frozen by the door. I could feel the rage bubbling up inside of me. I knew I should have left. I didn't. I just started talking.

"You liked the movie, didn't you?" I asked, more like a challenge than a question.

"I loved it," he answered with total oblivion.

"I knew you'd like it." I walked back and forth, trying to find a spot in the room that was welcoming. I couldn't breathe so well. My insides were twisting with spite and rage. Of course he liked it. He loved it. Anyone would love to watch a movie about himself.

"You say that with so much spite." The more confused he looked, the more I wanted to kick him in the shins.

"Because that movie makes me mad at you." I folded my arms.

"The movie?"

Kick him in the shins.

"The movie, the book, all of it. Mad. Mad!" I was regressing right there in his cheap apartment, standing next to a bar mirror on his wall. The neon light from the mirror hummed in my ear. I walked away from it. I hoped Susan's retinas bled nightly from the Guinness billboard in his living room.

"It does?" He laughed.

"Yes, it does." I wasn't about to be mocked.

"Why?"

I inhaled. "I really don't think you need me to tell you why the movie makes me mad. And if you do need me to tell you why the movie makes me mad at you, then I'm *really* mad at you for not knowing why I am mad at you. You should be apologizing."

"Um . . ."

I tried speaking slowly so he'd understand. "I knew the movie would get me riled up. I knew it, but I also knew you'd really like the movie. And you rented the damn thing. I had no control."

"I did really like it."

"I *knew* you'd really like it."

"I'm sorry."

"No, don't be sorry. I love that movie. Just like the book. I love that book."

"Right." He sat down, defeated. I stood behind his couch, near his kitchen. I was still holding my jacket. I wasn't looking at him. It was as if I was talking to his refrigerator.

"I threw that book across the room when I finished it. I loved it."

"Right."

"But the end makes me want to scream."

"How about you tell me this while I walk you to your car?" He was walking me away from his breakables.

We walked and at first it was quiet. I didn't appreciate him cutting me off like that, like he had decided our evening was over even though I was in the middle of a conversation. He wasn't going to get the last word. Not if I could still breathe.

I stopped him suddenly, grabbing his arm. "Why do men think that being with someone who loves you is settling?"

"Oh, man."

"And why did Laura have to be so boring? She was just there to love Rob and understand Rob and be confused over Rob. Couldn't she have her own passions and desires?"

"I really liked Laura. I thought she was charming. And she did get to have her own thing, like when her father died and she's sad at the funeral. I thought she was normal. Just the most normal person in the movie." He took a step back from me.

I jumped onto the trunk of my car, stomping a bit too hard on the bumper. My brown boots made a decisive clack on the metal. "She's only sad at the funeral so they can have sex," I said.

"To be honest," he continued, "I thought she was a lot like . . ."

Don't say me. Don't say me. Say me and I will throw myself into my side-view mirror. I am not like that weak, boring girl. I am infinitely more interesting than that woman. I'm my own person and not an object for you to validate.

". . . Like a normal person."

But I wasn't listening to him anymore. I kept talking. "I hate that theory where the guy's like 'Well, I'm an asshole. That's my *thing*. I screw up every relationship I've ever been in, and that's how that works. I'm going to be lonely and miserable forever, and occasionally moan about "Me Da" while I down a pint and no one is ever going to love me.' Meanwhile, someone loves him and he doesn't even notice."

"Me Da?"

"You know, like in those Irish books, like Frank McCourt. Always raising a pint to Me Da."

"Jesus, you're hard to keep up with tonight."

My hands flew up, palsied in front of my face, and then slapped down on my thighs. "And Rob's not even learning anything from these relationships. And I hate 'Well, things are going too well with my relationship right now, so there must be something wrong. I bet you don't love me anymore. Or I don't love you. Oops! I just thought it, so now it's a fact. We're breaking up.' "

He wasn't looking at me. I wasn't talking about *High Fidelity* anymore and he knew it. I wanted him to admit that there was nothing wrong with us and that we broke up because he got tired of being in a relationship. He got tired of being two people.

I lit a cigarette. I made myself calm down. "I'm not mad at you. I'm mad that you can identify with the film so easily.

Because when I watch it I think of you and I wish I didn't. I don't want Lloyd Dobler all grown up and miserable because Diane slept with some French boy when she went to Europe."

"What the fuck are you talking about?"

He couldn't possibly understand. He didn't watch films searching for the kind of person to fall in love with. He didn't understand the power of Lloyd Dobler. He didn't even know about my fake Lloyd Dobler who sent letters in the middle of the night.

"I hated how Laura's new boyfriend was such a loser. Laura should have gone out with someone Rob could have a *real* problem with. But since he was lame, Rob's only concern was if she had slept with him yet. Not her happiness. Not if the new guy made her coffee the right way. He didn't want to know if he was funnier or richer or if he stole the covers. But he wasn't worried that someone was loving her better, he just wanted to make sure nobody had sex with her yet."

"He does love Laura." Ian said it quietly, looking down.

"How? How do we know that? Why? Because he finally figured out after two years how to make a mix tape? Buddy, if you didn't know that eighteen months ago—give it up. He wooed her with a mix tape, for fuck's sake."

"But he didn't just move on to the next new thing. He loved Laura and stayed with her."

"He settled."

And there it was. The basis of our breakup, spoken out loud. Ian said he loved me, but then he wasn't sure. Then he decided he was sure, which only succeeded in making me unsure. So then we both weren't sure. I didn't want Ian settling for me. I didn't want to just be "good enough."

Ian lit a cigarette and sat down next to me on the back of the car. I could hear him crafting his sentence. "He didn't settle. He realized that he liked what he had. And other girls might be exciting, but they wouldn't be Laura. You understand?"

"I guess so."

"Then why are you so riled up?"

Because I'm never going to be good enough. Because we missed our chance. Because I'm the only one still in our relationship. Because I'm the only one who remembers how good it was. Because I'm in the past. Because I'm lonely. Because maybe he was the one. Maybe I should have let him settle.

"He's not settling," Ian said again, as if he could read my thoughts. "He's realizing what he has. And he knows it's good."

"But not great."

"He didn't say that."

"Whatever."

Somehow he let me end our conversation with that. He kissed my cheek and held my hand as he searched my eyes. He walked away quietly, that final "Whatever" still floating around my ears. My dismissive tone ended the first conversation we'd had about us in a long time, even though we spoke in fictional characters. It was appropriate, since I'd recently turned our relationship into a work of fiction.

I sat in my car alone. I was afraid to turn the key. I was afraid to drive away. I was afraid of what I'd do next.

When I finally drove home, I read over all the entries I'd posted, looking to see the difference between Anna K and me. Would Anna K settle? Had I made more out of my relationship with Ian than there really was? Or was it possible that the two of us were so good together that it made people like LDobler want just a taste of it?

I felt like I was reaching backwards, desperately trying to find something to hold on to. Suddenly settling didn't seem like such a bad idea. At least settling had a forward motion to it.

000027.

Smith handed me one of her Marlboro Lights.

"You owe me, like, a pack now," she said as she lit up. She gave a quick glance around to make sure we were safe. I couldn't see anybody. We had been sneaking off behind the track bleachers during breaks. A crumpled pink hall pass was half-jammed into Smith's jeans pocket. I couldn't remember how Smith had first convinced me to write out a handful of hall passes, but it felt like she'd been cutting more and more homeroom classes and I had been taking longer and longer breaks as I'd continually bummed cigarettes off her for the past few weeks.

"I can't believe we do this," I said for the tenth time that month. "When did I join the Pink Ladies?"

"You love it," she said with a smirk.

I had to admit that I did. Smith allowed me to play the bad girl. She was my favorite thing about my job. I wish I had been like her when I was in high school. I would have been the one studying in the library while Smith skipped homeroom. Hell, I still was.

I liked hearing about her troubles. There was a comfort in high school woes, a reminder that worlds can shrink and grow depending on how much you let yourself see. Smith's entire world revolved around her college fantasies and she used me as the big sister to debate her new ideas.

"I'm breaking up the group," she said to me. She leaned over the track railing and spit in the dirt near my toes.

"You say that every week," I said.

"For real, Miss. I hate those bitches."

The Action Grrlz were getting larger and larger, but Smith still hadn't found a direction for the group. Every meeting ended in arguments. Smith tried taking the lead by deciding they were going to protest the dress code, and then quickly changed her mind when she realized the dress code wasn't strict enough nor enforced often enough for them to make a fuss. If anything, it'd make the school more aware of the constant violations through-out the student body.

"Everyone's fighting all the time," she said. "I don't think that I should have to choose which direction the group goes in. I like that everyone likes different things. It's all that different shit that makes people interesting. It's boring to all talk about one thing."

"That's a good point," I said.

"Says the girl who only thinks about one thing," Smith teased.

"Then have your group be about making change."

"I want to have a rally to get people motivated to talk to each other about important stuff. Issues. That's what I'll do. I'll have a rally to get more people to join Action Grrlz. It'll be about hav-ing an opinion and expressing it. And in our meetings we'll, like, discuss topics and current events and exchange ideas and theories to stimulate change and shit. Is that a group?"

I put out my cigarette with my toe and smiled at her. "Smith, I think that's a damn fine group."

She smiled back, the rubber bands in her braces giving a quick flash of yellow. She saw something behind me and quickly put out her cigarette. "We gotta go. Coach Butler's coming over here and he'll bust us."

We ran back to the library.

000028.

"I think they broke up back in October."

I watched Dale drink his Cosmopolitan, which he made me order so he didn't have to. He ordered a martini. The Cosmopolitan switch-off had been happening for over a year. Once Dale realized I could order things he was too embarrassed to admit he liked, he made me order everything from salads and chicken nuggets to drinks with umbrellas to IHOP's Rooty Tooty Fresh and Fruity.

Dale handed me an olive and searched my eyes. "It's November. You know that, right?"

"I don't need you to tell me what month it is. And I don't care if they broke up. I mean, I care. I care very much. But I'm not supposed to care, so I don't care." We were on our third round of drinks. "Let me ask you something, Dale. If they broke up back in October, why didn't Ian tell me that when we went out?"

"I don't know. Maybe they hadn't broken up yet."

"Maybe not. But maybe they broke up because when we went out and Ian realized that I'm much more fun that Susan Suckass."

"I like her new last name." Dale lit a cigarette for me.

"I like it too. I made it up myself. I'm special."

"Oh, honey. I know."

I smoked my cigarette and looked around the bar. This was our favorite little hangout on Fourth Street. We liked it because it was dark enough that we'd recognize people who walked in before their eyes could adjust to the darkness. We could slink back further into our booths or even duck out the back door if we needed to.

"You really think you broke them up?"

I exhaled the smoke through my nose as I mulled it over. "Don't you think it sounds like it? Two dates with Ian and suddenly they're Splitsville?"

"I'm going to pretend you didn't just use the word *Splitsville*. And maybe Susan broke up with Ian."

"Because she's jealous of me."

"Ooh! When did you develop an ego?" Dale asked, leaning toward me conspiratorially.

"We can change the subject."

"No, I love the ego. It's about time you started thinking of yourself with some worth. Is it because of Mister Internet?" he asked.

I felt myself blushing. I had finally broken down about two weeks ago and told Dale about him so I wouldn't explode.

"He does help with the ego, yes."

"Well, I think he's a stalker."

"He's not a stalker."

"A stranger writes you letters all day long and you don't consider him a stalker? Didn't you say he quit his job for you?"

"Not for me. For his painting. He had some money saved up. Besides, I write him back. It doesn't count as stalking if I write back, does it?"

"Have you asked him his real name yet?"

"Can we talk about something else?" I didn't want to talk about LDobler too often because I was afraid I'd talk myself out of everything. Seeing how Dale found it freakishly fascinating made me wonder if I should be embarrassed. It was all so narcissistic already. I hadn't ever been so self-absorbed before, my head in a laptop all day long talking about myself to the world, sharing secrets with strangers.

"Hey, tell your dad Happy Birthday for me, okay?"

I choked a bit on my martini. "Shit, you have a good memory. And thank you. I almost forgot to call him before he went to bed." I'd called twice before, but both times he was at the doctor's. Mom told me to try again at night.

"How could I possibly forget when his forty-ninth birthday was one of the strangest weekends I've ever had?"

"It was just golf!" I shouted as I grabbed my cell phone from my purse and headed toward the door.

"It was creepy! I got a rash!"

I walked outside to the front stoop of the bar. Mom answered on the first ring. "Hello?" she whispered.

"Mom?"

"Hi, honey. I thought it was you."

"Is Dad still up?"

"No, you just missed him. He knows you've been trying to reach him."

"Damn." It would have been nice to hear his voice. He was so rarely awake when I called home.

"I'll make sure he calls you tomorrow when he's awake." Her voice was empty, dull, like someone had scooped everything out of her. I imagined her hunched over the table, a cigarette resting on an ashtray, the smoke making worried lines around her head as it rose.

"Mom? Are you okay?"

I heard her make a noise. A crackling sound. I thought my cell phone had cut out on us, but I realized she was just moving her mouth closer to the phone. Her voice had an urgency as she said, "Dad's going to have to go back to the hospital for a while."

I sat on the curb. "Ma, is he okay?"

Mom sighed. "I don't know, Anna. I hope so. He's going to need a blood transfusion and a few tests. We'll have to see what the doctors say, okay? I'll call you when we know."

"Okay."

"Honey, I have to go. I'm just so tired." I could hear her yawning as we hung up the phone.

Before anything could sink in, Dale was beside me, holding my purse.

"Becca called from Spaghetti Warehouse," he said. "We have to go see her."

"Dale," I started to protest.

"The bride-to-be is very testy. Besides, I have to talk to her about renting some more equipment. She wants me to film this wedding from more than one angle, and somehow she doesn't realize that requires more than one camera."

"Dale, I really don't want to. My mom . . ."

"Tell me while we walk."

Dale tucked my coat under his arm and rubbed his hand through my hair. "I'm starting to really love Betty," he said with a smile.

"I thought hair was supposed to grow faster than this," I laughed.

Dale and I were breaking rules by going to Spaghetti Warehouse. We promised each other long ago that we'd never eat in a place with license plates on the walls. Dale added the extra rule of never eating at a place that's also a warehouse. They were pretty good rules. But I had to put in an appearance with Becca since I hadn't returned her last few phone calls and she wanted to discuss the wedding.

When I got home late that night, still slightly drunk from bad wine, I couldn't fall asleep. I was thinking about Dad, wishing that we had more of a history together. I wanted to go back to when things were simpler, when being a daughter meant just doing as I was told and keeping straight A's. Being a daughter had nothing to do with watching someone slip silently away. I wanted to go back to when a father was someone big and strong, an invincible man who never let anything get in his way. I wanted a tough, fearless dad one more time.

000029.

Father Knows Best:
A Lesson in Automobile Maintenance

13 NOVEMBER

I got my first car when I turned seventeen: an '85 Renault Alliance. It was beige, I think, and was very stained and sad and scary. The speedometer didn't work. Once you hit 45 mph, it would kick in and point the needle to 98 (the highest number on the dial) and would make a noise like you were revving the engine. The seats didn't recline, but instead worked like those chairs that lift you when your knees give out. The heater smelled like maple syrup. The stereo didn't work, and a friend of mine offered to fix it. He removed the entire front panel to get to it, and never was able to put it back on correctly. The battery would die every other week. We'd jump the car, charge the battery, and it would die again. We'd buy new batteries, but they'd still die. All of those things I could put up with, but when the brakes started to fail, I got scared.

Initially you'd hit the brake and it would fall all the way to the floor. The car wouldn't slow down at all. You'd have to feverishly pump the brake pedal and eventually it would click with something and jerk the car to a stop. The emergency brake was used in near-death situations.

I told my dad about the brakes and described the "pump action" I was using to stop the car. He informed me that my cylinder needed "repumping" and he had the perfect solution: Drive the car backwards and pump the brakes, "resetting the cylinder."

"I'm not driving home backwards, Ferris Bueller," I said.

"Anna K, I'm serious. You pump the cylinder back up when you do that," Dad insisted, the pop culture reference flying right over his head.

"Dad. I've fallen for many of your tricks. I thought that the reflectors on the street were so blind people could drive. I thought a land shark ripped through downtown Los Angeles, chewing on poodles and killing innocent blondes in bikinis because you told me you saw it on the news. I even for a quick second believed you when you told Shannon the number of spots on a Dalmatian signified how long the dog would live. But this I'm not buying. I'm not driving backwards."

My father has a look that he gives when he wants to prove he's not lying at all. His eyes widen and his mouth opens just a bit. Usually his fingers will extend and his arms will go out, like he's in shock. The look says, "How could you even think for a second that I would deceive you?"

The problem is that Dad is good at faking this look when he is actually lying. If you still say he's lying after he's delivered this look, you enter into Phase Two of Dad's "I am not a liar" dance. The mouth snaps shut. The hands come back down to rest on the chair. He usually kicks the recliner back up and snaps the television on. He'll stop looking at you and merely say, "Fine. Do whatever. You're going to do what you want, and if you don't want my help, then that's fine. See ya."

It's the "See ya" where you know things have gone sour. This is the point where you have to do whatever it is, because you're about to be grounded.

I drove the car to the end of my street, right by the stop sign. I stopped the car, took a deep breath, and popped it into reverse.

I try to imagine this scene from my father's point of view. Dad walked out to the front lawn as I was passing at thirty-five miles an hour, my head cranked sharply to the left behind me, trying not to hit any of the cars parked in the street. I had a wild look, and the scream that he heard as I drove past must have been: "Waaaaaaaaaaaaaah! NOOOO BRAKES IN REVERRRRRRsssse! Aaaaaaaaaaaaaa!"

I stopped the car by slowly rolling to a stop on the curb of a neighbor's yard.

I walked back to Dad, who was standing on the lawn with his hand on his chin.

"Were you really pumping the brake?" he asked.

"Dad, I can't feel my knee, I was pumping so hard."

"Huh."

"You wanna try it?"

Sometimes things work out in your favor. Sometimes you get to see that "Well, I'd like to see him try it" image that you want so badly. Dad must have really convinced himself that this was the way to fix the brake problem, because he took the keys and walked over to the car.

I ran inside the house shouting, "Mom! Dad's gonna drive backwards in my car with no brakes because he doesn't believe me!"

"Oooh! Oooh! Let me see!"

We watched Dad drive all the way down the street and slowly stop the car by the stop sign. In order to do this, you had to grind the pedal like you were putting out a cigarette.

I do wish I had a picture of my dad's face as the car went traveling backwards down our street. He craned his head back and forth, up and down, forward and backward again, fear frozen on his face in a look that screamed, "I'm going to crash and they're going to laugh at me."

He hit the curb with the back of the car much harder than I did. Once the car stopped, he calmly stepped out, walked up to me, and handed over the keys. He never stopped walking away as he said over his shoulder, "You should get the car looked at. There's something wrong with the brakes."

He went inside, and there was never another word spoken about it.

Happy birthday, Dad. Thanks for showing me that you can control the truth as long as you believe in it hard enough.

Love until later,

Anna K

000030.

Subject: You're back!!!!!!

Anna K!

I missed you! You're back! You're back! You're back!

You hadn't written in over a week. Never go away that long again! It made me very sad to be without your words. You are what I do when I don't want to study.

Guess what? I'm in Austin this weekend. I know that you
might be busy getting ready for Thanksgiving, but if you're not
too too too busy, I'd love to get a cup of coffee with you and
meet you face to face! Please? It would make me so happy.

If you're busy, I understand. I'm happy you're writing again.
Anyway, I hope you're well. How's Ian?

Love,

Tess

Replying to e-mail was one thing, but meeting someone that
read my journal? I didn't feel ready for that. What if she saw
right through me? What if I was disappointing in person? What
if I found out that my biggest fan was someone I couldn't stand?

Subject: re: You're back!!!!!!!

Tess,

I'm afraid I'm really busy with work and getting ready to go
home for the holidays. I hope you understand.

-AK

Subject: re: re: You're back!!!!!!

AK,

I understand. It's just that I would really like to meet you in
the flesh. I want to know what you look like, since you're my

hero these days. My friends all tease me for talking about
you so much, but I feel like I've known you for a long time.
Just one cup of coffee. Please? Consider it an early
Christmas present!

-Tess

How bad could she be, anyway? The girl loved me. An hour of
coffee and praise couldn't hurt a Friday afternoon. She was probably harmless.

And, okay, I was really curious to test out a fan. If all went
well with her, maybe I'd be bold enough to meet LDobler someday. If he wanted to. If we wanted to.

So there I was, just under a week later, sitting out in front of
the large, open garage door of the Ruta Maya Coffee House, listening to a jazz trio from inside on the tiny wooden stage. A win-
try wind whipped past my face. I sipped my mocha and tried to
guess which girl was Tess.

She was wearing a green beret. Green like she was about to
sell me some Thin Mints. Green like I was supposed to think of
her as a child. She walked toward me, zoning in on my face,
smiling like we were lovers meeting at an airport after a long sep-
aration. How did she know it was me?

"Look! Famous shirt!" She pointed at my chest. I was wearing
a shirt I had written about a couple of days ago, saying that the
coffee stain on it makes it look obscene.

"It does look like the cat's flipping me off!" she said, her eyes
wide, her finger inches from my chest. I instinctively leaned back
in my chair.

"Go get some coffee," I said to her, smiling my friendliest smile.

"Do you think it's going to rain?" she asked as she looked up.
When her eyes met mine again I saw that she was pouting. The
girl was so young and aggressive. She never even said hello—just

launched into conversation like we'd known each other for years. I wondered if her heart was racing as fast as mine. I worried briefly that she'd brought a gun and she was going to kill me right here next to the couple playing chess.

When she came back with a cup of coffee steaming in her hand, I tried to start over in a more recognizable getting-to-know-you pattern.

"Hi, Tess," I said. I was still nervous, afraid of saying the wrong thing around her. Then I said with a start, "You're name's really Tess, right?"

"Yep." She laughed. Her eyes got wider. "You don't mean your name's not Anna, do you?"

"No, it is." I liked her smile. She had very large green eyes. It was like her entire face was exaggerated. Her cheekbones were rounded. Her hair was blond and short, and flipped at the ends. She looked exactly like what she was: a young girl finishing college who hadn't had anything really horrible happen to her yet, who thought the best about everyone and wanted to "do good" in life.

I smoked cigarette after cigarette, letting her do most of the talking. I started to calm down. Since she was chatty, I felt less like I was on display. To the common observer this would look like a couple of girlfriends getting coffee after work and not the winner of the Win a Date With Anna K contest that I was terrified it had become.

Tess was funny. She'd talk faster than she was thinking and she'd sometimes lose her sentence halfway through. She took big gasps of air before she talked, as if she was about to go underwater to tell me a secret. Her hands moved constantly, and she had a habit of tucking her hair behind her ears over and over again, like it wasn't staying where she put it. Sometimes she'd talk so fast that she spit.

"Did it cost a lot to get your bed fixed?" she asked. "You never said."

"What?"

"The bed. The bed where you and Ian . . . y'all broke it with the . . ."

"Oh! The bed! Yeah!"

Three months ago I had written an entry about us accidentally breaking our bed during a particularly heated night of sex. I guess there weren't enough Post-Its to prepare me for this meeting. She was going to catch my lies eventually. I just hoped I was ready with more lies to patch up the holes when she found them.

"I can't believe you'd forget that."

"I didn't forget it," I said. "I forgot I told all of you about it. No, it's fixed. Sorry."

Tess giggled into her café au lait. "I know all sorts of stuff about you. I guess you would forget some things that you tell us."

Us. Like she was the leader of my fans. A representative. Like I was leading a nation. A tribe. A cult. It was so unreal.

"I thought you'd be taller, Anna." She had her head tilted as she sized me up.

"I thought you'd be younger."

"And you're quieter than I thought you'd be."

"You're wearing a beret."

"You're making fun of my hat?"

I started laughing. It probably wasn't appropriate, as it was too early to be mocking her clothes, but I couldn't help it. There was tension and anticipation and that anxiety that comes with not wanting to disappoint someone. I couldn't get over how I was someone with fans, and I was meeting one of those fans and the entire thing sounded like something that happened to someone else.

Tess pulled the hat off her head and looked at it. "I wasn't going to wear it, but I didn't know how else you'd pick me out of a crowd. I mean, everyone here in Austin is pretty young. Except for you, I mean."

My mouth dropped open. "No, you didn't say that!" I shouted.

"I did! I said it! I'll say it again. You're old."

"You wear ugly hats."

"Oldie." She tossed her hat on the table.

"Hattie." I lit another cigarette.

"Okay, I take it back," she said, as she leaned in to bum another cigarette, this time without asking first. "You're what I thought you'd be."

"And what's that?" I asked her.

She smiled with her head down. Her eyes looked up at me as if she was scheming as her mouth formed the word.

"Fun."

000031.

Subject: I'm terrified of thunder.

Anna Banana (AKA AK),

I promise to never use that nickname again. I was trying it out. I hate it. I feel safe in assuming you do, too. I know you're having important girl time with a new girlfriend. I hope that's going well. I have to tell you, it's strange having you so busy entertaining guests. I'm also jealous that some other fan gets to meet you first. I'm glad to hear you two have hit it off. (Does she get to see your apartment? Do fans get a tour if they come visit? I'll book a flight for the first weekend in December, if that's the case.)

Back to what might be considered a point, I was thinking about how I feel very strange about this. There's no reason in the world that I should physically miss you right now. You're exactly as far away from me distance-wise as you always are. You're also a woman I've never met. But for some reason, not having you there to read my letter as soon as I send it makes me feel like you're away on vacation or off on business. You're "away," even though you're where you always are every day that we've known each other. How is it possible that I miss you?

You'll probably write to me later on tonight, or Monday morning from work, and chances are I'll only get two or three fewer letters than I usually get from you in a weekend, but I can feel those missing letters. It's the damdest thing. (Damndest. Damnest? Damnmdest? Shit. That's what I get for trying to sound proper when I write. The spellcheck on my computer tells me you spell it "dandiest." So there you go.)

Anyway, I guess this all means that you've somehow become a part of my life. You're a part of my day. I think about you, I think about what I'm going to say to you, I wonder what you'll say to me. I have an image of what you look like, what you sound like, and what you smell like. And even though this relationship will probably never mature beyond electronic pen pals, I wanted to take a moment to say I'm really thankful that you're in my life. That's what we're supposed to do this week, right? Be thankful? I mean, I probably won't be able to e-mail you on Thanksgiving, since my parents own what might actually be a Tandy from the late 1980s. I'm thinking it probably doesn't have Internet capabilities since it still uses giant floppy disks (I'm not even sure I'm staying with my parents. I hate sleeping on the couch. My sister has room, but she also has a kid—my niece, Arial, whom I love, but she's young and noisy. So I might go home after dinner, in which case I may very well write to you. Not that you care

about any of this. I'm thinking aloud here. Closing
parentheses, moving on).

Pretend this is your Thanksgiving letter. Happy Thanksgiving.
I'm glad you're here. I'm glad you wrote back to me back in
the day. I'm glad you're my friend.

I just thought of something. What if that girl is actually a crazed
fan and she's already stabbed you with a knife and that's why
you haven't written? What if she's smothering you with a pillow
right now while I'm blissfully smacking my keyboard, blah-
blahing about how cool you are? What if you're dead? I'm a
bad friend. This is why I should have your phone number. Not
that I want it, but just so I can call it and make sure the
message doesn't say, "Hi. Anna K just got killed by her crazy-
teenaged-stalker fan. Leave a message at the beep."

If you are dead, you'll never read this, will you? Wait. If you're
dead, you're a ghost, right? You're already a ghost? So
potentially you could already be visiting me? Here in my
apartment? If that's the case, I'm sorry I'm not wearing any
pants. It's sort of messy in here and rude to be in this state
the first time you see me. I swear, if I knew you were going to
haunt me, I would have taken a shower or something. Put gel
in my hair. Something.

Wait. You don't know where I live. Whew. Safe.

For now.

Sweet dreams, sweet friend.

-LD

000032.

"I need you to wait out here," I said to Tess as we stood at the door of my apartment. "Just give me a second."

"How messy could it be, Anna? I'm sure it's fine." She looked excited, ready to see proof of my private life. My afternoon with Tess had flown by. We kept talking and suddenly we were out of cigarettes, out of cash, and ready to flop on a couch in comfy clothing. I had invited her back to my place for pizza and movies.

"It's not fine," I said, jamming my shoulder into the door as I unlocked it. I slid myself inside before Tess could see anything. "It's beyond messy."

"You're being silly!" she shouted as I closed the door in her face.

The place wasn't just a mess; it was a single girl's mess. The apartment was completely void of anything Ian. I rushed straight away to the recycling bin and found a few empty beer bottles. I left them in random places in the apartment—the bookcase by the futon, the television stand, and my bedroom windowsill. From my bedroom closet I pulled a box of Ian's old things from the top shelf. I dropped his things in their old familiar homes. A pair of his boxer shorts on the floor in the bathroom, right behind the toilet. Another one in the living room, near the bookshelf. A can of shaving cream on the sink. An Oxford shirt on a chair. I didn't have enough guy things. As I walked to the door to let Tess in, I hoped she wouldn't notice.

"Okay, I'm coming," I shouted.

"Finally." Her voice was muffled through the door.

As I put my hand on the doorknob, I looked back over my apartment. It looked like a busy, hip couple lived here, a couple with too much going on to worry about cleaning up. They might have even had sex on that futon recently. The room had a tousled coolness to it.

That's when I spotted the Post-Its of Lies that had grown to mural proportions on my wall. A multicolored explosion of fibs stared me in the face. I frantically found the Weezer poster that used to be taped there, tripping over Taylor in the process. Nursing my stubbed toe, I once again stuck the poster to the wall, shoving random Post-Its underneath the paper. My lies were now safely covered—lies like my parents lived in Houston and that I took ballet for a number of years.

Tess knocked on my door. "Anna, I'm starting to feel rejected!"

I took a breath and opened the door. She looked around and squished her face into a doubtful squint. "I thought you were cleaning," she said.

"Trust me, it was worse," I said, noticing I was a little breathless.

Tess walked around my apartment like she was touring a place she'd been studying in school. She carefully looked over framed photographs, and each time it filled me with anxiety. What did I tell her about that person? Had I mentioned that friend?

"God, is this Ian? He's a total hottie. I knew he would be." Tess was holding a picture of Dale.

I laughed. "No, that's really *not* Ian."

I took a photo album down from a bookshelf. I opened to a picture of Ian and me with our arms around each other. We were at a wedding of a friend of his we both lost touch with. Kevin-something was his name. I think.

"Oh, he's even cuter. You're so lucky. Where is he?"

"On a business trip."

"What does he do?"

"Sales." Sure, why not? Sales. That was nice and vague.

Her eye caught the discarded boxer shorts. I could hear my pulse in my ears as I waited for her response. She looked back at me, her mouth open, her eyes squinted, her tongue touching her bottom teeth. She had to have known. She must have figured it all out. I was about to be exposed.

"Boys are dirty," she said quietly.

Tess and I talked through the night, giggling over stories like we'd gone through five years of school together. She told me about her crazy boyfriend that dumped her by saying she turned him gay. I told her about a boyfriend I had that decided to become Ringo in a Beatles tribute band. We didn't know which one was a more embarrassing story to tell. After a detailed comparison list where we analyzed how those relationships affected all future love affairs, Ringo won. When we finally looked at the time and saw it was after two in the morning, I insisted Tess crash on the futon.

I woke up from a bad dream around four. I dreamt that LDobler was at my high school graduation, and he was telling everyone I had cheated on my Biology final. LDobler was, of course, John Cusack in my dream, and I was trying to explain everything to him. Then he was crying, telling everyone that I ran over his dog with my car. My mother was there, and the bloodied, dead dog was in her lap. She was holding it close to her chest, looking up at me with tears in her eyes. "How could you?" she shrieked.

I couldn't fall back asleep. When I was little, Mom always told me to turn my pillow over if I had a bad dream, because the other side would be cooler. It was the hot side of the pillow that held the bad dream, and by smooshing it back into the bed you could get a fresh dream. But flipping the pillow wasn't working, so I quietly walked through the house to the kitchen for something to drink, as Mom also suggested a very cold glass of water to clean away lingering nightmares. Why all of her nightmare cures involved cooler temperatures I'm not sure.

When I opened the refrigerator door, I jumped. I saw a shape on the living room floor. It was Tess.

She was asleep with a blanket pulled around her. The laptop was open in front of her, but I didn't remember leaving the computer on. I gently placed my hand on Tess's knee.

"Tess?"

She stirred and for a second didn't know where she was. "Oh, Anna. Sorry."

"Why are you on the floor?"

"I couldn't sleep, so I was surfing the net for a little while. I guess I fell asleep here."

"I'm sorry my futon's not so comfortable."

"No, it's great, Anna. It's great. I love that you call it a 'futon.'" She stumbled over to the couch, clutching her blanket between her legs. "You're so technical. It's hilarious."

I noted how tiny she was, seeing her in my high school choir T-shirt and another pair of Ian's plaid boxer shorts I had exhumed from the box. As she curled into a fetal position, Taylor jumped up to sleep on her feet. Tess smiled and closed her eyes.

I heard her rhythmic breathing a minute later as I left with a glass of water. It was only then that I noticed my photo album was off the shelf on the floor by the computer.

The album was opened to a picture of Ian and me on the swing set at the playground near Ian's parents' house. I'm on the swing, and Ian's holding me back against his chest. I'm pleading for him to let me go, and he's holding me back by the swing chains. He's laughing and my face is frozen in a half-terrified grin.

It was then I saw that a yellow Post-It note had fallen off the wall and was on the floor by the album, my own handwriting scribbled across it. "Possible wedding next year?"

Even if she had seen it, she probably didn't know what it was. Of all the Post-It notes to find, at least this one sounded like I was working on a story. Or even if I was talking about myself, it wasn't like it was completely impossible. Maybe Anna K needed to remind herself that she might want a wedding next year. If I were Tess and I found this Post-It, would I think anything about it?

I had to stop worrying and get some sleep. If Tess was really curious, she'd ask me. If she had figured it all out, I'd know in the morning. There was nothing I could do. I picked up the Post-It and crumbled it into a ball. I carried it with me as I closed the album and put it back on the shelf. I picked up the computer, placed it back on my desk, and momentarily debated checking my e-mail. LDobler would have written another letter. I decided to save something for my Sunday afternoon once Tess had gone home. I turned off my laptop, grabbed my glass of water, and quietly made my way through the dark back to my bed.

Again I couldn't sleep. I flipped the pillow a few more times, but by then the entire thing was cool. I changed to a different pillow. I kicked the covers off. I pulled them back on. I took off my pajama bottoms. It wasn't that the nightmare was lingering, I was just completely awake.

In my head, in my dreams, in my fantasies (and even my nightmares) LDobler is John Cusack, dressed as Lloyd Dobler, wearing the outfit he's wearing when Lloyd asks Diane out for the first time. He's wearing a Clash T-shirt and his hair is tousled and he's warm and strong. He's watching me—watching me write him letters. I'm at my computer and I'm reading his words and I'm laughing. I start writing back to him and John Cusack's reading over my shoulder and he begins to laugh, and just as I sit up shocked that someone is there, he's suddenly around me, pressing against my back and shoulders. My bottom feels warm and tingles run down the backs of my legs to my feet. He's kissing my neck from behind. His teeth graze my skin. His tongue slides up to my earlobes. He's sucking and biting gently, but with just enough pressure. My arms are out straight, clutching the sides of my desk as he cups my left breast with one hand and his other hand lowers to my crotch. He pushes against my clothes. His hand is strong and insistent. I push my body into his hands. My back arches to push into him deeper. I can hear his breath in my ear, against the side of my face. I'm hot and I can feel my face turn red as I feel him wanting me. I can't see him but I can feel him. I can hear him. I can feel how he's craving me. I tilt my head back because I'm sure I can't breathe. He's sucking my neck and squeezing between my legs and I'm warm and wet and his tongue is in my ear and his hand is on me and I'm grinding into him and his skin feels good and he smells so good and I feel so sexy and I'm rocking and I'm coming and I fall asleep with my hand still inside my underwear.

000033.

Subject: you probably already know this

Anna K,

I feel dumb because you don't know me and I've never written to you before, but there's this girl that has a webpage, and she says she met you. She's talking some pretty candid things about you and Ian. I didn't know if you had seen it, so I thought I'd let you know.

If you've already gotten fifty letters like this, or if you're friends with this girl and told her it's okay to write that stuff, then I'm sorry I said anything. But if you want to see her webpage, it's at http://tess.diaryland.com

Hope you're doing well and Happy Thanksgiving.

Just some girl in Atlanta,

Christine

000034.

tess's stresses (the journal of a girl)
today's entry:
meeting anna k—(it's what everyone wants, isn't it?!?)

Oh, my God!!! I'm in Anna K's apartment!!! Right now! She's asleep and I'm all alone in her place, pretending that I'm her, writing at her computer in her apartment. Yay!

First of all, I want to say that Anna K is totally cool. I met my idol, and I have to tell all of you about it, sweet readers, because I promised myself I'd use this webpage to talk about everything that happens to me in my life.

She met me at a coffee shop first, which was probably because she didn't know if I was going to be a stalker. I wore the hat that I talked about in last week's entry because I was wondering if she was secretly reading my journal. She didn't ask if it was Sara's hat. Instead she made fun of it.

I didn't bring her down by telling her that my little sister had left it on my bed before she died. I let her make fun of it and I made fun back. It's not her fault she doesn't know about my journal, and I didn't want to start our meeting on a sour note. Besides, I can wear the hat without thinking about Sara. Actually, it makes me feel like she's with me, and that's a good thing.

Anyhoo, we totally hit it off and before I knew it I was at Anna K's apartment! I was at Anna K's place! Her apartment is so cute!!! Ian was out of town, but she showed me pictures. He's a total hottie, y'all. I don't know why Anna K never mentions that in her journal.

Whoa! I totally fell asleep right there at Anna's computer! Ha! She woke me up and tucked me back in. Aw, isn't she sweet? Now I'm writing from back in boring Denton. Boo.

She was so cool about having me stay over and I can't wait for when Anna K's going to come visit me. I'm going to make sure I'm in town if she's ever in Dallas, because Anna K told me about this time that she and Ian were supposed to be house-sitting for a friend and they ended up having sex in their friend's bed. Ew! Poor friend! Unless they want me to be in the bed at the time! That's so hot!!!

And I'm not one to gossip, but I'm pretty sure there are wedding bells in their future, possibly next year!

I got to pet Taylor, and I even used Anna K's shampoo before I left. My hair still smells like her. She uses this great shampoo that smells like Orange Dream Machine Jamba Juice.

She was so much like a sister to me in those few hours we were together that I wanted to run into her room and jump into bed with her and cuddle like Sara used to do with me. I wanted to stroke her hair and have her tell me a story as I fell asleep to the sound of her voice. I stopped myself from knocking on her door, though. That was probably a good thing.

Oh, God. I almost forgot to tell you. CrushBoy and I have been chatting late at night on IM. I'm so in love. I've totally forgotten about BarBoy from last month. Who? That smelly boy? Hee!

Later, lovelies,

Tess

000035.

Dale came over immediately to read Tess's webpage for himself.

"I should have known it'd be pink. God, what a girlie-girl." He made a gagging noise and leaned away from the laptop.

"I'm pissed off. Should I be pissed off?" I asked.

"Yes, you should be pissed off." He reached over and grabbed a string off my shirt. "Just who does she think she is? More importantly, who does she think *you* are?"

"I don't know."

"Well, she's nobody, so probably nobody read it, right?"

"Yeah." I sat down and stared at my shoes. I felt so dumb. I felt dumb for letting someone in. I felt dumb for caring. Why did I want to make friends with her? Why did I trust her with my personal life?

"This is the Internet. These are invisible people, Anna. They can't hurt you. They don't even fucking know you."

Dale was right, but I didn't know how to stop feeling like I had lost a friend. It all felt so shameful, getting exposed like that, getting used for a good story, having someone gush over me instead of actually becoming my friend.

"Dale, this is all my fault."

"No, it's not. She took advantage of your trust."

"This is why I don't have any girlfriends. Bitches, all of them. Lying, bragging, backstabbing bitches."

"This is why you don't have any girlfriends that are still in college." He pulled his cell phone out of his pocket. "I'm calling Becca. We're going out with all of your real friends and you're going to forget all about this. She's a stupid girl that made a fucking fool of herself." He sat down and stared at the monitor while he listened to the phone ring. "I mean, look at this. Pathetic. Just a little girl who wants some attention. You're lucky you found out about this before she went all *Single White Female*."

It would have hurt worse if I had been more attached to her.

Dale held his hand over the receiver and leaned toward me. "Congratulations on your upcoming wedding, by the way." He gave me a wink.

"Shut up."

Later that night after a few drinks, we wrote Tess a letter together, Dale and I. We told her that she was a stupid little child and she needed serious therapy. Then we deleted it and wrote another letter pretending to be a lawyer informing her of a possible restraining order. Then we deleted that and wrote Tess a letter from Ian, telling her that he was so sorry to have missed her because he wanted to meet her and maybe screw her brains out. Then we made him go on and on about how he's a giant fan of her journal, asking her to keep it a secret, since Anna K knew nothing about it.

That's when Dale hit "Send."

"What did you just do?" I asked, clutching his shoulder from behind.

"Oh. *Oh*."

"Oh, fuck!"

"Are you sure I didn't hit the delete button?" Dale kept clicking the mouse, as if that was going to send us back in time.

"No, Dale, you clicked 'Send.' She's going to read that, Dale."

"Yeah. I'm really sorry about this." He was smiling.

"Shit. Now I have to apologize."

"No you don't."

"Yes I do. I can't have her thinking my boyfriend has a thing for her."

"Sure you can. Just for a week. You're never going to see this girl again, and she fucked with your private life. You have to get her back. Come on, it'll be fun."

"She may not have thought she did anything wrong writing that entry. She's young."

"Fine. Then you can use this to find out how two-faced she is. See if she really thinks of you as a friend. Wait to see if she writes back to Ian. See if she even brings it up to you. And she's not *that* young."

"Shit. I can't believe we created a fake e-mail address for Ian." I was pacing.

"If she flirts back you can tell her that it was you the entire time, and you were seeing if you could trust her."

"I don't know, Dale." I bit a fingernail, a habit I thought I had broken last year.

"Anna. It's already been sent. The ball's in her court. If she really looks up to you, she'll politely thank Ian and let it go. Or she'll ignore it completely. I can see why you've been staying inside all this time. You've got your own Ricki Lake in here, don't you?"

000036.

Break
It's not you, it's me. Well, except for *you*.

20 NOVEMBER

I'm taking a little holiday. Don't worry about me. Have family fun and be safe.

Oh, and in case some of you found a little webpage that discussed my private life? Don't believe everything you read. Ian and I would only have sex in someone else's house if they paid us.

Aren't those of you who have no idea what I'm talking about terribly upset now? There's hot Anna K sex being discussed somewhere else? Scandalous!

Love until later,

Anna K

000037.

I was happy to take some time off to go home for Thanksgiving. I wanted to give myself some time away from technology. I was looking forward to playing a little pinochle with my parents and watching bad movies with my sisters.

Tess hadn't responded to Ian's love letter, and she also hadn't written me to apologize. The Tess Mess, as Dale named it, was a good lesson to get early on. I shouldn't open myself up to a person just because we had an e-mail relationship or because of hero worship. I should have been more careful. I should have had a talk with her, explaining what I did and didn't want to be public information. I shouldn't have treated her like an old girlfriend when the truth was she was the newest person in my life.

I was packing when the phone rang. It was Meredith.

"When's your flight?" she asked.

"Tomorrow morning."

"You need to change it, Anna." She took a breath. "Dad's sick."

"How sick?"

"Sick, like, you need to come here as soon as possible."

I called the hospital. I got Mom.

"He's already sleeping, Annie. We don't want to wake him. He was in a lot of pain earlier and it took a while for him to fall asleep."

"Why didn't you call earlier?"

"It all happened very quickly, honey. We've only been here for a few hours. Shannon's on a flight right now. I'm sorry, Annie. I'm sorry."

"Stop, Ma. Stop apologizing. Are you okay?"

"I'll be better when I've got all my girls home."

I got my flight changed to eleven that night. I'd get into Hartford around four in the morning. Meredith was going to pick me up and drive straight to the hospital. I called Mom back to tell her the time changes.

"Okay, Annie. I'll see you soon. I'm sorry you had to change all of your stuff. Are you going to be okay with work and everything?"

"Mom, stop worrying about me. It's Thanksgiving. I don't have work. Are you okay?"

"Hurry, baby."

My flight was in four hours. I was all packed.

I had two hours to wait before Dale picked me up. I was alone in my apartment. The stillness and the silence crashed inside of me like angry waves of terror. I had never felt so far away from home. I needed to see my father. I needed him to need me. And just as strongly, I wished I could just stay in my apartment and wait until it was all over. I felt like a bad daughter, wishing that none of this had happened, wishing I had never gotten that phone call. I wanted to go home to a house filled with warmth and love, turkey cooking in the kitchen, board games set up in the dining room, and a dog barking in the backyard. I wanted everyone to smile as I walked through the door, to be enveloped in hug after hug as everyone welcomed me home.

Those angry waves slammed against my brain again, reminding me that I can't have back what I never had in the first place. That wasn't my family. That wasn't my home. And now that one of us was probably leaving for good, it would never, ever be my family. We would never have the chance again.

000038.

Subject: too sad for turkey.

LD,

I don't know when I'm going to get a chance to write again. I thought I should let you know what's going on. I'm about to fly out to see my parents for Thanksgiving. The problem is my dad's suddenly very sick, and from the way my sisters and my mother are acting, I might be flying out to tell my father good-bye.

I don't mention my family much, and that's because we're a family that keeps to ourselves. We're very polite around each other. My mom is constantly apologizing for things that aren't her fault. We apologize to each other for being in the same room, for possibly bothering one another by our presence.

I'm scared. I'm scared that my father is about to die. I'm scared because I don't really know how to feel about it. We're solitary people, and the result of that is my father and I haven't really talked too much over the past few years. He keeps mildly updated on my life, and I stay mostly uninvolved in his. We talk through my mother.

Of course I love my father. Of course he loves me. We love each other in that way that fathers and daughters love each other. But here's the thing: He's this sick, and I'm trying to figure out how I'm supposed to feel. Isn't that wrong?

Shouldn't I be screaming and crying or throwing things or clutching the bookcase as I tremble and wail? Shouldn't people be here consoling me? Shouldn't my sisters want me to talk to them? Shouldn't my mom want to talk to me? Shouldn't I be talking to someone about something? Instead I feel cold. I've put on a sweater. I'm wearing two pairs of socks, because I know it will be freezing when I get to Hartford. But it's not cold here in my apartment. I'm just cold. I keep shivering. I feel like it's the first day of school. That's the empty feeling my stomach has. Like I just ate oatmeal against my will. Like I'm about to feel very lonely and left out.

I may not write for a few days while I deal with all of this. I hope he's going to be okay. I hope that this is just another false alarm and when I get there he's watching television, complaining about the glare from his window or something. I hope that they let him go home and he carves the turkey and we all sit down and quietly eat without getting in each other's way. I hope we can act like the family we are, and not have to bond together and create this loving, strong family that we have no idea how to be. It would feel fake and wrong, pretending to have these emotions for each other, wailing against each other. We don't do that. I don't know how we are supposed to learn it all in one day.

I'm waiting for my friend to pick me up to take me to the airport and instead of having my thoughts filled with my father, I'm wondering if you're going to be okay without me for a couple of days. I wonder why I'm thinking about you instead of the family crisis I'm supposed to be consumed with. How did you get so far inside of me?

I don't know what you sound like or look like. I don't know your real name. How ridiculous is that? I don't know you. But

I'm telling you things here I've never told anybody. I continue to pour my insides out to you like some kind of free therapy, hoping that when you write back you tell me that it's okay, that you feel the same way, that you understand me and that everything is going to be just fine. You've somehow become my closest friend in all of this. Why? Why don't I tell my real-life friends about these things? Why did I tell my friend not to interrupt his dinner with his boyfriend, but to come and get me later? Why didn't I want to intrude on anyone else's life? And if they're my "real-life friends," does that make you my imaginary one?

I'm probably dwelling on you so I don't have to deal with the real pain that's sitting next to me on the couch. That's where it is. Just outside my body, right next to me. I can see it. It's a little girl named Anna, and she doesn't know if she's ready to say good-bye to a father she's never really said hello to.

Dale's here. Gotta go.

I'll keep you posted. Hope to have good news soon.

God, why am I ending this like some sort of interoffice e-mail?

I'm sad. There you go, LDobler. I'm scared and sad and I don't know what's going to happen.

Happy Thanksgiving. I'm very thankful for you, too.

-AK

P.S. I'm packing my laptop. Something tells me I might need you around this holiday weekend.

000039.

When you smell a hospital, you know that things are bad. That smell is so tightly linked to Bad Things. Maybe if I had a baby. Maybe then hospitals would smell like We're Gonna Have a Baby. I hadn't been to a hospital often enough to have any good memories attached to the experience. The first time was when I was seven and I fell off a swing trying to look up at the sun during an eclipse. The recess monitor lady screamed at me to stop looking up. I panicked, fell off the swing, and broke my wrist.

The second time was a year later, when I had to say good-bye to my great-aunt, a woman I'd only seen at family reunions. She had a stroke. I hid behind my mother, my face buried deep into her side, as Auntie Moma reached her hand out to me. "Jennifer," she kept calling me. "Jennifer, give me back my cupcake."

I thought it was pretty funny, because when you're eight the funniest sentence in the world to come out of an old lady's mouth is "Jennifer, give me back my cupcake." She was angry with me for laughing and then with everyone else for contradicting her. They eventually had to take me out of the hospital room. My Uncle Sammy took me to McDonald's. I got a Smurf in my Happy Meal.

As the sliding doors opened in front of me and I smelled that hospital smell, I realized that this was the third time. The third real time. I think I'd been every once in a while to visit a friend or get my hearing checked or something, but this was my third emotional experience in a hospital. The smell was soaking into my skin. I felt like I was made out of latex.

I kept weaving around the hallways, afraid to peek into the patient rooms where the doors were open. I was afraid I'd see horrible things inside. Every room held someone sick, someone sad that someone was sick, and someone trying to fix the sick person. There was so much sadness on my father's floor that it felt like the whole building was about to break down into sobs. Other than hearing a few beeping noises, I was surprised at how quiet the place was. Just a heavy sadness and a tense hush like someone was trying to fall asleep. It looked like everyone there was waiting to clean up after the sadness was over.

In the hallway outside of Dad's room, I ran into Shannon. Her eyes were red and she kept wiping away tears with the back of her hand. She grabbed me in surprise. Her breath rushed out of her in a noise that sounded like "Whoa." She pulled me into a hug. "I'm so sorry," she moaned.

I hugged her tight and whispered. "It's okay."

"I'm sorry. He's gone. He's already gone."

Gone. The word people use when it's too fresh to say "dead." Too soon to use real words. Gone. Like lost. Missing. Not there. Gone.

And that was it. The packing, the frantic phone calls, the planning, the changing of plans, the calls to Meredith to say I'd catch a cab so she didn't have to leave the hospital, getting to the airport, reassuring Dale that I was going to be okay, letting him hold me as long as he needed to feel like he had done something, checking my bags, the flight where I couldn't sleep and an Ed Burns movie tortured me from the ceiling of the cabin, the bumpy landing followed by baggage claim, hailing a cab, the silent drive to the hospital as I hoped everything would be okay—all of it was for nothing. Because I'd never get to hear his voice again.

"We tried calling you when we knew it was the end, but you were in the air and we didn't want to leave a voice message."

Then my tears started. Someone put me in a chair.

I knew my mouth was open. I heard my voice say, "Oh." But I wasn't controlling anything. I wasn't aware of anything. I was sitting in the corner of the room and what was left of my family watched me cry.

Meredith put her face in my lap. It was a strange move, and she did it so quickly that the smell of hospital whooshed up from her hair and into my face. She put her arms around my waist and held me there. She started rocking as she cried, sounding like she was six again. She cried like she had lost her favorite stuffed animal. I saw myself put my hand on her head and pat it. Like she was my dog.

"He said to tell you that he loved you," Mom said.

"He woke up? He talked to you?"

"Only for a few minutes." She said it like another apology, her head down, avoiding eye contact. "He seemed to know. He opened his eyes and said good-bye. That he loved us and he loved you and that he'll miss us."

"And then he sighed. It seemed very peaceful, Anna," Shannon said, her voice gravelly from crying. She was holding an unlit cigarette in her hand. I wondered how long she'd been holding it, as it had become wet from the palm of her hand and turned up at the ends.

"How long?"

"Two hours." My mother smoothed down my hair and wiped her face with her other hand. "Why don't you go and say good-bye? I have to do some paperwork."

Then I was in there, alone. Just Dad and me. My dead dad. How the hell did all that happen? I didn't have a dead dad yesterday. I didn't have a dead dad two hours ago. Now if someone asked how my dad was, I'd have to say he was dead. I couldn't do that. Dads aren't supposed to die. They sit in living rooms and wait for you to call to discuss books and movies and the state of the economy. They don't die while you're on an airplane.

I didn't want to be in that room. I didn't want to be the only living person in that room. I stood with my back against the wall, my father's body in front of me. He was no longer alive in that body. I felt so small it was as if I could crawl inside his mouth and look for him.

I took a step closer and felt a chill. A breeze. Then everything was very still again. I looked up and saw the curtains in the room move just a bit.

My body relaxed, and my breath rushed out of me. "Thanks for waiting, Dad," I said to the room. I smiled. "I'll miss you."

My right hand felt warmer. I closed it into a fist, to hold on to whatever it was that was touching me at that moment. I stood quietly and closed my eyes. I breathed in the last moments of my father that lingered in that room.

That's when I was able to really look at him. He was so tiny compared to the last time I saw him. His cheeks had emptied out, and his skin seemed darker, like he had just gotten back from a vacation. His hair was thinner, his skin looser than I remembered. My father was much older than I ever realized he had become. When did all of that happen?

When I walked out a few minutes later, my body felt different. My face, my bones, my back—everything had suddenly aged. I felt much older. I looked at my hands. The skin seemed tighter. Weathered.

It was Thanksgiving morning, and I was thankful that my father's spirit was strong enough to wait for me.

000040.

I didn't know just how solitary my family could be until that first day home without Dad. We walked in the house and tossed our luggage in different corners of the living room. All four of us stared at each other, standing in silence. Only Shannon was still crying. We stood in this living room that none of us grew up in.

We'd spent only a few holidays there, and it was rare for us to be in that room at the same time. I didn't remember the room being so big before, so full of furniture I didn't remember. It looked like someone else's house. Only Dad's recliner, all hunched and worn in the corner, felt familiar.

Mom spoke first. "I want to be alone. Are you girls going to be okay?" Her voice was different, mechanical. She looked past us toward the stairs.

We nodded, and Mom went up to her bedroom. Every once in a while we could hear her sobs and the sound of moving upstairs.

Meredith went straight to sandwich making. Mere ate all the time, so it wasn't inappropriate for her to pull out some turkey and cheese and ask if we wanted anything.

"I want soup," Shannon said. She was mostly speaking to the pantry, which contained no soup at all.

"How's school, Shan?" Meredith asked as she cut the crusts off her sandwich.

Shannon was a junior at Rice University in Houston. All three of us spent our high school years in Texas, but only Meredith moved up north a year after my parents did. Mere was always close to my father and openly Dad's favorite, but none of us minded.

"School's school," Shannon said, as she opened the cabinet where Mom kept the junk food. "Pringles? When did Mom and Dad start liking Pringles?" She opened the can and sat at the kitchen table.

"Who's going to cut the turkey?" Meredith whispered. Shannon and I looked at her.

"Are you kidding?" I asked.

"Can we not right now, Mere? Huh?" Shannon put the lid back on the can of chips and stood up.

"We should probably go to bed," Meredith mumbled.

"It's daylight," Shannon said. It was close to ten in the morning. I could still hear my mother weeping upstairs. I knew I wasn't going to be able to sleep. I didn't want to sleep ever again. What would a nightmare feel like in the middle of all this sadness?

"I'm not tired," I said.

"Me either," said Shannon.

Meredith got up and hugged Shannon. "Well, I'm going to go to sleep. I'm exhausted. I was at the hospital much longer than you guys were."

She walked out of the kitchen. Once we had heard her close the upstairs bathroom door, Shannon whirled toward me, whispering feverishly.

"She's such a bitch. Like she worked harder or had a sadder day because she was there longer? We're bad daughters because we couldn't fly in any sooner? Because we're not psychic and didn't come home yesterday?"

"Just ignore it, Shannon."

"I hate her so much. She's so self-righteous. With her perfect job and her perfect little friends and her perfect little apartment."

I realized I was drinking coffee out of the mug I bought Dad for Father's Day a very long time ago. It said, "Daddies Are the Best!" The lip of the mug was chipped and I ran my tongue over it.

Shannon pulled back her hair and I saw how much she looked like my mother. Her eyes had that tired look around them, as if she'd been worrying about the entire world all day long. Her hands were older than she was. Shannon was an engineering major at Rice. I really had no idea what she did, but I knew she was good in math and physics. She tried to explain once, but I actually fell asleep while she was talking.

"Let's go smoke," I said.

"Brilliant."

We walked into the backyard and sat on the swing set.

"I need to bum one," Shannon said.

"You always do."

We smoked and stared up at the bright blue sky. I squinted against the sunlight glaring off everything around us. My eyelids were heavy from crying. My face felt swollen, my tongue rough. It was cold out, but the cold felt really good, reminding us how crisp life can feel. How opposite of dead we were right then. The irony of smoking a cigarette at that moment made me laugh.

"I miss Dad," Shannon said quietly. She wasn't crying, just staring at her feet, breathing heavier than normal. I hated feeling so helpless. Worthless. What were we all going to do in that house all weekend? It felt like everyone wanted to be alone to mourn. We were keeping each other from feeling anything.

The swing set creaked under the weight of our bodies, moving back and forth. I could see my breath long after I exhaled the smoke from my cigarette.

"Are you going to write about him?" It almost didn't sound like Shannon. Her voice sounded younger. Soothing.

"What are you talking about?"

"Your webpage. Your journal. Are you going to write about him?"

I stood up.

"It's okay if you don't," she said. She wiped her nose like she'd been crying, but her eyes were dry.

"How did you know?"

"Oh, please. It's the *Internet*. You know you're one of the more popular journals out there."

"I am?"

"There are links to your page everywhere. Of course I was going to find it."

"Wait. When did you find it? What other journals? You read other journals? Why didn't you tell me you'd been reading? I can explain."

"Calm down. I think it's funny. I was reading some girl's weight-loss journal and she linked to that Billy Blanks thing you did. I read it and laughed and read another entry and you were talking about Ian, and then I knew. I knew I was reading my sister's diary. I totally freaked out."

"Holy shit." I sat back down on the swing. "Really?"

"No. Dale was just going to explode if he didn't tell some-body about it. But don't tell him I told you. I promised not to say anything. Anyway, once he told me about it, I read the entire thing that night. I wanted to call you, as if you somehow didn't know other people could see it."

"I can't believe you didn't tell me."

"I didn't want to face the wrath of Dale. And it's really none of my business. It's not like you were writing about me. Now the Ian thing's a little weird, that you pretend you're still dating him."

"I'm starting to feel bad for lying about it."

"Don't be. Those people don't need to know the truth. You don't owe anyone anything. At least you sound like you. You're not really lying anyway, since you actually dated him. You should see the other journals out there. One girl is writing about how she's a stripper with a drug habit. It's such bullshit. You know she's not, because if she was really doing all of the drugs she was bragging about, then she'd be too blitzed to figure out how to post a webpage. Actually, hers is really more like a blog."

"What's a blog?" I asked her.

She looked at me, amazed, her eyebrows shooting upward toward her scalp. "You really don't know anything about this, do you? Didn't you read any journals before you started your own? Did you think you were the only one doing this?"

I hadn't even thought of it. "Why would you read something like that, like the stripper website?" I asked her.

"I take study breaks," Shannon said as she blew out another puff of smoke. "I get bored. They're like soap operas. I can't stop reading some of them. I can't wait to see how they're going to mess up their lives next. There's this one guy who is totally stalk-ing his ex-girlfriend, and he doesn't seem to realize it. He keeps going on about how much he loves her, posting shitty poems, and the next day he's whining about some restraining order she's filed. It's hysterical. I love him because he's so clueless."

"That sounds awful."

Shannon kicked up her feet and started swinging slowly. She was wearing a pair of my shoes that I thought I had lost two years ago. "It's so much fun. Either you're reading someone like you, who writes about everything you can identify with, or it's this total train wreck you can't stop reading about. You just read about their pain and thank God you're someone else. It really puts things into perspective knowing you're not some poor bastard fired from his job because of a porn addiction."

"There's a journal like that?"

"There's a journal like that. And he has a thing for you."

"Gross." I wondered how strangers described my journal to their friends and family. Was I one of the train wrecks? What would Shannon think if she knew about LDobler?

Shannon laughed and lit another one of my cigarettes. "Anyway, it's fucked up."

"Do people feel sorry for me?"

"No. You're one of the other journals. You make people feel better about themselves because you tell them it's okay to dork out. Like your Betty haircut. That entry you wrote about breaking up with her? So funny. Look at me, all proud of my big sister."

"I get fan mail."

"I don't doubt it."

"Thanks."

"Dad would have been really proud of you, too."

I smiled. Shannon patted me on the back. "Hey," she said, leaning in. "Can we scan those baby pictures of Meredith in the bubble bath and put them on your website?"

The turkey was ready just before midnight. It was already carved when Mom brought it to the table.

000041.

Having a holiday weekend without a family member felt like putting on a sweater that had an extra arm. Nothing fit right and there was all this extra fabric and you just wanted to be normal again. Not that I'd ever worn a sweater with an extra arm, but I'd never had a holiday with a dead family member before, either.

I was in the living room when Mom brought me a cup of tea. "I was thinking," she started, carefully.

"Yes?" I was ready to listen to her talk for a while, to help her grieve. I wanted to be a good daughter, to be there for her when she needed me. I felt bad that I wasn't going to be able to stay for as long as she might need and was glad she was able to talk to me about all of this so soon. "Sit down, Mom." I patted at the couch I was sitting on.

She stayed where she was and smiled nervously. "Have you called Ian?"

"No." I said it quicker than I wanted to. Angrier.

"Don't you think you should?"

"Why?"

"Honey, you were with him for a long time. Your father liked him a lot."

"He did?" That was certainly news to me.

Mom took a breath. "We all did," she said, not bothering to hide the guilt trip. She left the room.

I grabbed the cordless phone with as much exasperated noise as I could. I made every movement as deliberate as it was elabo-rate, so from whatever room Mom had snuck into, she could hear that I was obeying her wishes, despite my best interests.

I got Ian's machine and stumbled out a mess. "Hey. Hi. Hey. It's me. Um, it's Anna. Hi. Hey, Ian. Um, this is . . . this is not what you say when you get an answering machine. Or is it a voice mail? Do we not say 'answering machine' anymore? Like, do I still say 'I got his machine'? You don't have to answer that. Hey, listen. My dad died. That's not a graceful way to say that, but there isn't really any grace in saying someone has died, and I hate saying the word *passed* like we ate bad chicken. I'm still talking. I should hang up. I'm in Hartford. My dad's dead. Happy Thanksgiving."

Classy.

Meredith flopped down on the couch next to me a few minutes later. "I hate these cushions," she said. "Why do Mom and Dad still have these stupid flower cushions?"

"They're from the last couch."

"I *know*, Anna. I'm not stupid."

Meredith was always three steps away from a fight.

"You asked," I said carefully.

"I hate their new furniture. I tried to talk Mom out of buying it, but she said that it was the first pattern she could find that Dad actually grunted about. She didn't know if it was a good grunt or a bad grunt, but the fact that he showed signs of life about a swatch of fabric gave her hope that she . . ."

Meredith stopped talking and lowered her head in her hands. She leaned forward and put her elbows on her knees. Her brown hair fell down around her arms. I put my hand on her back.

"I don't need you to do that," she said. It sounded like she was crying.

"I don't mind."

"Oh, well, *thanks*. Don't want to put you out." She flipped her head up and I could see that she wasn't crying. Her face was flushed and her brown eyes were sharply focused in anger.

I bit my upper lip. "Meredith? I'm just trying to help, okay?" My voice had risen and we were already in a fight. I didn't want a fight. These things just happened with Meredith.

"I know. You're always trying to help, aren't you? But you and Shannon are going to leave here in two days and go back to your lives and I'm here with Mom. I have to take care of her now."

"Mom will be okay, Mere."

"No, she won't! Nobody's going to be okay!"

She stood up and grabbed a handful of Skittles from Mom's candy bowl. I hid my smile. Shannon and I find that bowl to be the most disgusting thing in the house. Mom never cleans it and it's always full of loose, dusty candy. Meredith was the only one who ate every piece.

"I don't know what else you want Shannon and me to do. Dad didn't want any kind of service—"

"I know that."

"I *know* you know that. I'm not arguing over how well you knew Dad. Jesus, I'm trying to comfort you and you're making it so fucking difficult."

"I'm sorry. It's all my fault I don't grieve the way you want me to, Anna. We can't all be *precious* like you."

I couldn't deal with her anymore. "Sorry I bothered."

I walked out of the house and sat on the front steps. I lit another cigarette. My lungs were aching from all of the smoking, but I couldn't stop. I didn't know what else to do. There was nothing left to do. I wish Dad had left us with some kind of option. He said he didn't want a funeral. He always felt that the only people that would really want to mourn his death were the four of us. All of his relatives had already died, and he didn't have many close friends. But because of this we had no reason to be in the same room with each other and no real reason to talk about our pain. This was his memorial service. Mom wandering with a lost look on her face, Shannon watching MTV up in her old room, and Meredith bitching out anyone who tried to comfort her. Rest in peace, Dad.

000042.

Subject: . . .

AK,

I'm so sorry about everything. I'm sorry you're in so much pain. I wish there was something I could do, something I could say. Fuck. It feels so helpless over here . . . close enough to do something, but too far away to do anything real.

Even though I never met your father, I know he must have been a remarkable man. Half of his genes created one of the most spectacular women I've ever known.

Take care of yourself. Let me know if there's anything I can do. At any time. I'm here. Always.

-LD

000043.

For Dad

21 NOVEMBER

Why is it that when we cry our mouths salivate? Is it because the back of the throat swells up? Is it to clean out our mouths—we cry when we're in pain and the tears are an antiseptic? Is it because our tongues swell and rest on a salivary gland?

I think it's so we have a harder time talking when we cry, to prevent us from saying things we don't mean when we don't know how to express exactly what we're feeling. It might also be a defense mechanism. People stay away because we're weepy, drooling messes. The ones who love us no matter what let the snot and drool get all over them while they hold us.

I've been pretty snotty and drooly this weekend.

My father died today, on this holiday when we traditionally give thanks, and I'm very thankful to have been this man's daughter. Because of this, I feel the need to tell all of you a little bit about him.

He was a good man. He tried to be a better man. He changed over the years. Became a quieter version of himself. I heard many stories about crazy things he did back when he was my age. Back before he had to be responsible and become an adult. Back before his daughters forced him to become a father.

I'm not going to go on about him because he wouldn't have wanted it. He wouldn't have wanted to waste your time. My father isn't the type of man who is going to be missed by hundreds of people. He kept to himself. He minded his own business. He made sure he took care of the people who mattered most to him. You can bet your ass that the handful of people he loved and cared for are going to miss him tremendously.

It's different here at home without my dad. He was a part of this house as much as any wall or room. I rarely saw Dad outside of this house over the past few years. In fact, I rarely even saw him standing. He loved sitting in the living room, his recliner kicked back, remote in one hand as he watched television, his head leaning back more and more as he fell asleep to the sound of football. He had his routines. He had things that made him happy.

He paid his taxes. He owned his house. He raised a family. We never starved. We always had clothing. We even had cable. He was good at his job, a job he never really bothered to explain to all of us. He was good at being a husband, a job my mother never really bragged about. My father was a man who did the things in life you're supposed to do.

Looking around this place he left behind—at my younger sisters all grown up, starting their own lives with determination and self-esteem, at my mother who doesn't have to worry about how to pay for the house or pay the bills, or me, his oldest daughter, who lives on her own over a thousand miles away—I'm starting to realize why he was so quiet those last few years.

He was testing us. He wanted to make sure we'd be okay without him.

He didn't want a funeral. He didn't want a group of people gathered in his memory. I'm writing this at the risk of disobeying him, but I wanted to tell the world that he existed. I want everyone to know that I had a father and I'm very sad that he is gone. And this is my diary. If I didn't write about it, I'd be saying it wasn't important to me. And reading back over these words, for the first time now this all feels very real. It's all sinking in. I'm telling myself as I'm telling all of you. My father is gone.

Hey, Dad. I don't know that much about the Internet, but I have an incredible hope that these electronic waves are made out of some of the same particles you're made of now. I know we didn't get a chance to formally say good-bye, but maybe you can feel these words and feel all of the love I'm shoving into them. I'm packing them tight with all of the things we never got to say.

Thank you for being a good dad.

Make sure they let you mow the lawn in heaven every once in a while. I know how much it'd mean to you.

Love forever,

Anna K

000044.

Subject: Condolences

Anna K,

Having lost my father three years ago, I know what you're going through is hard. I don't even want to say that I know what you're going through because this is a very personal journey you're about to embark on. Just know that so many people love you and we're patiently waiting your return. Take good care of yourself.

Travis Robinson

Subject: prayers are with you

anna k i am really sorry about your dad i hope everything gets better for you soon happy thanksgiving and spend it with your family who love you we'll be here when you are back bye from mexico

-goosie123

Subject: I'm so sorry.

Anna K,

I'm very sorry. About everything. About what I did to you. You
have to know that I meant everything I said in the nicest way.
I admire you, that's all.

None of that matters right now. You take care of yourself. I'm
sorry you had to suffer such a loss this holiday season.
You're in my thoughts and prayers.

Love, Tess

Subject: loss

Anna,

There is nothing I can say to make it better. I want you to
know that everyone feels your loss because when you're
sad, we're sad. We love you and our thoughts and prayers
are with you. Take care.

-Michelle

There were at least fifty e-mails when I checked a few hours after
posting my entry. All from people I didn't know. All from people
saying they were praying for me. They were sorry for my pain. So
many people from all over the world stopping for a moment to
pay tribute to my father, a man they'd never met. A man who
knew nothing about them.

By Friday evening the house was too quiet for me. People had stopped coming by earlier that afternoon. Our fridge was full of food we didn't feel like eating. Shannon decided to go out and see a movie by herself. Mom retreated back to her room. Meredith went to her apartment.

It was only ten.

Subject: sad.

AK-

Oh, Anna. I just read. Again, I'm here. For anything. I'm so sorry.

-LD

Subject: re: sad.

LD-

203.555.4302

-AK

p.s.: hurry.

The phone rang three minutes later.

"Hello?" Did I sound nervous?

"Hi, can I speak to Anna, please?"

"This is she." Why was I being so formal?

And then it was quiet. His voice was deeper than I thought it would be. I put on my coat and walked out back with the cordless phone to sit on the steps.

"How are you?"

"I don't know," I said. I laughed. "I guess I'm okay. Am I allowed to be okay?"

"Are you at your Mom's house?"

"Yeah." I lit a cigarette. "Everyone's doing something and I felt weird being all by myself. I want to go home."

"I'm sorry."

"Yeah—me, too."

"Is Ian there?"

"No." It wasn't a lie.

It was quiet. I could hear his breath. The muffled sound of a television.

"So, I guess you're a real person," I said.

"Looks like it. You're not a man, which was my biggest fear."

"You don't know. I could have a high voice."

"Well, it's a nice voice. For a man or a woman."

He listened to me complain about how strange it was being at home, about my problems with Meredith and how Shannon had been reading my website. I told him about those final moments at the hospital. I talked until the sound of sirens on the other line stopped me.

"Sorry," he said when they died down. "Go on."

"Are you in an ambulance? Did I bore you to death?" Death. Too soon for that word.

"I live very close to a hospital." Too soon for that word, too.

Another siren on his end of the phone snapped me back. "That's so loud," I said.

"You get used to it."

My fingers were freezing, but my face was warm from blushing. I couldn't believe I was speaking to him for the first time in my life.

"Can I ask you something?" I asked.

"You can," he said.

"What the hell's your name?"

He laughed. How absurd that all of this had happened without us learning each other's names. "It's Kurt. Kurt Worschauser."

"Well, hello, Kurt Worschauser. I'm Anna Koval."

"Nice to meet you."

"We'll cover learning how to spell your last name the next time we e-mail."

We talked about the painting he was working on. He had found an old picture of his great-great-grandparents, and he was doing something with that. I understood the words *composition* and *balance,* but that was pretty much it.

"Where are you?" I asked him.

"I was going to stay at my sister's, but I had to leave. Arial was screaming. My niece. I can't stand it after a few hours."

He told me about the snow outside his window, and I told him about the ice crunching under my feet as I wandered to the swing set. He told me to take my cold ass inside. I went in briefly, but Shannon was back from seeing a movie, and she wanted me to get off the phone to keep her company. I asked her to give me another ten minutes.

"You're like my imaginary girlfriend who's away at camp," Kurt said before we hung up. "I only have to read your letters when I'm bored, and I write back when I feel like it. We don't argue because we never see each other."

"Plus," I said, "we don't go on dates that cost you cash, and we don't have an anniversary where you have to buy me presents. We never have to argue about where we're sleeping. I don't know if you're a shitty driver or a bad tipper."

"I might be a bad tipper."

"I might be a shitty driver. It doesn't matter."

"How perfect are we?"

"Perfect," I smiled. "As long as we never, ever meet."

"It would ruin everything."

Later that night, I couldn't sleep. I went back out into the backyard and smoked cigarette after cigarette, wondering what I was doing. I could tell Kurt was interested in me and I was very much interested in talking to him, but I was too scared to tell him who I really was. He liked Anna K. He might not like me. What did I think was going to happen? Why, of all the people in my life, did I want to talk to Kurt, whose name I didn't even know until he called?

As I stubbed out my last cigarette, I decided I shouldn't talk to him on the phone anymore. I didn't want to have my heart yearning for someone I couldn't have.

000045.

The next afternoon, I was happy to be tucked into Dad's old reading chair with a blanket around my legs. I was in my parents' bedroom, which was now just my mom's room. Nothing belonged to Dad anymore, I reminded myself. It was so cold outside I could hear it ringing in my ears. I was very comfortable upstairs in the heated room. I instinctively looked for Taylor to curl up with. I yearned for the comforts of home again and wanted to be back in my apartment. The sadness started seeping into me, stinging my eyes, making me wish the days would speed up so I could fly back home.

"Anna!" I heard Shannon shout. "It's for you!" I hadn't heard a phone or a doorbell. "Someone's here for you!" she shouted again.

Wiping my tears, I quickly fantasized that Kurt somehow figured out where I lived and had driven here from Pittsburgh to see me in the flesh. I pushed my blanket to the floor and rested my book beside it.

"Dude!" Shannon's head poked in the door. "I called you. What's your problem? You've got company."

"Shut up." Again my stomach fluttered and I felt myself grow hot. I didn't want to fall for one of Shannon's tricks. But how did Kurt do it? How did he find me here? He might just have been as perfect as I'd been hoping.

"Here he is." Shannon beamed as she backed out of the door. Another body filled her place.

Ian. Clean-shaven, wide-eyed, Oxford-shirted Ian. He held a cup of coffee and wore a look of absolute compassion I hadn't seen since the time I sprained my ankle on a camping trip. Ian had carried me all the way down from the top of the cliff with that same stoic look on his face. Ian the Protector.

"Hey, baby," he said.

"I'll leave y'all alone," Shannon said as she shut the door.

"What are you doing here?"

He squatted on the floor in front of me. "I thought you might like some company."

"How did you get here?" I asked him.

"A plane. I got a new credit card. That's what new credit cards are for. Trips you can't afford but need to take."

He pulled me into his arms. I fell forward, off the chair and into him, my blanket tangling around my feet. I was surprised at how easily I fit back into his chest. How comforting the smell of him was in my head. My face felt warm against the cotton of his shirt. I could hear his heartbeat. I didn't know how much I had needed physical attention. My hands found his belt loops, and I hooked my fingertips in them. My eyes closed and I felt my body relax. "Thank you," I whispered.

We spent most of the day with Shannon and my mom. Ian was good at fixing things, so Mom had him do a few things around the house that Dad never got a chance to do. He was fixing the garage door when my mother called me into the living room.

"Are you two back together?" she asked, her smile taking up her entire face.

"No, Ma."

"He's obviously here because he loves you."

"Just because he's here doesn't mean that he loves me."

"Oh, you know he loves you. Just like you love him."

"Mom."

"Why don't you two just get back together?"

"It's not that easy."

Mom jumped forward toward me suddenly.

"What's wrong?" I asked her.

"Did you see how close I was standing to *The Tommyknockers?* Lord, how scary."

The rest of the day my mother conspired to get Ian and me alone. Mom and Shannon decided to eat dinner at Meredith's, and Mom told us that there wasn't enough food for the two of us. It was so lame that we had to pretend to understand so we didn't have to talk about how my mom was trying to get her daughter back with her ex. I was embarrassed for both Ian and myself. Shannon had whispered "Hang in there" into my ear before she left. Mom actually winked and gave me a thumbs-up as she closed the front door.

We watched television in the living room with me on one side of the couch and Ian on the other. He pulled my feet into his lap and started rubbing them.

"You don't have to do that," I said.

"I know. I want to. Is that okay?"

I nodded.

We kept our focus on the television. Ian didn't so much rub my feet as he just held them in his hands. He'd absently squeeze them every few minutes, but it wasn't anything like a foot massage. Eventually the whole thing felt forced, so I pulled my feet away. He quickly grabbed them again.

"Is something wrong?" he asked.

"No, I just feel like I'm making you do that."

"I asked to do it."

"I know, but . . . you're not even rubbing them."

"Sorry," he scoffed, and started squeezing them tight. "You shouldn't complain about a free foot massage." He pinched my pinkie toe too hard.

"I'm not complaining," I said as I sat up straight and pulled my feet out of his lap. "I'm saying you don't have to do anything. Any of this."

"I know I don't."

I sighed and looked up at him. "Why are you here?"

"I thought you might need somebody." He said it to the television and not to me.

"Why are you really here?"

He turned away and looked down.

"I don't know," he said.

I just stared at him, waiting for him to continue.

"Susan and I broke up," he mumbled.

"I know. Does that mean you want to get back together?"

"Does it have to mean that?" Finally he was looking at me.

"I don't know! I'm following your train of thought here. I thought that's why you told me."

"No, I was just telling you!"

I was sitting up straight, but Ian was sinking further and further back into the couch, like I was berating him. I hated when he did that. I hated feeling like a mother punishing a child.

"Sit up."

"Sorry."

Sorry, *Mommy.*

"Or don't sit up. I don't care. Shit." My hands were trembling.

"I'm sorry, Anna. I don't know. I thought you'd be sad. I wanted to be here to make you feel better. I thought you might need someone. I know how your family gets at times like this."

"I'm sorry my mother is trying to make us get back together."

"It's okay."

"No, it's embarrassing."

He grabbed my hand. He was sitting closer to me now. "It's understandable. We were good together."

"Were we, Ian?"

He had pulled my hand into his lap and his fingers were tracing the inside of my arm. "I thought so. Didn't you think so? I still do."

"See? What does that mean?"

"Why does it have to mean something? Why can't I say that and have it be something I said?"

There wasn't any logic in that sentence. I knew that. But at the time it made sense to both of us, and it was the logic we followed all the way until our mouths found each other and we made out on my mother's couch that Meredith hates. We kept following that logic until we moved into the guest bedroom, where we made love for the first time in a very long time.

It wasn't too fast. It wasn't too hard. It wasn't rushed. We moved together. We never spoke a word. We just kept breathing and moving, holding each other. We kissed and touched. It was dark, so dark I couldn't see his face. He felt thinner in parts, wider in others. I wondered if I felt different to him. He held my breasts more than he used to. He kissed harder than he used to. Then my feet twined with his like they always used to as he grabbed me by the hips and pulled me in just like he used to and we made love just like we used to. Like we were used to. There was an incredible comfort in that.

Afterward he fell right asleep, just like always. I stayed up, which was different. I listened to his breathing in the dark and tried to push myself back in time. I pushed myself back two years ago. I was in bed with Ian and it was dark and we had just made love, but it was two years ago. I tried to see if I was happy. I wanted to see if anything was different.

There was a change. I was feeling guilty. I kept thinking of LDobler, or Kurt, I guess. I felt like I was betraying him. I pushed those thoughts out of my head and snuggled in tighter with Ian. In his sleep he lifted his arm and put his hand around my waist, just like he used to. I felt his skin against my cheek and inhaled the smell of him. He smelled like home.

I reminded myself that Kurt was a man I'd never met who thought I was right where I was at that moment—in the arms of Ian. At least I wasn't lying to him anymore.

000046.

Quickly

25 NOVEMBER

Thanks to everyone who has sent very nice words of condolences about my father. My family is doing okay and I'm touched that so many of you stopped your day to think of me.

Love until later,

Anna K

Subject: hi.

Anna,

I've been staying away because the last thing in the world you need to deal with is me, but I haven't been able to sleep thinking about what I did to you. I'm so sorry to have abused your trust. I never meant to hurt you. My therapist says it was just because I was excited to meet you, is all. She says I wanted to brag to others to prove my existence worthy. Or something like that. Anyway, I hate not being able to write to you or talk to you. You've become one of my best friends, as stupid as that sounds.

I'm so, so, so, so, so sorry. About everything. I miss you.

-Tess

000047.

My next week felt three months long. If I wasn't sleeping, I was crying. If I wasn't doing either of those things, my head felt as if it was stuffed with cotton, a dull haze fell over my eyes, and even the slightest movement would leave me exhausted. I didn't answer the phone or leave the house. I wouldn't have even changed my clothes if it weren't for Dale, who came by three times a day to feed me. He also brought over his DVD player and kept me in full supply of movies that had nothing to do with families or dying family members. He would rub my back as I cried. I made him talk about mundane things as I zoned out in my bed. I listened to the latest gossip at his job, problems with Jason, or the most recent news on his screenplay. He was almost finished with it, and I couldn't wait to read it. He was trying to figure out who should play the lead girl and I planned on suggesting Smith.

Through all of this I knew Dale wanted to ask me about Ian. It shows the caliber of friend he is that the subject never came up.

Ian had left the morning after, before I had even woken up, and I hadn't heard from him since. He left so quietly—like I was some kind of mistake, like there was shame in what we had done. I didn't have the strength to get upset over it yet; I wasn't even ready to think about what it all meant. I just wanted the heavy sadness to lift out of my bones. All I did was sleep until I couldn't stand the sight of my apartment any longer.

I eased back to work the next week, mostly because I wanted to see how Smith was doing. It was the first week of December.

We were at our spot under the bleachers when she said, "I'm really sorry about your dad." The Action Grrlz had all signed a card for me. They were up to fifteen girls. It must have been comforting for them to all sign something that had a definite purpose.

"Thanks. Are you nervous about the rally?" I asked her.

"Hell, yeah. I can't believe it's on Monday. I wrote my speech."

"I can't wait to hear it."

She squatted down to tie one of her shoelaces. It was purple and long. She yanked on her shoes like they were being punished. "Are you sure you don't want to bail on it? You've had a pretty rough couple of weeks."

I leaned my head against the cold metal pole I was holding on to and closed my eyes. I was still tired from everything. My body ached with sadness. It felt like my joints creaked with every motion. I kept seeing my father's body in the hospital. I heard Kurt's voice in my head. I saw Ian's body over mine.

"You haven't been listening to a word I've said, Miss." Smith punched my arm.

"I'm sorry." I opened my eyes and focused on her. "Tell me again."

Smith squinted for a second. She looked away. "Forget it," she said.

I didn't know how to tell her that I wanted to listen. I just couldn't keep my head in one place.

"I can't believe you fucked your ex-boyfriend. Haven't you seen *High Fidelity*?"

"Seen it and read it," I said, burying my face in my sleeve, wondering if John Cusack was making royalties off the number of times he'd been referenced in my life recently.

"You two getting back together?"

"No. Let's talk about something else."

"Anna Koval doesn't want to talk about boys? It's like the entire world has just shifted, Miss."

I must have looked miserable at that moment because Smith quickly reached out to me. She leaned into my side and put her arm around me. I could feel her small fingers on my shoulder. Her skin felt cold through my sweater. She didn't say another word. She just rested her head on my arm. I hadn't expected such a gentle touch from Smith. I wasn't sure if I was supposed to allow it, but it felt so good to have someone touch me, to quietly tell me it was okay to be sad. It wasn't like a man's touch, which can be hard and can get inside of you, pulling everything out. This was tiny, like when my little sisters and I would twine our bodies together on the couch Saturday mornings and watch cartoons. I pretended Smith was one of my sisters. I closed my eyes and felt my breath catch in my throat. She tightened her grip on my arms and pulled me against her as I tried not to cry. All I could hear was the wind whipping under the bleachers and the sound of flagpole chains clanging in the distance. My head was swirling and my heart was aching. I didn't know what I wanted. I didn't know how to feel like myself again.

It's not like I thought Ian and I would get back together. I didn't want that. I wasn't ready and I didn't feel like my father's death was an appropriate reason. I wanted to be able to tell Ian that I was flattered by his interest and grateful for his comfort, but I didn't want anything more to happen. I wanted to be the one to break it off. I wanted to tell him no. I wanted to leave *him* for a change. But he never let me be the strong one. Instead he left before I got a chance to say anything. I was never the one in control of us. Not the last time and certainly not this time. I didn't even have the control to stop myself from falling back into his arms and letting him make love to me. I was so weak that I didn't care about risks or who he had slept with since the last time we were together. It was weak to even want him again, to look back at him and take him again.

I was at square one all over again.

When I got home that afternoon I grabbed my CHANGE list. NEW HAIRCUT had been crossed off. I crossed off LOSE WEIGHT. It seemed like such a stupid thing, to worry about my weight when my entire life was fucked up. I had made a list based on impressing someone else. Not one of those items was for me. Was I so self-hating that I needed to write down things that were wrong with me? Why would I do that to myself?

I wondered if my ass was still tall enough to get on roller coasters.

DRINK MORE WATER. I couldn't believe that was a resolution. As if drinking a few liters of water would give me a brand-new perspective on the world, make me one with the universe, and allow me to finally understand calculus. It was just hydrogen and oxygen, not a master's degree.

I crunched the paper into a ball in my right hand. I wasn't going to live by a set of flaws. I was going to live my life without feeling like a daily failure.

000048.

Subject: re: re: re: Don't tell anybody—I hate the Indigo Girls

AK,

I hate that I only have your mother's phone number. I'm thinking of prank calling her until she gives me your number.

Are you afraid that our long-distance bills would be too high? Is that why you're playing telephonic hard to get?

Today I shoveled my sidewalk. That is how exciting my life is here. I also realized that Christmas is very soon. Just a few weeks away. What would you like? Wait, are you Jewish? See? So many things to learn about you.

Last night I went out to this bar where I go sometimes because everybody inside it is always the same. It's been the same four guys at the corner of that bar for the past ten years. They served me before I was old enough and now I feel very loyal to them. It's a good place to go when you want to see how far you've come over a period of time. Just check in. They haven't seen you in months, so the questions they ask tell you how much your life has changed.

"How's Heather?" they asked. So I hadn't been to the bar in over a year.

"She's getting married to a Frenchman," I replied, and they paid for my beers all night long in exchange for their opinions. Apparently I look thinner, seem happier, and am better off without that bitch that they never liked.

Then I met the most beautiful woman while I was waiting in line for the bathroom. She loves Ben Folds Five, knows how to use chopsticks, and has an extensive art collection. She has two dogs and speaks three languages fluently. She can pick up a bar of soap with her toes and knows all of the words to the theme song from *The Great Space Coaster*. She thinks I'm witty, charming, and handsome. I took her back to my apartment and we made love slowly until the sun came up, where she made me crepes while wearing only a pair of high heels. She fed me breakfast as she sang all of the songs from Bob Dylan's *Blood on the Tracks* in order.

Are you jealous? Well, don't worry. Turns out I just fell asleep at the bar.

But come on, you have to admit, if I found some girl like that you'd be insanely jealous, wouldn't you? You'd have to come to Pittsburgh and punch her in the face, right? Because from where I sit, that imaginary girl might be the only woman in this world that could beat your place in my heart.

Ignore what I just said there.

-LD

000049.

Tess showed up at my apartment the following afternoon.

"Hear me out, okay?"

She was wearing a green coat and brown corduroys. She wore a ski cap. Her right foot was twisting inward at an awkward, nervous angle. She was holding two cups of coffee. A bag was crammed under her arm.

"Are those for me? Because if they are, you're starting off on the right foot."

"Is Ian here?"

"No." I was sick of the sound of his name. Sick of all things Ian. I needed Anna K to break up with him soon so I didn't have to talk about him anymore.

"Please, can I come in?"

It felt like years had passed since Tess posted that entry. It was the same feeling as when Meredith and I fight when I come home for holidays. The next time we saw each other, there'd be a faint ache from where we used to be smarting, but it was too dull to remind us what the fight was all about.

I let Tess in and took a coffee from her. She dumped out the bag. Cookies and packs of cigarettes scattered onto my coffee table.

"Merry Christmas," I exhaled.

"I have a proposition."

She started talking very quickly, moving her hands whenever she stopped for a breath so I wouldn't have a chance to interrupt. I sipped my coffee and listened.

Tess had written a paper on Internet diaries. It was part of her thesis, and she had submitted it to a web conference. They liked her paper and what she had to say and had invited her to come and speak at the conference that weekend. They wanted her to bring someone who wrote a web journal to answer questions and discuss what the next wave of journalism might be if these sites gained a greater audience.

"How many people visit your website a day?" she asked me.

"I don't know, Tess. It's been more expensive lately, though. The hosting company has been charging me out the ass. Something about the bandwidth."

"You don't know? You don't check your stats?"

I stared at her until she walked over to my laptop and pulled up my website. She asked me a few questions, typed a few things, and pulled up a page. She made a hissing noise through her teeth and turned the laptop toward me. "Did you know over five thousand people read your site every day?"

"Is that a lot?"

"It's not huge if you're a company. But if you want to compare it, about fifty people read my site, and I'm dancing over it. That means I don't suck."

"So, what does this make me?" I asked.

"A writer."

I tried to imagine what five thousand people looked like. I wondered how many of them were just like Kurt. Was that possible? Could there be more than one of him out there? Maybe I could find someone else, someone who lived closer to me. My head started aching. Five thousand people. What did they all want from me?

In all those five thousand people, how had Kurt stood out? How did he break past that faceless pack? What made him take an extra step forward, allowing him to be whole and human in my mind? Maybe I had added qualities to him that he didn't really have. I might have just elaborated and exaggerated until I imagined a real relationship between the two of us. I could be the only one feeling this, reading into his words and deciding we had more than was even possible.

"So, will you come to the conference with me and speak?" Tess lit a cigarette. "You're qualified, and the fact that you know nothing about the community you're in is incredibly fascinating."

"I have to answer questions?" My mouth went dry. "I don't really like talking about this thing, Tess." Maybe I could send Shannon in my place, since she spent so much time reading journals. She was much more of an expert.

"I know it's not glamorous, but it's a free trip, a free hotel room, a free rental car, and a chance to get away. You can do your Christmas shopping in a different part of the country. It will be fun."

"I don't know, Tess. Does the hotel have a pool?" I joked.

"I'm pretty sure Pittsburgh is the last place where you'd want to swim these days. I can see about moving the conference to Green Bay if you want to totally freeze your ass off."

"Pittsburgh?"

She booked my ticket that instant, from my computer. The conference was just days away. Days. I was going to see him in days. I had to see what he looked like. I couldn't ignore the pull inside of me any longer. I had to find out if it was real.

000050.

While making the final descent into the Pittsburgh International Airport early Friday evening, I went over my Post-It list again. I was smarter this time and had written out two lists: one for Tess and one for Kurt. I wasn't going to make any mistakes. I was going to try to weave all of my lies into at least semitruths by the time I said good-bye to both of them.

I was pretty comfortable with the Tess list. I wasn't so emotionally involved with her that I might slip up, and I wasn't too worried about what she'd think if she caught me. I'd explain to her that there were some lies I told early on to protect myself, back when I felt more vulnerable to strangers interested in my life. Was that a good enough excuse that Kurt would buy it as well?

I waited to tell Kurt I was coming until yesterday. Originally I wanted to surprise him, sending an e-mail from some local café telling him to meet me there. That entire ordeal was way too *You've Got Mail* for me, though, and I figured he deserved some preparation time.

Besides, I needed him to have his schedule completely free so I didn't end up sitting between him and some girl he'd known for years. I was asking him to cancel all plans immediately and drop everything to wait for me to bust in on his city. I was fine with how selfish that was. I felt I'd earned it in thousands of half-flirting words over the past four months.

I was happy to be flying alone, as the conference had already booked Tess's flight when she invited me along. We were meeting in Baggage Claim. I wasn't even in charge of getting the rental

car. I leaned back and tried to imagine that this was just a vacation and not potentially an enormous disappointment.

I shifted in my seat away from the sleeping woman leaning
heavier and heavier on my side, and my mind wandered to the
other night, when Becca almost kicked me out of her wedding.

She had met me for drinks, saying she had a "delicate matter"
to discuss. After the uncomfortable small talk she finally said that
Ian told Mark about us sleeping together in Connecticut. Now
Ian wanted to skip out on the wedding so it wouldn't turn into "a
scene." Becca and Mark didn't want a situation on their wedding
day, but Ian was one of Mark's best friends, so they didn't want
him to leave. Basically they were asking if I'd be nice enough to
bow out of the wedding and let someone else be a bridesmaid. I
was mortified to find out that Becca and Mark actually had to sit
and talk about Ian and me having sex, how Ian had run out on
me afterward, and which one of us was more important at the
ceremony. Everyone at that wedding would soon know that Ian
wasn't talking to me because he flew to Connecticut for pity sex.

"I understand, Becca," I said quietly. "I won't come to the
wedding."

"I hate that they're making me do this," she told me as she
dropped her head down to the bar. "I'm so sorry, Anna."

"Don't, Bec. That's dirty. Your hair's in beer."

"I don't care. Shit, I paid thirty dollars for a shampoo with
beer in it. This is just as good, I'm sure."

She wiped her forehead back and forth on the bar. She was
wearing her hair down because her stylist had told her that she
was ruining her hairline by wearing it up so often. Becca didn't
want to be a bald bride. She moaned from under her hair as the
ends lapped in puddles of beer.

"She can't do that here," the bartender said to me.

"Thanks, dude." I nodded at him. "Good to know."

"I can do what I want, Mr. Bartender Man. Don't you know
the bride always gets her way?"

It wasn't that she was drunk; I think Becca was just at her breaking point. So many things to deal with and now she had to fire a bridesmaid? I couldn't imagine.

I grabbed her purse and held her on the shoulder as I paid the tab. "She's had a rough day," I explained to the bartender.

"Do you want me to call a cab?" he asked. He was cute. Blue eyes, big hands, and a tattoo at the base of his neck on the right side. A word I couldn't read. I briefly imagined us naked on the bar counter, shattering beer glasses all around us as he drove my hips into the counter and pulled on the back of my hair.

What was wrong with me?

"We're fine," I told my brief boozy lover as I pulled Becca into my arms. "Let's go," I said to her.

"I'm sorry about Ian," she whispered into my ear.

Once outside the bar, Becca whipped around so quickly that her purse smacked me in the thigh. She grabbed both of my arms and looked into my eyes.

"You're going to be my bridesmaid," she said with an intensity I'd never seen before.

"Becca, you don't have to do this."

"I'm not letting Ian tell me what I can and can't do at my wedding. That's bullshit. He'll have to suck it up and be a man. You're our friend too, Anna, and he's got no right to threaten to pull out of the wedding just because he's too much of a baby to deal with the decisions he's made in his life. You're *my* bridesmaid and fuck him if he can't be mature enough to deal with it."

Why couldn't I say things like that? How did Becca know how to sum up my feelings in one speech of fury? I wanted to be the one saying all the right things for once. To validate my own feelings for a change.

Ignoring our plans to meet in Baggage Claim, Tess was waiting at my gate when I walked off the plane. She pulled me in for a hug. She smelled like sugar and flowers. She had gotten a haircut in the few days since I'd seen her. Glittery clips pulled her blond bob back on the sides, bringing out her giant green eyes even more.

"Yay! Yay! You're here! It's freezing outside."

Tess chattered on about her flight and the hotel and the itinerary as I stood in Baggage Claim waiting for the moment when I could smoke again. The conference was tomorrow afternoon and we'd be treated to lunch before Tess spoke. I was going to sit next to her at a table until the question-and-answer period. Then Tess would explain who I was, show pictures of my website, and then let people ask me questions.

There was a problem with the rental car. Tess was too young to rent it, so I handed over my credit card and did it myself. Tess was apologetic, but it wasn't a big deal to me. I was anxious to see Pittsburgh for the first time. Kurt's Pittsburgh.

It was nothing like I'd imagined. I thought I'd be walking into a city that had a sky black with soot that smelled like hard work and sorrow. I'm sure the Christmas season helped. It was sparkly and pretty with tinsel. There was a warm holiday sheen about the town. The houses and bridges had a history not found in Texas cities. There were layers and hills and old buildings that had been there forever. Large buildings jutted toward the sky and water surrounded everything. It smelled good. I love the smell of cold. It feels like it's cleaning out your insides.

Our hotel rooms were nice. Thankfully I didn't have to room with Tess. I told her that I was feeling a bit tired and made plans to have dinner with her in a couple of hours. I checked my e-mail.

Subject: holy fucking shit.

AK-

I'm freaking out, just a little. I was walking to get coffee this morning and I realized you were on a plane that was rushing

over here and soon you'd be here in my city and there's
nothing I can do about it. You'll be here and we're going to
meet and this thing is actually going to happen. We're going
to meet each other.

I need you to calm me down. Or don't. Maybe you're just as
freaked out. I'm not making any sense. What if you don't like
me in person? What if I disappoint you?

I'm ldobler23 on Instant Messenger. We can write there and
it won't be as intimate as the phone and won't take as long
as these e-mails. Don't tease me about my IM name, please.
I only have it to talk to a few people, like my sister. And you,
if you want.

This is terrible. I hope you're nervous, too. Why am I
nervous? This is so stupid. Ignore this. I can't wait to hear
from you. To see you. To meet you, for real.

Ignore that, too. Or don't.

-LD. Wait. Kurt. I'm Kurt now, huh?

-Kurt

I was too anxious to nap, so I forced myself to watch the
Weather Channel until I fell asleep. Tess called to wake me up a
few minutes before ten. "Are you almost ready?" she giggled. I
was sure she was about to knock on my door. I asked for a few
more minutes and threw on my clothes.

I looked myself over in the mirror. My eyes looked tired, but
that was from the plane combined with the very short nap. Betty
was unhappy, so I splashed water on my comb and ran it

through, pulling my hair into a ponytail. I dabbed on lip gloss. I looked closer at my skin, checking for wrinkles. I looked closer at my face, checking for lies.

It was time to start fixing things.

000051.

I was freezing by the time we found a diner. Every restaurant was closed at that hour, and we finally settled at a Denny's, the smell of warm grease melting our numb fingertips.

Tess and I sat across from each other. She started once our food had arrived.

"I'm really sorry about hurting you with my website."

"It's okay, Tess. You don't have to keep saying that."

She shook her head and looked down. "I've been wanting to say this for so long. I'm not writing because you do. I mean, there are other journals out there. But yours was the first that made me trust myself enough to try my own."

"Because mine's nothing special?" I brought the mug of coffee to my lips. It felt so good to have something warm inside of me. I felt the coffee all the way down as it traveled to my stomach. My body relaxed and my toes unclenched for the first time since I got off the plane. Even my nap had been tense, filled with fretful dreams of not being good enough, of not getting the truth out correctly.

"You made me want to try it, too. Anyway, again, I'm sorry. I should have told you I was going to write about you."

"I haven't exactly been honest with you all the time, either, Tess."

I could have brought up Dale's e-mail from Ian and apologized and moved on. I didn't. I couldn't. I wanted to see if she'd mention it. I wanted to see what she'd do with it.

"I didn't have a sibling that died at camp."

Tess sighed. "I'm so glad to hear that."

"Yeah. It was a stupid thing to tell you. Sorry."

"No, I feel better because I lied to all of my readers and told them that I had a younger sibling that died, too."

"Sara?"

"I made her up." Tess bit her lower lip and smiled. "I wondered if they'd all buy it. They did."

"So did you," I said.

"How many of us are making up fake dead people?"

"I don't know."

"We're terrible!"

Her eyes widened. She hesitated before she asked, "Your dad?"

"No, he's really dead. But I've never taken a ballet class in my life."

"That's okay. I never did a show on Broadway."

"I didn't buy that lie for one second."

"Like I believed that you really stole a CD from Borders because they didn't have the book you wanted in stock."

"Okay, that didn't happen."

"I know!" Tess shouted at me. "It's way too lame to be true."

"Bitch!" I shouted back. We were quickly back to how we were the night we first met, even though I still felt a little reserved. I wasn't willing to let her have as much of me as I did that first time.

"When are you going to tell everyone about Ian?" she asked.

I looked up from my fries. "What do you mean?"

"I mean how you've obviously made him up. Nobody would put up with all of your shit. Unless he's really ugly."

Only her smile told me she was teasing.

"You've clearly made him up and I'm hurt that you'd make all of us think that you're something you're not, Anna Koval."

She laughed. I laughed. I sipped my coffee as she continued. "Besides. He totally wants to fuck me, and you know it."

I looked back up at her. "That's so gross, Tess."

"No, he told me. He's in love and we've been writing in secret and he told me that he's terribly jealous that I'm with you this weekend instead of him. He wanted the three of us to mug down on your futon."

Was this a trick? Was she trying to make me confess everything? Or was she testing to see if I knew about Ian's e-mail? Maybe she already figured out that I sent that e-mail and she wanted to see if I'd fess up.

I didn't say anything. Any word seemed like the wrong one.

"God. You should see your face," she said as she tossed her napkin onto the table. "Calm down. I'm kidding."

I hated it that I didn't know which part she was kidding about. I hadn't checked the fake Ian e-mail account in a while. I wondered if she had written him back after Dale's prank.

Again I realized I barely knew this girl sitting across from me. She was too young to be friends with me. I didn't want a relationship with Tess. I came on this trip for Kurt. I just wanted her to know the truth so she didn't waste her time with me or get hurt. I needed her to know that people aren't always who or what they say they are. I wanted her to learn something from this. I figured I could test out telling the truth to her to see how bad the reaction would be. If she wasn't upset, maybe Kurt wouldn't be either.

"I'm not getting married next year," I started. "There's no talk of it at all." I looked down as my mouth kept running. "My parents don't live in Houston. I don't have an ex named Devon. I never skipped a grade. I was never in a holdup. I didn't write a book of poems that were almost published. I'm not in a play right now. In fact, I haven't been in a play in a long time. I sort of gave up acting but I'm too afraid to tell anybody. I'm afraid everybody will find out I'm a fake. I'm torn because I don't care what most of my readers think, but I do care very much about a couple of you, so I keep lying for the benefit of the entire group.

I'm sorry I wasn't more honest with you. I didn't want to disappoint you."

When I finally looked up, Tess was staring at me with a huge smile. "Congratulations, Anna. You're as fucked up as the rest of us."

000052.

annakannak: Hello?

Idobler23: Hi.

annakannak: Am I doing this right?

Idobler23: I don't think there's a wrong way. Hi.

annakannak: This feels really stupid.

Idobler23: I know.

annakannak: How old are we?

Idobler23: Too old for this, I'm sure. Thank you for doing this.

annakannak: It's okay.

Idobler23: Where are you?

annakannak: I'm in my hotel room. I'm supposed to go out and meet my friend for drinks soon, but I told her I had to call Ian. So for the purposes of right now, you're Ian, okay?

Idobler23: Okay. Hey, baby. When should I change the kitty litter?

annakannak: That's good. Very convincing.

Idobler23: Thanks.

annakannak: You could give me your phone number.

Idobler23: Nope.

annakannak: Why not?

Idobler23: Because the last time we talked on the phone you didn't want to talk to me again ever. So I'm respecting your wishes. No phones.

annakannak: You're being stupid.

Idobler23: You're the stupid.

annakannak: I was going through some bad shit. I'm sorry you felt like I was ignoring you or abandoning you. I wasn't. I promise. I'm sorry. Look, I'm here, aren't I? Hello?

Idobler23: You're only here for the conference. Don't try to sound like you're here for me.

annakannak: I know you like your town and all, but trust me, Pittsburgh isn't a place you hope you get to go to. I didn't jump up and down about the conference because I was getting to see the Tower of Knowledge.

Idobler23: The Cathedral of Learning.

annakannak: Whatever.

Idobler23: So why are you here?

annakannak: To meet one of my best friends.

Idobler23: Who?

annakannak: You.

Idobler23: Me?

annakannak: Yep.

Idobler23: Wow.

annakannak: Yeah.

Idobler23: Thank you.

annakannak: Well, it's true. Ta-da.

Idobler23: Now I feel like an asshole for making you go to a chat room to talk to me. I should be man enough to use a fucking phone, for fuck's sake.

annakannak: Nice language.

Idobler23: I cuss when I'm nervous.

annakannak: I can see that.

Idobler23: Aren't you nervous?

annakannak: Of course I am.

Idobler23: Is it because you're ugly?

annakannak: Asshole. What if I really am ugly?

Idobler23: Well, I think it's only fair to tell you now that I'm really, really ugly.

annakannak: Oh?

Idobler23: Hideous. Children running in the street, pointing and screaming.

annakannak: That's too bad.

Idobler23: I know. I tried hiding with my parents my entire life, but eventually my mother got so depressed having to look at my face boils every day that she kicked me out.

annakannak: I can understand.

Idobler23: Me too. But I wish she hadn't given me her family's nose. It's huge and gets in my way.

annakannak: In your way?

Idobler23: When I talk. Sometimes my upper lip catches on the end of my nose. Every once in a while you'll have to detach my lip from my nose. You don't mind, do you?

annakannak: Why can't you do it?

Idobler23: Because my hands ooze from all of the sores, and they're afraid it'll spread to my face if I touch it.

annakannak: What a horrible way to live.

Idobler23: You get used to it. Look how far we've come already. I appreciate how you love me for who I am and it doesn't matter what I look like. You can see the real me.

annakannak: That's because I know what it's like.

Idobler23: You do?

annakannak: Of course I do. You don't spend half your life with this body without learning a thing or two about how cruel the world is to the hideous.

Idobler23: You're hideous, too?

annakannak: Yes. I'm gigantic, but just in parts. Bad glands. I'm swollen in these strange areas. Like my left thigh. My other thigh is fine, but my left thigh is enormous. Sometimes it's so swollen that I can't wear anything on that side, so I wear tiny skirts. It wouldn't be such a bad thing if I didn't have a swollen right ass cheek.

Idobler23: That sounds awful.

annakannak: It's really only awful for the man in my life that has to drain it once a week. It gets really pussy.

Idobler23: That word is very different when you write it out. You do mean full of pus and not that your ass is a vagina, right?

annakannak: Hee. Yes.

Idobler23: Good.

annakannak: Anyway, I was discussing my hideousness. The huge thigh and huge ass aren't really what you end up noticing about me. See, my nose bleeds all of the time, and it drains into my gigantic lower lip. I've got no teeth, so it falls into my mouth where I make loud sippy noises and gulp my nose blood all day long.

Idobler23: Ew.

annakannak: What? How is it that I'm the one that went too far?

Idobler23: You're gross.

annakannak: Shut up.

Idobler23: No, seriously, I don't want to meet you now. I'm afraid I won't ever be able to sleep again.

annakannak: This was your game to begin with. Dammit.

Idobler23: So what do you think of Pittsburgh?

annakannak: I think it's fucking cold. And why can't I find a place to eat?

Idobler23: I'll show you a good place.

annakannak: Promise?

Idobler23: Well, I would have, before I knew how gross you were. I'll e-mail you a list or something instead.

annakannak: Very nice of you.

Idobler23: I try.

annakannak: Are we gonna do this? Are we gonna meet up?

Idobler23: Do you want to?

annakannak: I do. Is that okay? Do you want to?

Idobler23: Yes, Anna Koval. I'd very much like to meet you.

annakannak: Good.

Idobler23: Do you want to meet me?

annakannak: I do.

Idobler23: Well, we should do that, then.

annakannak: Okay.

Idobler23: You free tomorrow?

annakannak: After the conference, yes. Dinnertime.

Idobler23: Dinnertime tomorrow.

annakannak: Or tonight.

Idobler23: Oh.

annakannak: But tomorrow's good.

Idobler23: You want to meet tonight?

annakannak: No, you're right. Tomorrow's fine.

Idobler23: I didn't know you meant so soon.

annakannak: Forget it. I've got plans anyway.

Idobler23: We could. I could come by the bar or something.

annakannak: No, forget it. We'll do it tomorrow.

Idobler23: You sure?

annakannak: Yes, that was stupid. I can't even stay up too late, since I have the conference tomorrow.

Idobler23: You want to stay up late with me?

annakannak: Shut up.

Idobler23: It's so soon. We haven't even met yet.

annakannak: Shut up.

Idobler23: Slut.

annakannak: Stop.

Idobler23: Heh.

annakannak: So, tomorrow night.

Idobler23: Sounds good.

annakannak: You'll pick me up or should I meet you somewhere?

Idobler23: I can pick you up.

annakannak: Okay. Good.

Idobler23: The hotel's not far from where I live.

annakannak: Okay.

Idobler23: Is seven good?

annakannak: Yeah.

Idobler23: Then I'll see your ugly ass tomorrow.

000053.

Who Am I, Anyway?
Am I My Resume?

12 DECEMBER

It's cold in Pittsburgh. I've probably said it 15,000 times since my plane landed, but I'm not done. It's cold. The coldest we get in Austin is, like, 23 degrees. Then we cry. We cry because we don't understand anything so cold. I feel like my bones and muscles have frozen solid. My ears feel like they're in boiling water. This morning after my shower my nipples froze and shattered into pieces that scattered across the floor. I'm nippleless. I'm hideous!

So today I'm speaking at a conference about this website. People are going to ask questions like why do I keep this website and what kind of people are interested in someone like me and why do I tell you about my personal life.

People seem to not understand why I would do something like this, but I think the answer is simple: You are always there for me.

I've met great people through this page. Remember when I wrote about Taylor's kitty litter problem? At least sixty of you wrote to suggest a different kind of litter that wouldn't stick to his ass when he was done pooping. You people care about me, my cat, and my cat's ass. That's more than most of my friends care.

I love that when something happens to me, it can become bigger because of this page here. I can share it with the world and we can all laugh when I'm an idiot. We can all cry when I'm sad, and I never feel all that lonely. I like that I get feedback so soon after I post. You guys can feel like family. You make me feel important, and that makes me feel happy about myself and the choices that I've made.

Like this play I'm in right now. I haven't talked much about it because I've been so busy and we've had some sporadic rehearsals, but in this play my character has been writing letters to a man she's never met before. She answers a chain letter, and one of the chain letter recipients sends her some money, and inside is a letter asking her to be his pen pal. Ten years pass and they share each other's lives together through these stories.

Ten years of their loves, their losses, their successes. They share each other's pain. My character has this monologue where she decides to go and see him. After all of this time, she has no choice but to meet him because he stopped writing to her suddenly and she needs to see if he's okay. It's the first time he hasn't written and she's scared that something bad has happened.

Turns out he was fine. He had just fallen in love. He was getting married and was about to send her a wedding invitation. His fiancée had found all of their letters and felt threatened by their relationship, so he had to break things off. He's sad, but grateful he's saying good-bye to her in person.

My character then sings a song about how when you lose the piece of your heart that's been beating for you, you cannot live your life the same way ever again.

She dies on his doorstep.

I've been thinking about the power of words and how our relation-ship—yours and mine—is based on a series of words strung together to tell parts of a story. You get the parts I share with you, and I get the even rarer parts of your own stories that you fill in for me when you feel you want to.

So when they ask me today why I do this, I think I'll explain to them that if I didn't write to you, if you didn't write to me, if all of this suddenly ended, I think I might just die inside.

But that sounds way too dramatic, doesn't it? I always get dramatic when I'm away from home.

Please send earmuffs.

Love until later,

Anna K

000054.

Last night I dreamed that I met Kurt. It was raining, and I held a newspaper over my head as I walked through the streets. I looked up at the giant buildings over my head and I couldn't read any of the names. Everything was written in a different language. I kept walking, turning down streets, running from giant dogs, hiding behind trash cans as bad men ran past me, hurrying around in a city I didn't know, searching for a building I couldn't find.

And then suddenly I was standing right there, at the building where I was supposed to meet him. I didn't have time to check and see if I looked okay. A bolt of lightning slammed behind me. I screamed and ran inside the building.

It was dark. I squinted to find teenaged kids sitting at my feet. Their clothes were old and dirty. They huddled together like they needed the warmth, bowing forward and speaking quietly. The place looked like it used to be a restaurant some months ago but was now abandoned. There were cobwebs and the lighting was very poor. I heard a fan churning somewhere.

I squatted to ask one of the homeless teenagers if he knew where Kurt was. I didn't get a chance to speak. He pointed at the shadow of a man sitting at one of the tables. He was the only person not sitting on the floor. I handed the teenager my newspaper as a thank-you, and I walked over. All I could hear was the rain hitting the roof. Everyone inside the room was silent.

I couldn't see his face at first, but I knew he was looking at me. I pulled back my chair. The legs made a horrible screeching noise across the floor. Everyone shushed me and I sat down quickly.

It was Kurt. He was in front of me.

Water was still dripping down from my hair into my eyes. He put his hand to my face and wiped some of the water away. I grabbed his wrist and held on to it. He pulled his arm back until his warm hand slipped into mine.

We stared at each other. We had finally met, and there were no words that we needed to say. We sat there watching each other. Kurt's face broke out into a smile.

When I woke up a few seconds later, I couldn't remember what he looked like anymore.

000055.

Inside Anna K:
I've Been Probed

13 DECEMBER

So, I'm still alive. I know you were worried about me. The conference is over and I can breathe now. I've been nervous all morning. Now that it's over, I know a bit more about myself and a little more about my friends.

I wore these shoes that I know look good, but they smell. I fill them with baby powder before I put my feet in them, but they still stink once I pull my feet out. The problem is they're clogs, so sometimes I absent-mindedly pull my feet out to play with the shoes and then suddenly I'll smell my feet.

I've taken them off before in mixed company and people shout, "Good Lord, what is that smell?" I have to put them on in the morning and never take them off until I'm home, and then I run into the bathroom and wash my feet because even I can't stand it. My feet usually don't smell. I've never had this problem before. And two days ago the shoes received another strike against them: The right one makes a small squeak with every step. Some sort of air seems to be escaping from the sole when I step down. I sound like the little housecleaner from *Poltergeist*.

So, I'm a musical stinkfest walking down the hallway at this convention, but I won't get rid of these shoes. I had to search forever to find a pair of clogs that kept my feet protected, looked good, and had a three-inch heel.

Because of this, I was already on guard as I sat down at this conference and my friend started talking about web journals and visitors and hits or whatever. Then I got nervous. What were all of these people going to say to me? What did they want to know? What made me so special suddenly that I was behind a table facing a crowd of people while someone else discussed me? Would my life be different now that I was not hiding behind my webpage anymore? Now that they could see my face. Now that I was meeting people who used to be strangers.

To keep myself from running out of the room, I had no choice but to imagine having sex with them. The short bald guy on the end—I teased him a little. I wiggled on his lap and watched him get excited for me. But I was already on to the woman sitting next to him. I straddled her waist and let my hair cascade over her shoulders. She was holding dollar bills in the air and whooping it up. The guy behind her kept smacking her on the back, congratulating her for getting a chair so close to the front. The guy sitting next to her was writing about me in his Palm Pilot and I got so hot with the technology that I attacked him. He smelled like Brut and his neck was raw from shaving recently, but I didn't care and I went to town on him. Everyone got excited and started ripping off their clothes, grabbing at me, wanting to touch a tiny inch of my perfect flesh, which smelled like plums, and everyone was moaning and sweating and licking each other, and that's when someone asked the first question.

I had to have them repeat it. They asked when I decided to start a website. I said it happened when I decided to teach myself HTML so I could get a better paycheck. I made a joke about the dot-com bust and everyone laughed long enough for me to mentally dress them all again.

The hot blonde who just moments before had been asking if she could suck the inside of my knee asked me if I minded having people know the intimate parts of my life. I couldn't very well answer that I'd already tasted her right nipple and ask her how that felt, so I told her that I didn't feel like I revealed anything I wouldn't tell a friend. I consider myself to be a rather open person. I trust people. I like people.

The guy with the nine-inch dick then raised his hand. I smirked. He asked, "What makes you think you're so special?"

Suddenly I didn't see his giant dick anymore. None of my orgy partners was looking all that fly. Everybody was dressed again and staring at me all full of judgment and spite. BigDick continued and said, "I mean, why do you think anyone would care about what you have to say? It's your diary. Why do I want to read your diary? Who cares what you think? Who cares what happens to you every single day?"

I didn't know what to say, so luckily my friend said it for me: "Thousands of people every day care what she has to say."

"Yeah, but are they lonely people with nothing to do? What do you want out of this? Money? Fame? Attention? Are you the lonely one? Are journalers just a bunch of lonely women trapped in rooms filled with cats looking for someone else to talk to?"

I cleared my throat. "Actually, we're all just hopeful singles who can't keep a relationship going or we're in an emotionally abusive one because of our daddy issues. We surround ourselves with pets and strange friends and project a hectic, fulfilling life when we actually can't stand the sight of ourselves in the mirror every single morning."

The room was quiet, staring at me. "In other words," I continued, "We're just like you. We're human beings searching for validation."

I hate it when I fuck someone who turns out to be an asshole.

I know that it's strange to put my life out there like this. I'm risking something of myself for all of you. And I don't imagine that we're all losers. Sure, I sometimes say I'm hideous and dorky, but I assume we're all operating under the same notion that in real life we're basically interesting, attractive people. Online we can be honest and tell each other that we're scared of looking like idiots.

After the question-and-answer period, a group of people from the same company wanted to know more. They approached the table and asked questions about my personal life—about where I live and what I'd be willing to do if I was paid. I didn't want to answer any more questions. Turns out they worked for those Webcam sites where girls play with themselves online for money. I felt cornered and didn't want to hear these people proposition me. I didn't want them to show me how easily my webpage could become a money-making porn venture.

I had only one way out. I slid my feet out of my clogs.

You can pretty much count to thirty-six. That's when the smell will hit them. But because I had been nervous and uncomfortable, you only had to count to eighteen this time. The two men and one woman stood up sharply and stared at each other. They sniffed a couple of times.

"What's that smell?" BigDick moaned. "Is that *feet?*"

My friend grabbed me by the hand and pulled me up. She said, "Don't follow us or we'll call security."

We started giggling the second we hit the door and didn't stop until we were on our third beer at the hotel bar.

Don't call me a whore. I'll assault you with my stank-feet before you know what hit you.

Love until later,

Anna K

000056.

Walking back to my hotel room, I was anxious to get ready to see Kurt. He was picking me up in about an hour and I still needed to try on the three different outfits I had brought to see which one I'd end up wearing.

Tess was still on my heels, still giggling from the conference panel. We had a couple of beers in the hotel bar afterward, and she found it amazing that so many people wanted me to turn my site into porn.

"Are you going to write about this?" she asked me.

"I guess so. I pretty much have to, don't I?"

"I'm sorry they ended up being assholes. I wanted you to be the rock star here." She pulled on a piece of my hair as I ran the key card into my door. "Let me make it up to you tonight," she said. "My treat."

"I can't tonight, Tess." I knew this was coming, and I wanted to get it over with as quickly as possible. "I've got plans."

"Oh," she said, looking confused.

"An old friend who lives here. I called her before I left town and we're getting together to catch up. I haven't seen her since high school." It seemed physically impossible to stop lying to her.

Tess pulled her hair back with one hand. "I understand," she said, nodding. "That's fine." She started walking away, toward her room. "I'll just see you tomorrow morning, okay?"

"Yeah. Thanks, Tess."

"For what?"

I didn't know. It just seemed like the thing to say. I was thanking her for not making me tell her the truth. "Thanks for inviting me on the trip."

"Have a good night, Anna," she said, and walked into her room.

The message light on my phone was blinking red when I entered my room. There was only one voice-mail message. It was Kurt.

"You're gonna hate me," the message played in my ear. "I can't come tonight, Anna."

I dropped my purse on the bed and sank to the floor, the smell filling the room as my feet slipped out of my shoes. I felt nothing as I listened to Kurt talk.

"I'm not ready. I'm scared that this is going to fuck everything up."

I twirled the phone cord around my ring finger until the end of it was stuck. I saw the tip of my finger turning purple. With my other arm I threw a pillow off the bed from behind me. I untangled my finger and lit a cigarette as he went on.

"I'm afraid of what will happen if we meet. I'm afraid you've blown into my town long enough for me to fall in love with you and then you're going to blow back out and leave me here all alone and miserable. I don't want to put myself through any more heartache. I'm not ready for you to mess up my entire world. It's like you've already moved in and you're asking if we can knock down a wall to make more room for all your shit. And I want to knock down walls and give you more room around here. That's the problem. I want you to take everything. But the fact remains I can't let you. And I'm not strong enough to pretend that doesn't bother me. I'm hanging up now. Then I'm going to drink. Heavily. Tomorrow I hope that I will feel like less of an ass. Then we can meet up. I'll take you out to lunch. I'll plan shit for tomorrow. You wanted a friend and I've given you drama. I'm sorry. Tomorrow. We'll fix all this shit tomorrow. Maybe daylight will be less romantic. Maybe in the daylight things will be calmer and clearer and I won't be such a jag-off."

The message ended. I hung up and stared at myself in the mirror. I thought about how strained his voice was, how he'd pause to breathe and I'd hear him gulp between words. I wasn't worth all of this. I wasn't even sure if Anna K was worth all of this. Meeting me tomorrow would surely be a disappointment for him. There was no way I was going to live up to his expectations.

I couldn't sit in my room waiting for tomorrow. I had to keep my head busy. I had to stop myself from finding where Kurt lived, walking over to his place, taking off my clothes, and letting him have me for as long as he wanted. I had to stop myself from thinking that he and I were a possibility, especially when I was surely going to be a letdown. I had to have a night that had nothing to do with a man.

I called up Tess's room. "My friend bailed," I said as a hello.

"We're going dancing," she said immediately.

An hour later I found myself at an eighties nightclub that was busy and full of people wearing clothes I'd never wear. Tiny little shirts and tight pants were grinding against other tiny clothes that held tiny girls. It was freezing outside. They had to have gotten dressed inside the club, as I couldn't understand how else they got there without losing body parts from frostbite.

I had a brief fantasy about jumping the bouncer and having him fuck me in the VIP room. I was worried about how dirty my head had gotten lately. I had inappropriate thoughts about the desk clerk, my bellman, the guy who made my latte in the morning, the guy who hailed my cab, the guy who drove my cab, and now the guy checking my ID. I didn't know why my head was so active and why my body was so craving physical attention. Maybe dancing wasn't such a bad idea after all.

Tess was one of those dancers who went away when she was on the dance floor. She stared straight out, breaking it only to glance at her feet from time to time, and her body grooved to the music. Every once in a while her gaze would catch mine and she'd smile, but mostly she kept to herself.

I'm more of a social dancer, and luckily there were a few other social dancers around me. We moved and swayed together, grabbing each other's hips and singing along to the music. Salt-N-Pepa's "Push It" found me face to face with a skinny boy with a good chest who pulled me in and pushed me out and turned me in the right ways. The song was silly, but the sweat was good. It was nice to be touched, to be held in the small of my back, to feel sweat running down the back of my neck.

The eighties music only lasted for about half an hour and then the vibe changed to a pulsing house beat. The room was dark and there were laser lights flashing around us. A fog machine was in the corner, which I thought was completely unnecessary. The fun group of dancers next to me left to get something to drink and was replaced by wiggly boys dancing to the trance music. Everyone was on his or her own now, spinning and jumping, twisting erratically, falling into separate worlds.

Once it was no longer fun for me, I walked away through the fog. The club had become so dark I couldn't see Tess. I walked to the bar for a bottle of water before I walked outside the club to cool off.

The air out in front of the club was brisk against my skin, but it was nice to be away from all of the noise. I lit a cigarette and checked my watch. It was only one. I opened my purse and grabbed my cell phone.

Dale answered on the second ring.

"Yay! You're not dead!" he cheered. "Stalker boy and stalker girl have yet to kill you!"

"Yes, I'm completely alive and still have all my limbs."

"Good. Wait. Are you trapped inside of a washing machine? What's that noise?"

"I'm at a club."

I couldn't hear anything because of the noise outside, but I knew Dale was laughing at me.

"Dale, I don't need this right now."

"It's just . . . I think it's cute you're hanging out with the kids again. Watch your drink, you might get some Roofies."

"I'm still not laughing."

After I recapped the web conference, he asked, "Did Tess say anything about Ian writing to her yet?"

"No, not really," I said as I blew out a puff of smoke. "She said something about him wanting to sleep with her, but then she said she was kidding. We need to check Fake Ian's e-mail when I get home."

"I don't trust that girl."

"You don't trust anyone."

"Hey, I haven't told you my good news yet. I finished the screenplay."

"That's great! When do I get to read it?"

"Wait. More good news. I asked one of my friends who works with Austin FilmWorks to take a look at it. She liked it and she gave it to someone else to read who gave it to someone else and that person wants to pay for it and—blah, blah, blah, Hollywood, blah—they're going to make my movie!"

"That's fantastic! I'm so proud of you!"

"So why haven't you met stalker boy yet?"

I took a breath. "He cancelled."

"Because he's actually a woman living in Arizona? I knew it. Jason totally owes me ten bucks."

"Because he thinks he's in love with me."

"Dammit! I hate when I'm far away from the good gossip."

I told him everything from the chat room to the phone call just a few hours ago.

"He's going to kill you," Dale concluded.

"He is not. He's just confused."

"Only crazy people tell you that they love you so much they can't ever see you. It's because they're trying not to kill you."

"He's not a crazy person. What if he really loves me?"

"Yes, well, it's too bad you're already attached to the perfect man. He called, by the way. Finally. Said he's sorry he treated you like shit and ignored you after you let him fuck you in your mom's house. Oh, wait. No. That wasn't him. That would have been *sensible* and would have been the *right thing to do*, but you're non-dating an *asshole* who's trying to get out of weddings just so he never has to—"

"I got it, Dale," I said, cutting him off. "Okay," I whispered.

"Tell your Internet boy the truth. What do you have to lose?"

I could lose everything. The potential to have it all. I could lose the first person in a long time who really thought I was something special.

The cold was starting to get to me, so I promised Dale I'd call him the next day to fill him in on everything.

I found Tess inside and told her that I wanted to go home. She was dancing with a boy who had a Glo-Stick in his mouth. She asked if I minded taking a cab. I wished her luck and was grateful to be on my way so easily.

I checked my e-mail when I got back to my room. For the first time in over four months, Kurt hadn't written. I went to sleep feeling that missing letter, wondering what percentage of my daily conversations happened with machines.

000057.

ldobler23: Good morning, Anna.
annakannak: Oh! Kurt? Hi. This thing made a noise and it scared me. I was just checking my e-mail. I didn't know that it automatically logged me onto this thing.

ldobler23: I'm glad it did.

annakannak: Hi.

ldobler23: Hi.

annakannak: Hi.

ldobler23: Do you hate me?

annakannak: Of course I don't hate you.

ldobler23: I can't believe I said all of that last night. Will you pretend I didn't?

annakannak: No.

ldobler23: Oh.

annakannak: It would be hard to pretend that.

ldobler23: I guess so.

annakannak: So, are you picking me up soon?

ldobler23: Yes.

annakannak: No pussing out today?

ldobler23: No pussing out. I promise.

annakannak: What are we going to do?

ldobler23: Fun things.

annakannak: Pittsburgh fun things, huh? If you say so.

ldobler23: I'll pick you up at ten. Don't eat lunch.

annakannak: Okay, I'm starting to get scared now.

ldobler23: Really?

annakannak: Yeah. What if this ruins us forever?

ldobler23: I'm sure it won't.

annakannak: You could hate me.

ldobler23: I won't.

annakannak: Promise?

ldobler23: No.

annakannak: Fucker.

ldobler23: I'll see you soon.

annakannak: How will I know which one is you?

ldobler23: You'll know.

000058.

I met Tess in the lobby an hour later.

"Do you want to keep the rental car?" I asked her.

"No," she said. She was wearing a Cure T-shirt and jean shorts with tights under them, a look I hadn't seen since I was in the ninth grade. "I'm going to have the hotel shuttle take me to the airport."

I had brought her a cup of coffee. She sipped it.

"You look nice," she grunted.

"Oh. Well, I haven't seen my friend in a while. You know how you always want to look like you're doing better than the last time you saw a person."

"Are you? Doing better?" She wasn't looking at me.

"I don't know."

"I'm sorry. I'm cranky this morning. I was up with that guy very late."

"Oh, yeah. How did it go?" I lit a morning cigarette and leaned in. "Did you do the nasty? Da butt?" I bumped into her hips and moaned, "Oh! Sexy! Sexy!"

"It's very early, Anna. Please don't dance before ten."

"Sorry." I giggled into my coffee.

"What gives you so much energy this morning?"

Only one more hour. One more hour. Just one more hour. Sixty minutes. Less than that by now. Even less by the time I realized that it was even less. The minutes, ticking by.

"Before you run off to have fun with your real friends, I brought you something." Tess was handing me a box that was wrapped with silver paper. "Don't freak out. I made them."

They were superhero action figures. One was obviously Tess, with the hair and the giant "T" on the chest. The other one was either me or Hester Prynne.

"I thought you might like to have some more updated Barbies," she said. "You know, with real sexpot superstars."

"I can't believe you made these." They looked incredible. "Do their legs bend all the way back?"

"I just took some old dolls, changed their hair and painted some new makeup on them. I made the clothes. I was bored one night and on too many Nō-Dōz. I had a French final I blew off. No big deal. You like them?"

I did.

"Thank you."

We hugged. We wished each other safe trips home. We promised not to write anything incriminating about each other. When she went back to her room, I saw her wipe a tear away in haste. "I'll miss you!" she shouted as she shut the door.

Fifty-two minutes later, I was standing outside the hotel. I couldn't wait in the lobby anymore. I had already gone over my list of lies, had three cups of coffee, eaten two pieces of gum and six Altoids. I had brushed my hair and applied lip gloss and put on moisturizer. I had run out of preparatory things to do and I couldn't sit still any longer.

I gave myself whiplash craning my head down the street as I waited for Kurt to pick me up. I didn't even know what kind of car I was looking for. Since he could be just about anyone, each person walking toward me went through an evaluation process. If the person walking toward me wasn't him, I'd choose traits in this person I hoped Kurt would have. I was trying to decide if Kurt should have a nose ring when I heard a voice from behind.

"Well, hello, Anna K."

John Cusack has dark hair, a tiny mouth, and looks like a good kisser. Kurt was tall, blond, with glasses and no nose ring. Still looked like a good kisser.

"How did you know it was me?" I asked.

"I didn't. Lucky guess." He smiled and looked up to the sky. "Very lucky," he said quietly. We both exhaled at the same time.

He took me to lunch at a little diner that he said was near his house. He ordered a club. I had a BLT. The table was blue, with this plastic lacquer type of thing over it. It had postcards decoupaged inside the lacquer. The postcards were of different shots of San Francisco. Alcatraz. Trolleys. Fisherman's Wharf.

The chairs we sat in were wooden and worn. The seats were too hard and unforgiving. The room smelled like mop water. The coffee was watery. The food was fine. Not that I ate much.

"You don't like tomatoes?" I asked him, noticing the food pushed to one side of his plate.

"No," he said.

"Oh."

"You want them?" He pushed his plate a bit toward me and a few fries tumbled off the side onto the table.

"No thanks," I said. "I've got a lot to eat here."

"Is it okay?"

"The food? Yes."

I had an incredibly hard time staring Kurt in the face. I don't know how I got so nervous. It was like I was waiting for him to ask me to dance. We gave each other the quickest answers to every question. Where were the jokes and the flirting we were so accustomed to? How did we end up scaring each other like this?

I grabbed the salt shaker and it fell out of my hand. As I lurched to pick it up, my elbow hit my water glass, sending it tumbling over.

I jumped up and cursed. Kurt was quick with the napkins, preventing the spill from pouring into our laps. Water dripped off the table to the floor. A busboy came up with a mop. People were staring. I could feel the tears beating in my entire face, waiting to make their move. He was right; we were ruining everything by meeting face to face.

Kurt looked up at me and made eye contact. "Let's get out of here, okay? I'm not hungry anymore."

We walked outside of the diner. I spoke first. "I'm sorry."

"We're nervous."

"Do I make you nervous?" I asked.

"I make myself nervous, Anna," he answered. He pulled off his glasses and started to clean them on the end of his shirt. He looked over my head, down the street. "I imagined our first afternoon together so many different ways, but I never thought it would be me saying stupid shit while you wished you were somewhere else." He was much taller than I was, and I could see a small scab on his neck where he must have cut himself shaving.

"Hey," I said suddenly. "Take me to your bar with those guys that tell you about your life."

He smiled. "I can't believe you remember that."

Two beers each later, we were much more relaxed. We were able to look at each other. We made jokes and even touched each other a few times. Avoiding talk about anything uncomfortable, we refrained from discussions of Ian, my father, his message last night, or his ex, Heather. We stuck to movies, sports, and music. We ended up arguing over which song is better for trashing a hotel room: Prodigy's "Firestarter" or L7's "Shit List."

"I can't believe your friends aren't here," I pouted.

"Wait long enough and they'll show up. There's one now."

An older man with a large, rounded stomach took his place on a stool at the end of the bar. He gave a small wave to Kurt. "Is that the girl?" he said loudly.

"Ah, jeez," Kurt said, lowering his head toward the bar. "I knew this was a bad idea." He looked back to the end of the bar. "Hey, Al."

"You did good, Kurt!" Al shouted back, his thumbs and fore-fingers forming two "OK" symbols over his head.

"Thanks," Kurt said as he led me by the elbow away from the bar. "Let's get a booth," he said.

"You aren't as short as you make yourself sound," he said to me after our next round. We were huddled together in the booth, the room quickly getting darker.

"Tall shoes," I replied. "You aren't as much of a loser as you make yourself sound."

"You thought I'd be a loser?" A waitress brought by a lit candle inside a Mason jar.

"No, but you talked like *you* thought you were a loser," I said.

"How does someone do that?" he asked as he sipped his beer.

"I don't know. With more whining? I kind of thought you'd be fat."

"Thanks. Because I'm a loser?"

"No. I just thought you might be fat. Your voice, I guess."

"I have a fat voice?"

"You speak with a fat accent."

He shook his head. He laughed.

His eyes were brown. His hair fell down in chunks around his face, but it wasn't messy. His hair had a natural wave that framed his face nicely. His face was clean-shaven, and I could see a few scars on his chin and one under his right eye. I asked about it.

"My sister. We were fighting over an Easy Bake Oven packet and she jabbed me with a pickup stick."

"That's a puncture wound?"

"I'm not really sure how she did it. She's strong. I couldn't have been more than ten. It wasn't even that bad of a cut—it just scarred for some reason. I like it because it's in the shape of a letter *C,* and my sister's name is Cassie. Cassandra, actually, but I like that she put her mark on me like she's Inigo Montoya."

I turned my hand over and showed him the inside of my right elbow. "Sisters always cause scars, don't they?"

"Theresa?" he asked.

"Who?"

"Theresa. I thought that was your sister's name. Shannon is the other one, right?"

As far as he knew. I tried to cover quickly, but I'm sure I looked caught. "We call her Meredith, mostly. Theresa is her middle name. I don't know why I told you her name was Theresa." Only the last sentence had any truth in it.

We shared an order of onion rings as we watched Al hit on the girl who sat next to him. She left seconds later, quickly cursing at him before bursting out the door.

"Hey, baby, you'll miss me when I'm on the moon," Al shouted at the closed door. The bar erupted in laughter.

"I'll miss him, too," Kurt said. "I never get to go to the moon."

"That's where all the really cool guys get to go." I looked up to see that the place had gotten quite crowded while we talked.

"What's the worst pickup line you ever heard?" Kurt asked, dipping an onion ring into a puddle of ketchup.

I thought for a moment. "He said to me, 'Hey, you know you could be Julia Roberts' stunt double?'"

Kurt laughed into his drink. "What does that mean?"

"I know! I look nothing like Julia Roberts, in the first place."

"I wasn't going to say that, but yeah, you look nothing like her."

"Thanks." I dug my straw into my Coke and rooted through the ice.

"Not that you're not pretty, but you don't look like Julia Roberts. You've got blond hair and she's easily a foot taller."

"If by a foot you mean five inches or so," I said. "But I get your point. Thanks."

"I'm not saying you're unattractive. You're very pretty." He was pleading for me to look back at him again.

I smiled. "But that's not the strangest part of what he said. He said I could be her *stunt double*. Does that mean I'm the burly version of Julia Roberts?"

"What did you say to him?"

"I told him that he looked like a poor man's Bruno Kirby."

"Nice."

"Thanks," I said. "What's your worst?"

"That a girl ever used on me?" he asked. "Well, once a girl handed me her phone number and told me to call her when I was 'done with' Heather. Because Heather is some kind of disposable item. She said it like she was asking me if I was done with these onion rings or something."

"What did you say to her?"

"I didn't get a chance. Heather slapped her in the face."

"Heather was *there*?" The waitress brought over another round of Cokes.

"The girl had a lot of balls," Kurt said. "Heather wasn't the kind of girl you pulled that shit around."

"What's the worst line you ever used?" I asked him.

"What makes you think I use lines on women?"

"Just taking a wild guess."

"Oh, I'm sure I once said something really stupid like, 'Are you a thief? Because you just stole my breath away.'"

"You never said that."

"Everyone's in junior high at some point, Anna."

"Lord."

"What line did you use?" He leaned in toward me and the scent of him filled my head. Warm, like a fire burning and someone drinking hot chocolate. A little spicy and warm.

"I'm a girl. We don't use pickup lines," I said, leaning into his smell. My head felt lighter. I bit my lip, aware of how much I'd been grinning.

"You just use your computer to pick up guys."

I leaned back. "I'm not picking you up."

"Come on," he said. " 'I'll buy the onion rings?' That's the worst line I've ever heard."

"I know the best line I've ever used." I smiled.

"What's that?"

"I'll kick your ass in Street Fighter."

"The video game?" he asked.

"Yep. Makes 'em melt every time."

"Do you really know how to play or is it just a line?" He leaned in toward me again.

"Oh, I'll kick your ass in Street Fighter," I boasted. "And then you'll be in love with me forever."

"I don't doubt it," he said quietly. We went back to our food. That line worked every damn time. I knew he was into me just as much as I was into him.

"What's your best?" I asked.

"I'm not as crafty as you are. I don't lure women into arcades to force them into loving me."

"Okay, you win for 'Less Desperate.' Now tell me your line."

"Ever since I first saw you I've been dying to know what it's like to lean into your body as I slowly make love to you all afternoon. I want the smell of you all over me. I want to do very dirty things to you until you're so weak you can't move anymore. And then I want to go get some ice cream."

I know he said things after that, but I didn't hear them. I was imagining what his apartment looked like and exactly where I'd be pinned as he slowly worked me over. Would we be in the kitchen? Would we be in a hallway near a bathroom? Was there a mirror where I'd spot myself smiling before I closed my eyes and allowed myself to fall into him?

I don't know if he even asked me, but within the hour we were at his place. I was surprised to see that it wasn't actually dark outside yet; the bar had tricked me into thinking it was late at night. It was still the afternoon, and the overcast sky gave everything a beautiful blue-gray haze.

His apartment was small. The floors were wooden, and there were signs of a dog.

"Heather's dog. She'd stay here sometimes because I loved her so much. The dog. Well, and Heather. In any event, she's not here anymore. Trooper. Or Heather." He showed me a picture of a big, floppy basset hound.

The painting he was working on was wonderful. It was the family portrait broken up into little squares, and inside each square was another painting of his family, and all of the squares added up to a larger version of the family. It was like a memory of a family gathering, how if you stared at something long enough, when you closed your eyes it broke apart in your head and you only remembered tiny squares of things.

I closed my eyes and saw his apartment as it shattered into tiny squares in my mind. His coffee table, where there was a very old *TV Guide*, three pens, and a 7-11 Double Gulp cup. The wall over his couch, where he had a framed Rothko print (it was blue and red). I could see the kitchen, where he had wineglasses and a stainless-steel refrigerator covered in photos and magazine clippings. In front of his television there was a guitar I hoped he wouldn't play. I saw his desk. The computer was off. I stared at the keyboard for a few seconds as Kurt went to get a glass of water. That was where he spent so many hours writing to me. That's where he wrote all about himself and asked questions about my life and probed into my head. That's where he thought about me, about who I was and about how he wanted me in his life.

I had been in this apartment so many times over the past year and yet this was the first time I'd ever seen it.

As Kurt handed me a glass of water, our fingers touched. I blushed for noticing it. Behind him was a section of wall, close to his bedroom, that would be a great place to get pinned against. I could hear my pulse and feel the blood rushing through my wrists.

"It's wonderful," I said, gesturing toward the painting as I sat on his dark green couch.

The room filled with the sound of an ambulance siren. Kurt laughed and pointed in the air, his awkward motions reminding me about the nearby hospital. Over his shoulder I saw a framed picture of a woman laughing. Was that Heather or his sister?

"I'm going to show you something," he said as he walked back to a stack of canvases against a wall. "Promise you won't laugh."

I walked toward him. "I can't promise a thing."

He pulled out one canvas and held it against his chest. His arms were wide as he gripped the sides. "I painted you."

I felt my eyes widen.

"Don't say anything yet," he said. "I didn't know what you looked like, so this is all wrong now that I know, but I was thinking about you one night and I painted what I thought you'd look like. It's dumb, but I promised myself that I'd show you this some day, and now here you are. So here."

He rested it in our laps. The wooden brace felt cool to the touch. The paint sat thickly on the canvas. A young girl was smiling at me. She had strawberry-blond hair—straight but full as it fell around her pale skin. She looked delicate, with a very small forehead that curved into a tiny nose that perked upward. He had given her dimples, and her chin jutted out in a smirk. Her hair hung down loosely, but one hand was frozen beside her head, pulling a strand of hair behind her ears, right beside her vibrant green eyes. There was a sparkle he had painted in them that was so sharp it seemed that the girl in the painting knew something about me that I didn't want her to know. She wore a tiny silver tiara. A banner hung over her head. "Love Until Later," it read. She might not have been me, but she was certainly Anna K.

"She's beautiful."

"I'll do another one now that I know what you look like. But I thought you might get a kick out of this anyway." Our legs were touching and his arms were over mine as we both held the picture.

"I love it," I said. I could feel his breath on my skin, next to my left ear.

"I'm glad," he said quietly. He leaned the picture against a table and looked at me.

"I'm glad to have met you, Anna K," he said plainly. "You are one very charming lady."

"Cool," I responded. *Cool?*

Kurt put the picture out of our reach and then moved his hand near mine. I went to put my hands close to his and ended up tipping my glass of water. I shot up and cursed. "The second time today," I moaned. "What is wrong with me?"

"You're starting to sober up," Kurt joked. He mopped the spill with a towel from his bathroom. "It's okay. Sit back down."

I sat near him and he put his arm around me. "Do you know what kind of nasty things I've spilled right here?" he asked.

"No."

"I'm not going to tell you. But I want you to know that this water puddle would be disgusted to know what it covered up. It's okay. Calm down."

He pulled his glasses off his face and put them on the table. He rubbed his eyes. He blinked as he refocused on me. He looked younger without his glasses. Smoother. His entire face softened, and I wanted to kiss his forehead so badly. Just pull him toward me and thank him for making me feel better so many times over the past few months. I was so happy to be right there.

He held my hand, stroking my pinkie with his.

"Is this okay?" he asked.

I nodded.

"I don't want to cross any lines with you," he said.

"You're not crossing any line," I said, as I moved my head to his shoulder. I was leaning my entire body against the side of him, hoping he'd grab me and pull me to him. I wanted him to take control and move me, clutch me, and make me forget we had met under these strange circumstances.

He stood up. "We should go," he coughed. He walked into his bedroom. He turned back around to say, "You smell very good. Now put your shoes back on."

In the solitude of the bathroom a few minutes later, I wondered how upset Kurt would be when I told him the truth about Ian. Would he be relieved to know that I was available or would he feel betrayed? I wondered if he was the kind to forgive easily. Was he even ready for something like this, so soon after Heather? I looked myself over in the mirror and fixed my lip gloss.

Kurt deserved to know the truth, and he'd want to know that I was actually a single girl who thought he was fascinating and sexy. Then we'd have a wild night in Pittsburgh. No pressure, no guarantees of anything, just one night (with the possibility of more). I'd put it all out for him to decide what he wanted. He'd see how vulnerable I'd become in telling the truth, and he'd want to take advantage of our remaining time together.

Kurt said it'd be cold where we were going, so he gave me an old sweater of Heather's as we left his apartment.

We drove for a while before we walked deep into downtown Pittsburgh.

"I like all the Christmas stuff," I said, looking up at the tall brick buildings.

"*Sparkle* stuff. Pittsburgh doesn't allow you to say Christmas. Or Hanukkah. Or Kwaanza or Ramadan or anything religious, because there are all different kinds, including atheists. So they made a city mandate and it's now called The Sparkle Season. We hate it."

"Who's 'we'?"

"Everybody."

Later down the road, Kurt pointed at a sign in front of a bar that read FUCK THE SPARKLE SEASON.

"See?" he asked as he shot me that smile, the one I'd always imagined but never believed I'd really see. And now there he was right next to me, within touching distance. Real. Flesh. A person. Anything was possible now. I felt giddy with anticipation.

He pointed out the new baseball stadium. As he stood at a statue of Roberto Clemente, I excused myself to find a bathroom.

I pulled my list out of my coat pocket. I had brought my lie list with me. I was going to remember everything I had said that was untrue and explain everything. I was going to come clean. It was time.

As I found my way back to Kurt, he smiled when he saw me. "Hey, you," he said. "It still trips me out that you're here, just a bit."

He kissed my cheek. "You're cold," he said. "Come on. Run with me. We'll warm up."

He started running down the street. I broke into a sprint. My feet found an ice puddle and I slipped. My hands flew out of my pockets to steady myself and my lie list flew into the air. I reached to grab it, but it swirled into the wind. Kurt ran back toward me to help.

"No!" I shouted. "Just let it go!"

He kept grabbing for the list, the paper twirling in the air just out of his reach. "No, I got it! I got it!"

I saw him getting closer and closer to the list of lies. He'd grip the edge of the paper right before another gust of wind would rush in and pull it away. He jumped and grunted as his gloved hands groped for the paper. Another gust of wind pulled the paper up and down the street.

"Just forget it!" I shouted.

Kurt pulled off his gloves and started running toward it. "It's going to go over the bridge!" he shouted.

I ran after him, screaming for him to stop. He was determined to be a hero. The paper was sailing toward the bridge. I prayed my lie list would suffer an icy, wet death.

The wind died, the list began its descent, and Kurt lifted his hand.

I threw myself into Kurt's body. My hands went around his waist and my mouth found his neck as I blew hot air on his skin in an exhale. I heard him gasp and saw the paper fly out of his hands and over his head. I watched it sail down to the water.

His arms were around me as he started chuckling. "I think you ruptured my spleen."

"Thanks for trying."

"Was it important?"

"No," I said, shaking my head. "Not anymore."

"I was worried it was your airline ticket."

"No, it wasn't. That would have been terrible."

"Not too terrible," Kurt said. He smiled at me with a smile that said I could never do anything wrong. He was absorbing me with his eyes, taking in all of me. I felt more beautiful than I ever had in my life. I felt captivating. Important.

He grabbed my hand and held it. He hadn't put his glove back on. My hand felt hot inside of his. I felt my face flush as he walked me down the street. It started to snow.

When you live in Texas, every single time you see snow it's magical.

I didn't want to tell him anything that would change the way he looked at me. The way his eyes searched mine, I felt he was fascinated every time I spoke. If I told him that I'd been lying, he might never look at me that way again. I wasn't ready to do that yet. I wanted more time on this pedestal.

We went to The Andy Warhol Museum. More specifically, he took me to his favorite room in the museum. The Silver Clouds room is quiet and white. It's filled with giant silver pillows that float and suspend. A fan in the corner of the room keeps the air circulating so that the pillows keep bumping into each other, gathering and separating, floating around the room like a giant space romper room.

As we stared into the room from the doorway, Kurt explained that there was a period in time when Warhol decided his art was over. He thought his career was coming to an end and that he was working on his last exhibition. So he decided to end it himself by making his art float away forever. He created silver Mylar pillows filled with helium. But the Mylar was too heavy for the balloons. Instead of taking off, they hovered in the air. Andy's art wouldn't leave even when he was trying to send it away.

The fans in the room tossed the clumsy, lumbering silver balloons in a hushed, beautiful dance. They were like elephants suspended and slowed down in time—moving and bumping, hoping for contact, repelling touch.

"You have to walk through this thing," Kurt said. I was nervous, so he pulled me by the hand into the room.

I saw our reflection in each pillow as it slowly floated toward us. Pillows were over my head; more were hanging out next to my feet. I kicked one accidentally and it bounced into another, and they both slowly floated away from me. Everything moved slower than the pace of life. It made everything seem quiet and small and still. I hesitantly reached out and touched one. It made a soft crinkle as my fingers slid over the smooth surface, my image distorted in the reflection of this exaggerated silver Pop Tart.

One pillow moved out of my way as the fan pushed it to my right. I looked up to see Kurt standing in front of me. I could see myself in the balloon to his right. I saw my face, red from the cold and smiling from the boy. I saw my arms reach for him. I saw him look down and then at me. I saw us hold each other by the waist. I saw us kiss.

I've never had a kiss that tasted as sweet as that kiss in that room with that boy. That feeling, right there, of everything falling into place—of mouths uniting two people who have been searching for so long for the perfect moment—I had never believed in it before. Standing against him, I was still the fastest-spinning object in the room.

We kissed as the silver clouds danced around us. We kissed as we moved to the couches in the lobby. We kissed until they kicked us out. We kissed every three steps in the street. We couldn't find the car because we were kissing so much. We kissed in an alley as the snow came down around us. We shivered into each other and held each other's skin under our clothes. It had grown dark and the streetlights illuminated our breath as it rose around our heads.

As we leaned against a brick wall, I pulled away to pull a stray hair out of my mouth. My face was wet and stinging from the cold. My jaw ached. My lips were chapped from the raw weather. We both giggled.

"You're a very good kisser." I smiled.

"So are you," he exhaled as he leaned in to kiss me again.

The next time we came up for air, he asked, "Are you okay? Is this all okay?"

I nodded, unable to talk. I was panting.

"If at any point this becomes not okay, you let me know and we'll stop. I don't want to do anything you don't want to do."

"I thought you didn't use lines on women." I smiled, surprised that I was able to fire enough synapses to crack a joke.

"You make me weak," he answered.

With each kiss I got stronger. Every time his mouth moved on my neck or his hands gripped my sides I felt more confident that I could tell him the truth.

As we drove home, I made him pull over five times to kiss on the side of the road, headlights whirring past us in the dark. I wondered how I was so lucky. I was kissing him and still nothing had screwed it up. Maybe it was because he didn't know everything about me or because I was something forbidden. Right then I didn't care to find out the answer.

We kept kissing until we got back to his apartment. We kissed against his front door. I was ready for anything, wanted him to do everything. I wanted him to steal me and keep me in his apartment forever. I had to let him have all of me.

Once inside his apartment I took off my coat and said, "I'd feel better if I wasn't wearing this sweater."

"You're hot?"

"No, it's Heather's."

He looked me in the eyes. "I didn't even notice, Anna. I just saw you."

It was time to tell him the truth. If he was going to have all of me, he had to know who I really was. I opened my mouth to say something, but he backed up. "I can't believe I said that," he said. " 'I just saw you.' That's what I said. When did I become so cheesy?"

He kissed me again. Full and strong. I lost my words.

"When I'm kissing you I can't say anything stupid. From now on, whenever I say something cheesy, I'm going to follow it with something gross about myself. Here: 'I just saw you.' I sometimes forget to brush my teeth before I go to bed."

"I need to tell you something," I said.

"Okay. Say something nice about me and then something awful about yourself. Something good; something gross."

He couldn't have set it up any better.

"I think you're an incredible person. And I'm a liar."

"Too vague. We're all liars." He kissed the base of my neck and said, "Try again."

I started falling to the ground as my knees weakened, my hands jutting out behind me to catch myself on whatever was closest. I felt him breathing into me, pulling me tighter to his body as he eased us to the floor. I wanted to tell him as much as I wanted to never speak again. "I think you're amazing," I gasped. "And I need to tell you something about Ian."

He pulled back from me. "Another rule," he said, holding up one finger and wiping his mouth with his other hand. "No talking about Ian."

"It's not like that," I started.

"I don't care what it's like," he said. "I don't want to hear his name. Is that okay? It's selfish, but I don't want to think about him while I'm with you. And I don't want to know that you're thinking of him while you're in my home. If we're going to keep doing this, I can't think about him."

"It's just, I . . . Kurt, we're not together," I said.

"I know. I know we're not together. I don't need you to remind me. I told you to stop if you didn't feel right about this." He stood up. "We should stop."

"No," I said, standing up and grabbing his hand. "I mean Ian and I aren't together. I haven't been telling you the truth."

"You mean you guys are on a break or something?" he asked.

I took a breath, ready to explain everything, ready to lose everything just to have all of the confusion over, when he said, "I don't want to know. I'm this guy you're allowed to be with because you're mad at him or you need attention or whatever the excuse is. You're not with him right now and that makes this okay for you. I get it. Don't justify it to me. I want you here. Please don't say his name anymore. I want you. I don't care about anything else. We'll deal with it tomorrow. If you want me, tonight I want you."

He pulled me toward him again and moved his hand to my breast. He kissed my collarbone as he whispered into the skin of my neck, "And Chinese food makes me gassy."

We climbed into his bed. He was on top of me. Our bodies weren't used to each other.

"You're on my hair," I said.

"Sorry," he panted. He moved to the right. "Ow!" he yelped. "That's my arm."

"Sorry," I whispered, and moved my elbow.

We both wiggled to fit our bodies into each other. He was tall, and when his hips moved against mine his head was well over me. I pulled myself up to kiss his neck, but I couldn't reach his face anymore.

"Hey," I said quietly.

He snapped his head down to kiss me and his chin hit the bridge of my nose. My eyes watered from the sting and he rolled off me, asking if I was okay.

"I'm okay," I said as I held my face in my hands. "Am I bleeding?" I held my head back for him to inspect.

"No blood," he said. "I'm so sorry."

"It's okay," I said. "You know, this is why dogs do it like they do. They get just as excited but do less physical damage to each other."

We started out slower and got better at it. By the time the night rolled around we were very, very good at it. We screamed over the sirens as ambulances passed. We talked and kissed and made love over and over. I had orgasms that made me blind. The arches of my feet were aching from having my toes clenched for so long. I kept craving more and more. I couldn't believe myself. All of those quick fantasies I'd been having over strangers were surfacing and he'd answer my cravings instantly with complete satisfaction. He hit every aching spot inside of me. I couldn't get enough of him.

I don't know when we fell asleep. I opened my eyes as the morning light crept into the room. He opened his eyes soon after. We stared at each other for a few seconds. We never said a word before we started kissing again, making love in the dim light, our bodies still aching from the night before. Quiet and hungry. Hushed and bittersweet. There were bruises and muscle cramps. My hips groaned at the weight of him, but I welcomed the pain. I wanted to feel him on me for weeks. I wanted him to leave a permanent mark.

We were quiet in the morning, knowing that our time was running out. There wasn't anything we could say to change the fact that I was about to fly very far away and he was going to stay here and what had happened between us was quickly coming to an end. My stomach felt hollow from the unexplored, the missing, the potential of us that might never be realized.

As I walked into the living room I noticed for the first time a shelf full of *Simpsons* figurines. "Oh!" I involuntarily said.

Kurt looked caught. "I didn't know if you saw those before."

"No, I didn't. Are they Heather's?"

"No, they're mine." He smiled.

"Can you tell me that they are Heather's so I can pretend you don't have a shelf full of Homer dolls?" Collections creep me out a bit, frozen people on display like that, but that these were from *The Simpsons* was an extra warning sign. It was possible that Kurt was one of those people who compared every funny thing that ever happened to a *Simpsons* episode. He'd speak like Comic Book Guy when a restaurant got his order wrong. He'd quote Ralph Wiggum lines when he was confused. *Simpsons* fans are their own kind of breed. It's like *Star Trek* except they think it's cool. They don't see the similarities.

I figured I owed him a few lies and secrets.

My insides were curling in regret as I reached the door of my rental. As the ambulances charged past us, screaming in urgency, Kurt held my head to his chest to guard my ears from the sirens. When the noise died down he kissed me and whispered, "Get out of my life."

"Everything is going to be okay," I said. "Things aren't exactly what you think they are. If you'd let me tell you."

"Don't, Anna. Don't say anything that's going to hurt. Just stop talking and leave. Give me a few days, okay?"

"But this is important," I said.

I wondered when I'd hear from him again. The romantic in me almost wanted to never see him again, have him be a one-time thing that got me over my self-esteem issues and helped me regain some confidence. A fling with a boy who showed me there were guys out there who could make me very happy. Just a boy in a city far away who was fated to spend one incredible night with me.

"It can wait." He kissed me one more time. "I don't want this to turn sappy, so I'm going to go. Wait. First: I've never had as much fun with a woman in my life. And I have zits on my ass."

I tried again to speak, but stopped when I saw the tears in his eyes as he said, "Go."

I drove quickly, hating every mile that grew between us, smoking every cigarette I hadn't thought to smoke while we were together. I made it to the airport with an unmistakable feeling overwhelming my body. It wasn't until I boarded the plane that I could name that desire, that craving, that instinct he made me feel all over.

I was thirsty.

000059.

Subject: my pillow smells like you.

A.-

Thank you.
You.
Sweet, wonderful you.
You've ruined my life. Forever.
I cannot thank you enough.
Now please go away so I can put my heart back together.
I'm not a homewrecker. I never wanted to be. I refuse to be.
Whatever you were going to say, I simply must say this first
so there's no more damage to our fragile bodies.
I hate this, but it must be done.
Go live your life with that man in Texas.
I'll live mine over here.
Everything is complicated. I know. I hate how fucked up it
all is.
Good-bye, darling.
Maybe someday we'll meet again.
God, I hope so.

-K.

Subject: Amusing

Hello, Anna K.

I've spent the entire day reading your webpage. I've read
every single entry. I think you're so talented. I've laughed my
ass off when I was supposed to, and I was sad when I was
supposed to be and . . . I'm gushing here. But I really
enjoyed it and wish that you were published all over the place
so I could brag to everyone that you're my favorite author.
Are you published? Because these essays should be
published. Tell me where and I'll go buy them. Write a book!
Something! I need more!

-Gretchen C.

000060.

When I got back to work on Tuesday, Smith didn't meet me for
our lunch break smoke. I walked down to the track bleachers,
figuring she was already there. It wasn't until after my smoke,
when I turned to leave, that I heard a voice from above my head.

"I'm fucking pissed at you, Miss."

She was sitting on the framework of the bleachers, her head
crammed between two slats, her feet dangling near my head.

"I wanted to kick you just now, but I'm too much of a pussy.
Don't tell anyone."

The blood drained from my face and my fingers went numb
when I realized I had missed Smith's rally yesterday. I couldn't
believe I had done that.

"Oh, shit, Smith. I'm so sorry."

She twisted herself over the bars of the bleachers and jumped down in front of me. Her eyes were red. "I don't give a shit about the rally, okay? It sucks to find out that you're not important. You're so caught up in all your boy shit that you don't look at anything. It's fucking stupid." She jammed her hands in her pockets and looked me straight in the eyes.

"I'm sorry," I said again. My brain kept going over the past week, wondering how I had let this happen.

"This was important to me," she said. "It's not like I think I'm your best friend or anything, but I deserve a bit of respect. Every day I have to hear you go on and on about Ian or Kurt or Dale or any of these boys keeping your head so busy. You don't ask about my life unless I point the conversation to where you have no choice. I'm sick of it, Miss. If we're not friends, then we're not friends, and you can be my adviser and I'll leave you alone. I don't want to be the person you wait to stop talking so you can talk again."

"We are friends," I said. "I like you so much, Smith. I'm really sorry."

"I like you, too. And I forgive you because I know you've been sad and you obviously got laid and that makes you happy and shit. But damn, Miss. I'm pissed you skipped out on the rally."

"You're forgiving me? You're a better person than I am."

"I know." She wasn't smiling.

"So, how was it?" I asked.

"It got shut down. I didn't have an adviser."

She lit another cigarette as I apologized again. "Nobody showed?"

"No, lots of people showed. So many that they made us break up the group before I could start talking because I didn't have an adviser. It wasn't sponsored."

"Can we do it again?" I asked. "Can you set one up for next week?"

"No, Miss! It's time for finals. And then we have winter break. I couldn't have another rally until February, at least."

My brain was working quickly. I wanted to make it up to her. "Okay, then we'll start working hardcore after winter break. We'll get everyone in Action Grrlz ready for another rally and I'll do everything this time."

She looked at me and popped her gum. "For real?"

"For real," I said. "It'll be huge. We'll just make it sound like the most important event of the year. Then, when everyone's there, you stand up and you unleash Action Grrlz. You tell them what you're about and you become the leader of the school's most notorious group."

"*Notorious.* I like that word."

"It'll be huge. Please let me make this up to you. I'm sorry I let you down."

"I'm gonna have to write another speech." She smiled.

000061.

Subject: It's Tess.

Ian,

I wasn't going to write you back because I thought your last letter was inappropriate, but I thought you should know that when I was in Pittsburgh with Anna she told me she was going to see one of her old friends, but instead she saw some guy. I saw him pick her up. She didn't come back to the hotel that night. She doesn't know I know all of this. She probably thinks I'm some stupid kid and that I'm not worth her time. I'm not as dumb as she thinks I am. I'm sorry if

this information hurts you, but I feel you have a right to know.
I think Anna's lying to lots of people, and I don't really want
to be her friend anymore. I bet she won't even miss me.

Let me know if you want to get together to talk about it. Also,
tell me if there's anything you need me to do. I'll be here.

Tess

Dale's eyes widened as he read the printout. "Wow, she's pissed."

"Yeah, I think so."

"She was too young for you anyway, Anna. And I was jealous
you went on a vacation with her instead of me."

We were Christmas shopping at Toy Joy, a tiny toy store on
the university campus. I was digging through a basket of plastic
fish, looking for an orange one to stuff in Meredith's stocking.
We've always called her "Fish Face" because she gives the worst
kisses. She puckers up all huge and it's wet and she loves to do it
and we are incredibly grossed out by it. Meredith will make the
perfect old lady someday.

"We shouldn't have sent that e-mail to her."

"Write a nasty entry about her, hinting you know she told
Ian. That'll scare the crap out of her and hopefully she'll be gone
for good. That's what I'd do. I can't believe she was hitting on
him in her letter. I mean, call her if he wants to talk?"

"Yeah, I noticed that, too."

"What a skank. I can't wait until you're a famous writer and
we don't have to deal with these losers anymore."

"Dale, if you keep talking about it like that it's only going to
hurt more when they reject me."

I shouldn't have told Dale that I had sent some of my journal entries to a few magazines. I wanted to see what would
happen. Probably nothing. Dale thinks *The New Yorker* will

pick one up for the Fiction section. I can't imagine, but it's still a pretty good fantasy. Who knows? I never thought the webpage would be as popular as it was, and it wasn't as if I was a complete nobody. I had just spoken at a conference. I was a confirmed writer.

"You're grumpy. Internet boy?"

"Still not talking to me."

"By 'talking,' you mean on the Internet, right?"

I looked up at him. "Yes. What are you getting at?"

"I wanted to remind you that you don't actually talk to any of these people."

"Well, I did a lot more than talk to that boy two weeks ago."

"You know there's no difference between this guy and Tess, right? They both want to wreck your relationships and have you all to themselves. It's just that one is a better lay."

"Well, as far as I know. Tess might be great in bed."

"She'd jump at the chance."

"How did this become my life?" I wailed at the ceiling.

"What did you send him for Christmas?" he asked.

"What makes you think I sent him something?"

"Because you're not in Pittsburgh right now standing outside his apartment holding a boom box in the air blasting Peter Gabriel."

"I sent him some paintbrushes, okay?" I didn't know anything about paintbrushes, but I hoped they were the right ones. The art store salesman said they were the most expensive. I hoped that also meant they were the best.

"And?"

"And a CD."

Kurt wasn't returning my e-mail. I got his number from Directory Assistance, but when I called his house, I got his machine.

"What CD?" Dale asked.

"A mix."

The nagging feeling that Heather might not have been out of the picture wouldn't leave me. Maybe that was why he asked for space so easily without finding out what I was trying to tell him. He must have known that if I came clean, he'd have to as well.

"What's the first track on the mix?"

"Our song," I answered.

"Which is?"

"Air Supply. 'All Out of Love.' "

"Why?"

"It was on in the bar the day we met. Pathetic."

"I love it."

"Oh, I know."

It wasn't like I was about to move to Pittsburgh, and I wasn't about to ask him to move to Austin, so what did I want from him? The long-distance thing was too hard. It's painful and expensive and feeds on paranoia, insecurity, and loneliness. Half the time I'd be wondering if our relationship was working because we were perfect for each other or if it only worked because it was convenient.

"Does he know that's your song?" Dale asked.

"No."

"I love it even more." He held up a punching nun puppet. "Buy me this," he said.

"No. You'll bring it to the dinner table and I'll never hear the end of it from my mother."

"I'm excited she's coming for Christmas. It's nice when everyone comes to you."

"I'm just excited you're making Christmas dinner. There's no pressure on my end anymore."

Dale put on a pair of X-ray glasses and said, "I'd like to remind you that I'm not cooking the dinner at all. Jason's the cook. I'm the eater." He grabbed a Santa Claus puppet down from a shelf. "You know, by sending him things you're violating his request for space."

"I know."

"So what else did you send him, Stalker?"

"A picture of myself."

"So he can paint a new picture of you?" Dale asked.

"Kinda."

"Wow."

"Don't look at me like that."

"And I suppose you're going to write him some kind of sappy entry that's just a big ol' message about how you might have fallen in love with him, right?"

"Want to write it for me?"

"Not if you paid me." Dale held the Santa puppet out in front of him. "Dear Mister Santa. I need a new ass this year. The one I've got's getting kinda fat."

000062.

It's Who You Know
(there's always more)

22 DECEMBER

You meet someone . . .

And even though you just met, you feel this history, a sense of belonging, and a sense of togetherness that you don't usually have with people. Maybe you can talk to her for hours, forgetting the time. Maybe you talk despite the time. The two of you laugh and order another drink and end up late for everything. The time you spend together is worth any amount of inconvenience later.

Someone meets you . . .

But you assume he couldn't possibly know you. You haven't given him enough time. She seems too busy. You are too busy. Maybe that person surprises you with a gift in the mail. A message on your voice mail. You bump into each other at the store and she asks how your cat is doing. You forgot that you told her about your cat's cough. It's almost nothing to you now, but she's been thinking about it. Someone outside of your world has been thinking about you. You've made an impression. You are a part of her. You let him in. Or maybe you didn't. Maybe all of this attention makes you uncomfortable. Maybe you decide you don't have enough time. Everything didn't come together just right. He wears too much cologne. She keeps shortening your name when you hate being called that, even after you told her not to. Maybe he's too perfect. Maybe if you know him much longer you will fall in love and you don't want to. Perhaps you don't want to put in the time. Sometimes you can be selfish. This is one of those times. Or not. Sometimes you get closer despite trying to stay away.

You know someone . . .

And you've known him forever. You know how he works, how he thinks. You know what he's going to do before he does it. You know all of her jokes before she says them. You know that scar right under his earlobe, you know the name of the dog that did it, and you know why it was his own fault it happened. You know the songs that make her cry. You know when he's in the other room crying and he knows you know. There's a quiet understanding between the two of you. A gentle reminder of each other, like when you visit your parents and the same stair creaks under your feet. A reminder that something larger than you remembers you and knows when you are around.

Someone knows you . . .

And you can say anything. You can wear whatever you want in front of him or nothing at all. You can laugh your stupidest laugh—she's heard it before. You can discuss the things you're ashamed of because you are safe. He will be honest with you. She'll cry for you. She ignores your Simpsons collection. He puts up with your ABBA obsession. He never runs out of coffee. He listens to you. He has a way of holding your hand that makes you shiver. He can ignite your entire body just by brushing his fingertips between your shoulder blades.

You love someone ...

And it is the hardest and most rewarding thing you've ever done. You ache with love. You cry sometimes, because you know two things: You know that you've never felt this good before. You also know that it couldn't possibly last forever. You want it to. You want it frozen. You want to stop time, right there, as she hands you your toothbrush, or as he pulls you back from the curb of the street for one last kiss good-bye. You want to be able to pull them closer than the hug, into your body, so you can keep the smell of them inside you, next to you, all around you.

You love someone and it hurts. You love someone and it's very, very good. Not only do you feel better about yourself, you feel better about people, life, animals, and the color orange. You find yourself doing ridiculous things. You clean under the bookcase for her even though she probably won't see under there. Just in case. You could end up in a passionate embrace by the CD player and she'll pull you down to the ground and you will know it'll be perfect. If you die right there with her, it will be clean. It will be clean for her.

You know yourself ...

And you know your limits. When she says the last thing you ever expected to hear—do you stop? When it becomes painful, too painful, do you let him go? When she's gone too far, or she's not doing enough and you're exhausted from dealing with her. When he doesn't return your calls and you're hoarse from trying to be heard, talking into nothing, screaming into nothing. Or maybe she quietly, very quietly, walked over and stabbed you in the heart. Or the back. Or right between the eyes. She waited until your guard was down. Or maybe not. Maybe she knew you were looking. Maybe she did it because you were looking. Maybe you knew enough about her that you should have known better. Maybe you both knew that. Maybe he wanted to see if he could do something you didn't expect. He might have been testing his limits. He wasn't thinking. Maybe he was trying to know someone else a bit more, just for that instant, just for a little while, just to be known by someone else, to know someone else. Maybe he doesn't want to know you anymore. It might hurt to know you. Maybe all of you are hurting. She's still getting to you, even when she's not around. He's still hurting you, even when he hasn't said a word to you in years.

You know everything, and you know nothing . . .

And in that there's this: You will always learn something new. About him. About her. About yourself. And in learning the bad, the uncomfortable, the messy—it's what you take away that counts. What will you do with that knowledge? Will you leave? Pull tighter? Ignore it? Use it to fall in love even deeper? That's when you learn more about yourself.

You aren't a bad person. You're a complex person. You're dealing with complex people. And there's always more to know.

Love until later,

Anna K

000063.

Mom looked tired. She didn't talk much and had brought a book to read. "I don't want to be any trouble," she kept repeating.

"Mom, you're not trouble," I insisted again as I brought a cup of tea to the table beside the futon. "I'm very happy you're spending Christmas with me."

It was two days before Christmas and 82 degrees out. A bizarre heat wave had hit Austin the day before and was predicted to hang around just until after the Christmas holiday. Everyone wore shorts and wished for a winter wonderland.

"And you're not upset that Meredith came too, are you?" Mom asked. Meredith had decided to come at the last minute and Mom had bought her ticket as a Christmas present.

"I'm not upset. I wish she hadn't made such a big stink about it though. She acts like she's doing us this giant favor having you buy her a ticket."

"Will you let the middle child have her thing?" It was unlike Mom to comment on Meredith acting out, but as she stared at me, her face showed nothing. She looked smaller. Her hair was grayer. Her clothes hung on her strangely, her tiny legs sticking out from her shorts. Her kneecaps seemed lost in pale, sad flesh.

"Sorry" was all I could think to say through my wave of guilt.

The front door opened and Meredith stomped into the room, the weight of the world in her last suitcase. "Where are we all staying?" she asked.

"Shannon is going to stay with Dale and Jason. Mom's taking my bed. You and I will share the futon."

"Lovely," Meredith moaned. "Oh, shit. I forgot about the cat."

Shannon walked in from the bathroom. "You aren't switching with me. I love Dale and we're already making slumber party plans. Besides, I'm helping Jason with dinner."

"Fine. I'll just be swollen for Christmas. I hope one of you put an inhaler in my stocking."

We called it an early night, Shannon walking straight over to Dale's. We spent the next day on our own doing last-minute Christmas shopping. That night after we'd wrapped everything and placed our gifts under my small Christmas tree, I found Mom drinking tea on my balcony. She was looking up at the stars.

"This was a good idea," she said. "I don't think I could have survived the first holiday in that house without him. It's good to get us out of Hartford. And cheaper for you and Shan."

"Are you coming to bed soon?" I asked her. "Santa can't come until you go to sleep."

She smiled at hearing the phrase she always used on Christmas Eve. "I don't think Santa's coming this year," she said.

"Mom," I moaned, dropping to the ground next to her. "That's so sad."

"I'm very sad, Anna."

"I know." I put my head on her knee. She ran her fingers through my hair.

"I'm out of cigarettes," she said. I lent her one of mine. I was back to a pack a day since Pittsburgh.

"Thanks," she said as she exhaled a stream of smoke. "Never get married, Anna. If you do, you're going to end up alone."

"Ma, don't talk that way," I said.

"Maybe it's different for you. You girls are all so independent and want your own lives. When I met your father, things were different. You got married and you became one person. You became a couple. My life became your father's life, and his life became mine. We eventually didn't see any other friends because we were too busy raising our family."

She was crying. A tear hit my arm with a small pat. I looked up at her.

"I don't think I'm good at being alone," she said. "I'm really lonely in that house."

I pulled her in for a hug. "Maybe you should take some time away from there. Go stay with Meredith, or come here."

Shannon walked outside and lit a cigarette. "Oh, are we all crying? I'll cry."

She plopped down next to me. "Mom, are you okay?" she asked.

"I'm fine," Mom said as she folded her hands in her lap. "I just miss Dad." I thought how strange it was that people lost their real names once they had kids. They no longer referred to each other by their first names. Everyone called her "Mom." He was "Dad," even to his wife.

"I miss him too, Mommy," Shannon said.

Mom wiped her tears with the side of her hand. "When I first met your father I didn't want to date him because I knew he was the man I was going to be with forever. I wasn't sure if I was ready. I was young and I thought that I might do some traveling. But your grandmother—your father's mother—loved me and kept asking your father to bring me around the house. One night he called and asked me to do him a favor and eat dinner with them that weekend so she'd get off his back. I knew that it would be the last time I accepted a date from a boy."

"And Dad proposed a month later," I said, finishing the story I knew so well.

"He certainly did," Mom nodded. "And I said yes." It was quiet before she added, "And now he's gone."

"I think he's still here, Mom," Shannon said, playing with the cuff of her jeans like we were in kindergarten. "I talk to him sometimes."

"I do, too. He helped me hide all of your presents here in Anna's apartment." Mom grabbed my hand and said, "Remember how your father and Ian would try and find all of their presents days before Christmas? Used to drive us nuts."

I laughed, remembering the time Ian accidentally locked the keys in the trunk of Dad's car when he was searching for presents under the spare tire.

"Ian is so much like your father," Mom said. "How is he doing?"

"Again with the Ian," Shannon said. "Give it up, Mom."

"Well, he came all the way up to Hartford when your father died. Obviously he cares very much about her."

I didn't feel like explaining to my mother that these days the thought of Ian made me exhausted, so I excused myself and went inside.

I went to bed hoping that Santa was going to bring me a simpler life for Christmas.

000064.

**Tiny Wooden Hand
(So Much Joy at Xmas)**

27 DECEMBER

This was the first Christmas that my family gathered without my father. My friend Dale tried to fill in as that missing male figure, which was sweet, but he was way too silly to carve a turkey with a straight face. I enjoyed the change of having Christmas in my own home, with friends and family traveling to be inside my doors. I liked decorating, talking in my Martha Stewart voice as I lit candles and made marshmallow treats.

Dale fell in love with the stocking stuffer I gave him. It's a wooden backscratcher. It's long, and at the end it has a tiny wooden hand shaped just for scratching. I'm sure you're thinking: "Oh, I have one of those, I love it too. It reaches all of the right parts."

Well, this wasn't exactly the same kind of love. Dale found this thing to be the funniest object in the world. It was his new best friend. I really cannot describe the love here. You see, the hand extends and retracts, and it does look just like a tiny hand, so it has become the source of great amusement. Perhaps you might want to get one for yourself. I had no idea how many possibilities were loaded into one tiny wooden hand. Why, you can:

• high five with a tiny wooden hand.

• grab objects from across the table with a tiny wooden hand.

• caress your lover's cheek without having to move from the couch with a tiny wooden hand.

• scratch your chin like an intellectual with a tiny wooden hand.

• pose like *The Thinker* with a tiny wooden hand.

• put a tiny wooden pinkie to your mouth and say "one million dollars."

• scratch the cat with a tiny wooden hand without getting fur on you.

• smoke a cigarette with a tiny wooden hand without having to bring your hand all the way to your mouth.

• drive like a low rider with a tiny wooden hand.

• brush back your hair with a tiny wooden hand.

• rough someone up with a tiny wooden hand.

- "raise the roof" with a tiny wooden hand.

- smack the back of someone's hand with a tiny wooden hand.

- give secret tiny wooden handshakes.

- have the world's smallest wooden hand stroke the world's tiniest penis (don't ask).

How could I possibly think of all of these uses for such a seemingly simple creation? Why, put the tiny wooden hand in a room filled with friends, family, and a pile of beer, and watch what happens! And if it's on a Friday night of a holiday weekend during a weird, humid, sticky heat wave? Well, then, my friend, be prepared for the height of comedy.

You can pay for pizza with a tiny wooden hand.

Somehow during the course of the evening, Dale put on Ian's old engineer's cap, some aviator glasses, and coveralls (Shut up. What's in *your* coat closet?). We had ordered pizza earlier. Of course, in our state of wooden hand giggles, the next logical progression was to share the love of the tiny wooden hand with perfect strangers, so they too could see what a genius invention it is. The scenario:

There is a knock on the door. Everyone hides in the kitchen, except for Dale in his outfit, tiny wooden hand in . . . well, hand, and I'm on the futon with an engineer whistle in my mouth. Everyone is silent. It is amazing how well this is going to come off. Dale opens the door—the pizza guy doesn't even bat an eye. He apparently delivers to train conductors each and every day. He stares at Dale and starts to hand him the pizza. Dale flicks out the tiny wooden hand, which has the money in its tiny wooden grip. The arm extends, and the hand reaches out to the pizza guy. This is too much for Dale, who is well aware of the comedic power of the tiny wooden hand, and he begins to giggle. He giggles right in front of the pizza guy, who now just wants to leave.

Dale invites the pizza guy inside with a creepy "Hi. You wanna come in?" This forces me to hide my face in the futon. I mean, come on, Austin's a small town, and I'm a performer. This pizza guy could be at my theater in a couple of weeks and yell out, "Her and her freak train conductor boyfriend tried to seduce me with a tiny wooden hand." Dale eventually closes the door and the party comes out of the kitchen laughing and blaming Dale for ruining what would have been "The Ultimate Pizza Guy/Tiny Wooden Hand Joke."

See, you probably thought that the lives of actors and writers were very glamorous. All Henry Miller and Anaïs Nin. Full of beer, drugs, sex, wild parties, interesting people. We get home drunk at the crack of dawn, thinking about how great the thunderous applause was that night on stage. But in reality we all sit around on a Friday night thinking up new tricks for the pizza guy. And while we do go home drunk at the crack of dawn, instead we think about how great the look on the pizza guy's face was when we extended a tiny wooden hand with a twenty-dollar bill crammed into it at his face.

It's been a hard holiday season for my family. It was really nice to see my mother laugh again.

Love until later,

Anna K

000065.

The letter came a few days later in a thin envelope and was very to the point: "Miss Koval, we're afraid we cannot accept this submission. We don't normally accept unsolicited material. Regardless, this particular piece does not fit our standards. It appears to be ripped from the pages of a teenager's diary and isn't something we'd find suitable for our readers."

Assholes. How'd they know it was from a diary?

The reality hit me: I wasn't a writer. I was a girl with a webpage. Anybody could do I what I did. In fact, thousands of people did what I did. How did I think I was special? How was I an appropriate writer for a *real* magazine with editors and standards and people trained to write real essays? I wasn't a novelist. I wasn't a celebrity.

I just wrote a diary.

The letter was short, but strong enough to put me back in my place. I didn't want to bother those grown-up magazines ever again.

There was a box outside my door as well. It was addressed to me in Ian's handwriting. I was sure it wasn't a Christmas present from him.

I opened the box. Inside were a few of my books, a sweater, and a stuffed animal that he must have forgotten I'd given him as a gift. I found an envelope at the bottom. Nothing was written on it. Inside was a card, the front of which was a naked baby holding his arms out. "Baby, It's Another Christmas!" it said inside.

Ian found cards that lacked a sense of humor to be incredibly funny. This was the perfect find for him, mixing naked babies with "baby" puns and a holiday greeting. His favorite card ever was a Valentine's Day card where a rabbit ate a carrot and on the inside it read, "I wanted to make you laugh, but I wasn't feeling too bunny. Happy Love Day."

Ian's handwriting was scrawled along the inside. "I'm sorry it's been such a shitty year."

I'd been wasting so much time. There wasn't anything wrong with me. Ian just didn't know how to love me.

I'd already known the truth for a while, but was unable to admit it until I held that empty box in my hands. I felt absolutely nothing for him, and I was free. I could accept what I had been too afraid to deal with. I didn't need Ian as my excuse anymore. He wasn't what I'd wanted in a long time.

I threw away the box with the stuffed animal still inside. I ripped his card in half. And why the fuck hadn't he returned my Beastie Boys CD?

We were breaking up.

000066.

Ian.

2 JANUARY

Relationships are very difficult. How two people grow with each other over the years amazes me. People change so much and sometimes when you change into two different people, you find that you aren't the team you once were. And no matter how much the two of you are in love, you just can't get things to feel like they're working.

We broke up. We've separated. We're on a break. We call it lots of things to cover up the pain that he's not here every day, reaching out a hand and stroking my forehead as he passes through the living room.

There was a boy. There was a girl. They created a life together. They decided to step back from it when it just wasn't fun anymore. It didn't make them happy anymore. They loved each other so much they couldn't stand making each other miserable anymore. This is life. This is what happens to people. We can trace a line of events, but we can't follow a series of emotions. Things change. We change. It is possible to love someone so much and still be unable to make him smile.

Sometimes the best gift you can give someone is space. That's what we're doing. "Merry Christmas," we decided. "Now go away."

I may talk a good game, but I have no idea what I'm doing, what I'm going to do, or what I'm supposed to do. I'm just here, trying to figure it all out.

I'm posting now, before I lose my nerve. Once I post this, the words are true. It's hard to have everyone know you're terrified.

Love until later,

Anna K

000067.

Subject: oh, no!

Anna K,

I'm so sad to hear that you and Ian broke up! It sounded like you two had such a good relationship. You're both funny and

he seems to really care about you. I'm very sad to hear that
you two are no longer together. I am thinking good thoughts,
and I'm sure you'll both work it out and get back together
soon.

-Marie Collier

Subject: GO GET HIM

Anna K,

You have to get back together with Ian! I love all of the
stories about the two of you! Now I'm so sad. There's no
hope for any of us now, I'm sure of it.

-Glenda

Subject: NOOOOO!!!

A,

I'm so sad to hear that you and Ian broke up. Ian reminds
me of a boy I dated named Ian and we broke up when I
cheated on him. He was the best thing that ever happened to
me. I don't know if you did something to lose your Ian, but try
not to act with too much anger. You'll hate yourself if you
lose him forever. Trust me. I will never have anyone love me
like he did. Some of us realize whom we love too late in life.

-s.

Subject: single?!?!?!?!!!!

Anna K,

I think your awesome and Ian's a idiot to let you go!!! I treat
you right. I drive a Jeep. My parents have cabin in Tahoe.
Give me a shot!!!!!1

-Keith

Subject: help!

An K,

I found a baby bird in a nest. I know that you like animals
and I thought you might know what I should do with it. I keep
feeding it grapes. What would you do?

-beth overton

Subject: I hope this is okay.

Anna K,

I've never written before, and maybe you don't know anything
about me, but my name is Stephanie, and I dated Ian the three
years before he dated you. A friend of mine showed me your
webpage a few months ago, and I quickly figured out who you
were. I originally started reading as a way to check in on him,
but I must admit I was quickly reading for you. I think you're
funny, talented, and smart. I can see what Ian saw in you, and
I know he must be hurting these days without you.

I also have the unique position of being perhaps your only reader who knows what it's like to break up with Ian. I sympathize with you. I know what that pain is like. I know that he will call you late at night to tell you that he's sorry for everything he ever did that hurt you. Then he'll say he's saying what he thinks you want to hear. I know that he probably owes you some money, but he still wants to have back anything you might possibly have in your apartment that's his. In fact, when he comes to visit you, you'll notice his head bopping around, searching your bookcases and CD racks, desperately searching for one more thing that's his. I know that his sister will write you letters, telling you that the family misses you terribly. Before you think it's a trap, I have to tell you that Ian doesn't know about the letters; Debra does that because she's genuinely a wonderful woman. How is she, by the way?

Ian will ask you to co-sign his next apartment lease by reminding you that it's your fault he's looking for one. I'm trusting you're smart enough to say no on that one. I hope you won't find his Box of Old Girlfriends that holds naked pictures of exes, perfumed letters, and love notes. Maybe you won't find him drunk on your doorstep at three in the morning, crying that he'll never find a person who will love him like you did and that he wants you to wait until he's ready to get back together.

I hope you won't let him keep you waiting to see what will happen next. Don't let him tease you with little bits of happiness, making you think that you might still have a chance. Don't let him keep you from falling in love with someone else because you think that the second you do he'll finally be ready for you. Move on quickly and love someone else as fully as you loved Ian. If you're lucky, Ian won't show up someday when you're sad and broken and just about ready to let yourself be loved again. He won't just show up and hold you and give you pity sex somewhere inappropriate (I can't go back to my high school ever again. Reunions are a bitch, I tell you) and then ignore you because he doesn't know how to talk to you. The breakup will be a knife in your side, just under the ribs, and every time you lean forward to stand up on your own, the knife will stick in you again, reminding you that you can't keep a relationship going. You aren't good enough. You failed at Ian; you failed at life.

He's a chaser, and the second you stop running, he'll run right past you. He wants what he thinks he can win. He never wants the prize he's got. It took me a long time to realize that I had done nothing wrong. That I was still a good person. It took almost three years for me to finally let someone into my life again. I'm happy to tell you that I'm now married and pregnant with my first child. Please don't tell Ian that you've heard from me. It took too long for me to leave him in the past. I'm ashamed to admit that I was still seeing him when he started seeing you. I don't know if he ever told you. We didn't sleep together then. He kept insisting there was some girl named Anna. I didn't believe him. Here you are. I'm sorry about that. I'm sorry that I kissed him a few times that night. I'm sorry I called you a bitch back then when I hadn't even met you. I'm sorry for a lot of things.

Having read your site for a while now, I know that you're strong, independent, and intelligent. Still, I wouldn't feel right if I didn't offer my support wrapped in a warning, since I'm also strong, independent, and intelligent. I'd hate to have been able to stop someone's pain but did nothing. I'm offering you support and a sympathetic ear if you need it.

Feel free to delete and ignore completely if you want. Write
back if it's exactly the kind of thing you need to bitch about
over a couple of beers. I live in Austin and I know a great
bartender.

-Stephanie Greenwood

Of all the people to read my webpage, I'd never have thought
that Stephanie "The Girl Who Broke Ian's Heart" Greenwood
would be one of them.

She was the reason for every fight Ian and I had early in our
relationship. I thought she had to be an evil, crazy woman, the
way Ian described her. Something she had done or said always
triggered some ridiculous reaction in Ian because he expected the
same behavior from me. This girl and I were not the same, but
her letter smacked me in the face with its familiarity.

Ian did so many of those things in the months after our
breakup. He would call at three in the morning and propose. He
said he just figured that was what I wanted.

Why now was it so much easier to look back on and judge?
Why wouldn't I see what was wrong back then?

His sister Deb did write. She wrote letters that would make
me sob. She'd remind me how I was a part of the family and how
much everyone missed me and how she hoped I'd be back soon.

Stephanie was right about more than just Ian's behavior. She
knew what I was doing to myself. I was scared to start up things
with Kurt because I was afraid I'd fuck it up. I'd fail again.

I had screamed, "I am not Stephanie!" to Ian countless times
over the course of our relationship. And now there I was, staring
at my monitor with only one thought: I am Stephanie.

000068.

Having a birthday three weeks after Christmas usually makes for some shitty presents, but having a birthday after an especially sad year makes for some really thoughtful ones. Dale gave me four CDs and a gift certificate for a day spa. My mother sent two books on acting and a framed picture of Dad and me. I'm in his lap and he's beaming down at me. I'm six months old. Shannon drove up from school to give me a six-pack of beer, which she promptly drank on my porch as she smoked my cigarettes.

Packages started arriving from website readers: books, CDs, candy, cards, photographs, and belated Christmas presents for Taylor. I was as flattered as I was amazed.

Kurt's package arrived the morning after my birthday. The deliveryman struggled with the large item so much that I felt the need to tip him five dollars.

Kurt had painted a collage of silver clouds, beer, puddles of water, horrible one-liners, and me right in the middle. Tiny silver hearts filled the background as the words "There's Still Time" were written in very small letters at the bottom. He sent a card. "I found some of your hair on my pillow," it said. "I mixed it in the paint I used on this piece." He named it *Love Lives in Texas*.

Three weeks later, I couldn't believe I was already trying on bridesmaid dresses with Dale by my side. The time was starting to fly by with the amount of work I'd been doing on Smith's rally in between updating my journal with Anna K's post-Ian lifestyle. It was very exciting to have her go out and have fun, to give her girlfriends and stories where she'd enjoy something about herself that Ian might have overlooked.

I was crunching candy hearts and wiggling around in my dress as Dale twisted the neckline around my bust. The candy hearts were from Dale for Valentine's Day. The dress was from evil dressmakers who have ordained that every bridesmaid will look like a second-rate woman in every wedding ceremony ever held.

"You're hurting my titties."

"Your titties are hurting this dress."

"Becca picked out a dress for girls with no boobs."

"You look obscene."

I looked in the mirror. I had cleavage practically up to my neck. "This won't do, Dale," I moaned.

"I know. I'll call Becca later and see what she wants to do about it."

"I can call her."

Dale took my hand. "Trust me. You want me to call. You stay away from the bride, if you know what's best for you."

"What did Jason get you for Valentine's Day?" I asked him.

"Oh. A happy/sad mask."

"That's nice." I smiled.

"Anna," Dale said, leaning in. "Don't tell anyone because I feel like an asshole, but if I get one more happy/sad theatre mask I'm going to kill someone."

"You've finally figured out that they're creepy?"

We stared at each other. Dale looked down. "Promise you won't tell anybody, but yes. God, they're hideous."

"Thank you!" I danced up and down.

"Please. Save the moves for the reception."

We stared back at the mirror. The dress was aqua and hung down to my toes. The sleeves were long and pointed at the backs of my hands. The dress was made out of a velvety fabric that had no give whatsoever. My breasts were trying to find someplace where they were accepted and loved, and optioned to pour over the top of the dress. I looked like I was ready to skank up a groomsman.

Dale sighed. "Always a bridesmaid wrangler, never a bride."

000069.

Poems for the Love-Challenged:
One for Every Occasion (Take That, Hallmark!)

14 FEBRUARY

i need you
i want you
i need you
i want you
i need you
i want you
i need you
to shut up.
i want you
to go home.

The warmth
In my mouth.
That rush
Through my veins
Making my heart race
My pulse quicken
My head—
Just a bit dizzy.
My legs—
Just a bit numb.
My tongue

Yearns for more

More of you

Right now.

Now.

I can't wait anymore.

This is torture.

Seriously.

I'm in hell

Waiting for you.

I just want to shout

To this giant crowd of people

"How hard is it to make a latte, fuckers?"

I love you, coffee.

Here.

It's for you.

No, it's just a little something I thought you'd like.

What is it?

Well, I was out getting some gas, you know?

And, uh, this was right there at the register

and it made me think of you.

Your sweet ass.

It's mint flavored.

Check it: It's both a rose and panties.

Isn't that cool as shit?

I bought you a panty rose.

Don't look at me like that.

Go put them on.

And sprinkle this Limon stuff on them, too.

Good morning, you.

This is my favorite time.

This time, right now.

When the sun is first starting to come up
and the light hits the flesh on your back just so
And the room still smells a bit like us
Our smells mingled together
Matching the taste on my lips
The feeling of your legs tangled with mine
The warmth of your breath on my cheek
The memories of our passion and yearning and groping still fresh on
     my muscles
The sound of your heart beating against my body
This is my favorite time
Because it is ours.
It's quiet.
I love you more than anybody.
But you'd better get up now.
And go back to your room.
Mom will kill us if she finds us here.

                    dear dre,
          bitches and hos be riding my dick like the Tilt-A-Whirl.
               but no one makes me feel like you do.
                         i love you.
                          Snoop

                    For the time you left my shoes out in the rain.
                      For the time you broke my favorite hair clip.
    For the time you hammered nails into the wall and called it a hat rack.
        For the time you tried to serve me a tea bag from the trash can.
                        For the time you put a match out in my car.
             For the time you woke me up by pushing me off the bed.
                  For the time you called me by your brother's name.
                        For the time you almost drowned me.
                     For the time you locked the keys in my car.
                    For the time you lost my Macy Gray CD.

All is forgiven.

All is worth it.

And on that last one, you were actually doing me a favor.

Happy Valentine's Day.

Happy Valentine's Day.

i'm sorry i've been telling everyone that you're gay.

it just makes me feel better.

you know. because you're a dick.

Hey. You.

Yeah, you.

You.

Call me.

I miss you.

I can't make it any simpler.

Love until later,

Anna K

000070.

It was windy on the track bleachers. Smith's hair whipped around her head as she stood watch over the quickly growing crowd on the field in front of her. She had dyed her hair cherry red for the occasion and looked like she had summoned a crown of fire. Her eyes were sharp, and I could tell that she was nervous. So was I. The crowd of Action Grrlz was sitting on the bottom step of the bleachers facing the audience, waiting for Smith to speak. Smith was just waiting for the crowd to be big enough for her.

I was standing just off to the side of the bleachers, near our rented amp. I was looking up at Smith with the rest of the waiting students. I could feel anxiety rising from the arches of my feet. I shifted my weight back and forth as I searched the field. I looked farther to the right, toward the back of the school building. Classes had let out fifteen minutes ago and large clumps of kids were walking toward us. They were loud and laughing, free with the release that comes at the end of a school day. We were lucky enough to score one of the five Texas days in March that has a cool breeze and a clear blue sky. Other states know it as "spring."

The students pushed each other playfully, keeping to groups of three or five; a random couple would wander at a slower pace. There were cheerleaders in uniform, other groups wearing the same T-shirts, kids dressed in all black, and boys already suited up for their after-school sports practice. I counted thirty-five kids in the first quick scan. Ten minutes later there were easily eighty.

Smith gave a small glance over at me and raised her eyebrows. She was surprised at the turnout as well. We had been petitioning and papering the school with fliers, but Smith wanted the specifics of the group kept secret. The Action Grrlz's fliers simply read: "YOU MUST BE THERE."

"Everybody at this school does what they're told all the time, Miss," Smith had said to me when we first picked up the stack of fliers. "They'll think this is some pep rally or something."

As I watched Smith adjust the microphone stand we had swiped from the A/V club, I became more anxious. I picked up the same vibe from the crowd of teens in front of me. We were all shifting, squinting into the afternoon sunlight, shielding our foreheads from the wind whipping our hair, turning the ends into tiny daggers that batted at our faces. We were all at attention, waiting to hear what that flier told us we couldn't risk missing. She hadn't told me what she was going to say. I asked her to keep it a surprise.

Smith smiled as she looked down to grab the microphone. I knew she was proud of herself. I couldn't stop grinning. I was proud of her, too. My few months with Smith had felt like years. She seemed older and smarter as she stood in front of that crowd. She held her head higher than she used to. She no longer hunched herself forward. She wasn't apologetic anymore.

"Move your giant head, Anna," Dale snapped. He was filming Smith's rally for her college applications. I moved over and got a different view of the crowd. They were so quiet. Even toward the back kids were standing on their toes, leaning forward, waiting to hear what Smith was about to say. I wondered if most of these kids even knew who she was. Smith coughed next to the microphone and started speaking.

"Okay, um, thank you all for coming," she mumbled, and a tweak of feedback pierced through her microphone. I gave a sharp glance toward the sound operator. Her name was Shelly, a junior in the group. She tossed a cigarette underneath her tennis shoe and adjusted a few knobs on the amp. There was a murmur of laughter throughout the crowd, and Smith looked a bit shaken. She looked upward, as if the sound of her voice had materialized into something thick in front of her eyes. She breathed deeply and leaned forward into the microphone again.

"Y'all, listen! We are the Action Grrlz!"

The twenty girls in front shouted and raised their hands in the air. The group had grown since last semester and now had a variety of girls of different sizes and races. The entire front row looked like a Benetton ad.

The crowd was now starting to lose interest. A few boys in the back shouted requests to see the girls' breasts.

Smith gave a quick glance around and continued. "My name is Smith. Okay, so to get into college you have to have all of these extracurriculars, you know? So I was looking for a group to join

this year and I couldn't find anything. Every group was so spe-
cific and school related. I wanted a group that people talked
about, you know?"

People were starting to break off and have smaller discussions under Smith's speech. A few of the Action Grrlz
screamed, "Shut up!"

Smith took a quick glance at me and then went back to the
microphone. "Hold on," she said.

There were moans from the crowd as Smith jumped off the
bleachers and walked toward me. I saw one of the other Action
Grrlz run over toward a small crowd headed back toward the
school. She curved around them like a sheepdog, her gestures a
mix of bargaining and threats.

"Miss, this is so stupid," Smith moaned to me. "Give me a
cigarette."

"No, you're doing really well," I said.

Smith turned back toward the crowd. "I should have written
it down." She looked at Dale pointedly and said, "I told you I
needed the notecards."

"Just be louder," Dale said. "And enunciate." He held up his
free hand, his forefinger touching his thumb. He punched it
through the air with every syllable. "E! Nun! See! Ate!"

Smith placed her hand in the mirror image of Dale's and
mocked him: "Oh! My! God! Shut! Up!"

Dale turned Smith around by the arm, pushed her back
toward the bleachers, and chanted, "Bigger. Faster. Go! Go! Go!"

I walked up to Smith and grabbed her hand. She turned
toward me. Her lower lip hung down, and I could see her bottom row of teeth as she bit her upper lip. I saw a hint of tears in
her eyes.

"You can do this," I said to her. "You know you can. Just talk
to them like you talk to me."

"I sound so stupid when I talk in front of people," she said.

"Smith." I smiled at her. "You're very charming."

She pulled her head back sharply, and I was instantly worried that I had somehow insulted her. "Nobody's ever called me that before," she said. "I'm charming?" She laughed a little and added, "Like a princess?"

"Exactly like a princess," I said. "Princess Bad-Ass. And you're losing your subjects." I turned her back toward the crowd. "Hurry!" I said, and gave her a little push.

She left my hands and I felt that surge of pride again. This time it was more sisterly than protective. As I watched Smith climb back up the bleachers, my memory flashed to the time I taught Meredith to ride a two-wheeler. She was eight and I was ten. I was holding on to the back of her pink bike with one hand and she had turned herself around in the seat to grab on to both of my arms. The bike was wobbling and I thought it was going to turn over. I had to hold the handlebars with my other hand. I was steering the bike as Meredith was clinging to me, screaming. I told her, "You already know how to do this." She did. She didn't realize that she hadn't been using her training wheels for a few weeks. She had wanted to ride her bike through the same grassy field I plowed mine after school. She had wanted to ride next to me and no longer wanted to be stuck on the same tiny sidewalk in front of our house anymore. So I got Dad's toolkit and figured out how to take the training wheels off myself.

The more Meredith squealed, the more I repeated to her that she knew how to ride. But she had to look at the street.

"Then you'll be gone!" she shrieked.

"I'm right here. I won't let you fall." She was heavy and my arms were getting tired of holding her and the bike upright. I wanted her to start pedaling.

"Promise me," she whimpered.

"Mere, I promise," I said.

She turned right around and pedaled. The bike whipped out of my hands and she was off down the street. She laughed, and shouted back, "Are you still there?"

I was running behind her shouting, "I'm right here!"

"You still got me?" she shrieked again as she started pedaling faster.

"Yes, Meredith! You're doing so good!"

"I know!"

She rode for another hour with me running behind her. She never turned around.

As we were putting the "horses" back in the "stable" that night—our ritual of wiping down our bikes, pretending to clean and brush our horses before they went to sleep—Meredith turned to me and said, "I know you weren't always right behind me because I was going so fast. But that's okay. I knew that you weren't ever going to let me fall."

Smith grabbed the microphone. "Okay, here," she said. She pointed at tiny Thanh-Mai sitting on the ground. "Thanh-Mai. Stand up. Come over here."

Thanh-Mai, a small Vietnamese girl in a green sweater and a plaid skirt, stood to join Smith. On the metal stairs, her steps sounded heavy for such a little girl. Her footsteps echoed over the crowd, clanking and scraping as she lumbered up to Smith. The crowd was getting more and more restless.

"This is Thanh-Mai," Smith said. "She's a sophomore here and she's in Student Council. She plays three instruments and can speak two languages. Thanh-Mai knits and is going to be a pediatrician when she grows up."

Thanh-Mai didn't seem to know the focus was on her. She was frozen. Smith turned toward her. "Tell them what you're passionate about, Thanh-Mai."

Thanh-Mai's mouth moved, but I couldn't hear what she said. The crowd didn't either, and people were shouting to have Thanh-Mai speak up.

"She said she cares about animal rights! Listen, y'all! Thanh-Mai is an active member of PETA. She protests the rodeo and the circus when they come to town. So does

Sandra." Smith pointed at Sandra and motioned for her to join them.

"Sandra is a junior and she's on the debate team. She cares about animal rights, the environment, and works at soup kitchens for homeless teens."

Smith motioned for the other Action Grrlz to stand up. They all formed a line on the third stair of the bleachers. They looked dazed. They didn't know that Smith was going to call so much individual attention to them. Smith stood over them. If she noticed they were uncomfortable, she didn't let on.

"Jenny raises money for AIDS research. Monica is drug free. Frannie is straight edge. Karen volunteers at a hospital for girls with eating disorders. Amy is a Republican. We're all different girls, but we all want to talk about what we believe in."

Each girl straightened up as her name was announced. They looked at each other and smiled. They hadn't thought of them-selves as activists before. Hearing their names and their interests announced over a loudspeaker made it sound more legitimate. Unfortunately, they were the only ones listening to Smith's announcement. The crowd was now openly ignoring Smith's speech. Some of them had their backs turned to the bleachers and were loudly joking with each other.

Smith gripped the microphone tighter and shouted, "And you don't give a fuck about us, right? You don't give a shit about who we are or what we do."

The crowd quieted. Kids turned back around as Smith's curses hung in the air. A few cheered. One kid shouted, "Not really." Another group laughed.

"And why should you give a fuck about us? We don't give a fuck about you, either. That's how we've worked it. We do our thing and you do yours. Nobody's inviting anyone to talk. Well, we're changing that now."

Smith took the microphone off the stand and sat down on a bleacher step. Her hair was still whipping around her face, and she held it back with her free hand. I could see her legs shaking as she said calmly, "The Action Grrlz want to talk to you. We want to open up lines of communication. We are inviting you in. And you will know us by our heads."

I never saw Thanh-Mai pull the clippers from her backpack, but suddenly the girls were cheering, the crowd was gasping, and Thanh-Mai was shaving Smith's head clean. Clumps of red hair floated in the air, drifting toward Smith's feet on the metal stairs as she stomped with excess energy.

"Did you know about this?" Dale asked.

"No!" I whispered. My voice was gone. My legs felt cold. I suddenly realized that I'd never met Smith's mother. I had a feeling I was going to very soon.

Smith stood with clumps of hair still attached to her head. Patches of white skin stood out as she yelled into the microphone, "We are the Action Grrlz! If you see one of us, stop and talk to us! We want to know what you think!"

I watched as twenty other girls took turns shaving each other's heads. Bits of hair picked up in the wind and swirled around us. It was a hairstorm. I realized that my mouth had dropped open once a curl floated to my lower lip. I looked over at Dale. He was smiling, filming the crowd. The crowd was cheering as clouds of hair silently floated over them. Smith picked up on the energy and continued over the hum of the clippers.

"Nothing changes if you don't talk about it. If you don't let new people into your life, you can't get new experiences. Every person you meet changes your life. You're supposed to meet that person for some reason, good or bad, you know? The Action Grrlz want to encourage those first meetings. Ask us what we're fighting for. Then we can come up with new ways to change things that suck."

Suddenly, girls from the crowd walked up the bleacher steps. Boys followed suit. Kids who had never met before were shaking hands and shaving heads. Smith was shouting her manifesto and I was amazed. She didn't stammer. She wasn't searching for words. She was huge up there, full of energy and passion. She spoke without hesitation. She had finally figured everything out.

"We're not freaks!" Thanh-Mai shouted into the microphone.

Smith laughed but was drowned out by the crowd below her. Girls were joining them, sitting on the bleacher steps, bending their heads to get shaved. At least fifty girls were bouncing with clumps and tangles of hair remaining on their heads. They giggled and squealed and wiped hair out of their faces. Boys shyly rubbed the backs of their newly shorn heads, unused to the air on their skin.

Smith turned and looked at me. "Miss?" she asked into the microphone.

"No," Dale said behind me. "Tell her I'm not fucking doing that."

"She didn't invite you, Dale," I said, walking away. As I climbed up the bleachers, I couldn't feel my feet. It was like I was floating up to her.

Smith grabbed my hand and squeezed it. "Thanks for being here, Miss."

I still couldn't talk. I didn't know what to say. Hair floated past my eyes in tiny black clouds.

"This is my adviser, Miss Koval!" Smith shouted to the crowd as she held my arm up. "She helped me form this group and she showed me that you have to take chances to move forward. You have to be willing to expose yourself to let others in. She's not afraid to be herself and she's not afraid to break rules to make people happy. She's the strongest woman I know."

Looking over the sea of freed hair at the crowd of kids cheering with every sentence Smith shouted into the microphone, I was swollen with pride. I also had no doubt in my mind that I was going to be fired on Monday. I didn't mind at all. At least I was getting fired for a reason. At least I'd done something real, something people saw, that they'd talk about. I was a part of something honest from start to finish.

I sat in the chair. I grabbed Smith's right hand and held it tight, her rings digging into the tender places near my knuckles. I lowered my head.

"You sure?" Smith asked me, holding the clippers over my left shoulder.

I took a deep breath and closed my eyes.

"Go."

000071.

When I got home I found Ian asleep on my futon. I never did get back my key.

The sound of my purse hitting the coffee table woke him. He sat up and lit a cigarette. I saw him grin and shake his head as he cleared his throat. He seemed amused with something. He turned my laptop toward me. I saw my webpage on the screen.

He said, "I want you to sit there and explain this and then I want you to explain it to me again. I want to understand how anyone could do something this fucked up."

I felt my stomach crash to the ground. "How did you find this?"

Ian laughed and ran his hands through his hair. "It's a great story, actually. I didn't want to come bragging to you over the past couple of months, but you may have noticed that I haven't been calling much. I wasn't avoiding you. I met a girl. I liked this girl. Shortly thereafter, this girl liked me. One night we got a little drunk and she got a little sad and she told me she needed to confess something. I figured she was about to tell me that her dad beat her or she had slept with someone else or she has a prison record or something with the way she was crying. Turned out she had to tell me that she knew me before she met me. That she knew who I was when I first started talking to her. She knew things that I'd never told her. And some of the things she thought she knew weren't true at all."

"Did you read it?" I asked.

"No, I didn't read it. I don't want to see it. I just want it gone, Anna. I can't believe you did this. You wrote a webpage, pretending we were still dating?"

"I broke us up a few weeks ago," I mumbled.

"Oh, well, *thanks*. This is unbelievable. This girl was initially attracted to me because of you. That's fucked up! She was mushy about some story you told that didn't even happen. It broke her heart when I told her you made it all up. I felt like an asshole. You made me an asshole."

I sat down next to him, finding my feet for the first time since he turned my computer toward me. "I only said good things. I'm sorry. I really am. I never meant for you to find it. I never thought it would become popular. I never thought you'd meet someone that read it."

"Yeah, well, it's weird. You wrote about our sex book?"

"I just wrote about how things affected me. I didn't spill your secrets."

"What's a secret anymore?"

"It wasn't supposed to turn out this way," I mumbled.

"Take that shit down."

I nodded. He walked out.

He never said a word about my shaved head. I was pretty sure he hadn't even noticed.

000072.

I liked that Smith continued our track bleacher tradition even when I couldn't be there anymore. I was mostly impressed that she didn't replace me with anyone and chose to spend her smoke breaks alone these days. I slinked into a shadow under the bleachers as she kept watch.

"I still can't believe you got fired for that, Miss. It's bullshit."

"I told you it was going to happen."

"Yeah, well, it's still bullshit."

"Maybe."

"Are you broke now?"

"Kind of. I have to find a job." I felt like I was purging my entire life. I was rid of Ian, the job that felt motionless, and I was slowly moving farther and farther away from my website, writing fewer entries from my heart, opting for quick notes rather than full stories. It felt good to keep some things to myself. Soon I'd have nothing from my old life. I'd be starting over. A clean slate.

"I have some money saved up for my college fund," Smith offered.

I took her hand and squeezed it. "I'll be okay. Thank you, though."

She smiled at me, as lines formed on the top of her head, making her look worried. "You sure?"

"I'm sure."

"Man, this sucks. I'll have the Action Grrlz rally until they hire you back."

"I'm going to look for something new. Besides, they'd never hire me again. Smith, fifty-seven kids shaved their heads. Do you know how many pissed-off parents that is?"

"I'm already sick of all the popularity." She popped her gum and puffed her cigarette.

"Poor you," I said.

Smith laughed. "The best part is this totally fucked up the skinheads. Now these people are walking up to them wanting to talk about racial equality and shit like that. Getting all political on their asses. I love it."

We watched a group of cheerleaders practicing. Tiny bald girls popped into the air, kicking and cheering, the sun glaring off the tops of their heads.

"It's all so beautiful," I said.

"I'm gonna miss you, Miss." She kicked me in the back of my leg.

"I'll miss you, too."

"When does Dale need me for the shoot again?"

"Next month. You think your parents will let you do it?"

"I told them I'm getting paid for it, so I don't see why not. I think it'll be fun to make a movie."

"You're going to be awesome in it."

We heard a screechy voice, a warbling birdlike caw calling out behind us. "Doris Smith? Are you smoking?"

We wheeled around to find Mrs. Langston, the cheerleading coach. We tossed our cigarettes far away simultaneously. "No, Miss!" Smith shouted at her.

"What class are you supposed to be in?" Langston asked.

"Homeroom," Smith mumbled.

"Then get there."

"Yes, ma'am."

Langston turned and stared at me for a very long time. I was the reason she was dealing with a double-bald basket toss. She turned sharply and stomped away.

I grabbed my things. "Call me if you want to hang out."

Smith hitched her backpack up. "Dale said we might all get together next weekend and watch the tape of the rally. He had one of his movie friends make some edits for my submission to Hampshire."

"Sure thing. *Doris.*"

She kicked dirt at me. "I rage against my name."

Langston was coming back toward us. We ran away in two different directions.

000073.

Subject: reason you might not like me anymore

Kurt,

I shaved my head. And if you ever see me again, I might still
be bald. I kind of like the way it feels when the wind blows on
the back of my neck. I like having people look at me twice. I
like that sometimes I don't recognize myself in the mirror
and I wonder who that girl is with the pretty eyes for just a
slight second before I realize it's me.

I'd like to talk to you, when you get a chance. I have many
things I'd like to say, if you're ready to hear them. Just call.
I'll be home all night.

-Anna

Subject: hi.

AK,

I don't know what to say about your head. I'm sure you look
stunning, but you always have.

I'm being a chicken shit here. I was going to call you. I can't.
I don't know how to say this, so I'm going to write it. We've
always written the big stuff. Right? I think? I feel like it's

easier to write the big stuff. That way I don't have to hear your voice. I'm a chicken shit. Deep breath. And . . .

Heather's back. She wasn't married. No French frogs. It was all untrue and now she's back here and coming over in an hour. I'm supposed to figure out what I want. She said it's going to be up to me.

Can you believe that? I waited all of that time for her to know what she wanted and in the end it's all about what I want. I guess she wants me. I guess she figured that all out in the time it took for my heart to shatter and mend itself. Isn't that just fucking great?

I'm mad at her. I'm mad she never called. I'm mad she waited so fucking long. I'm mad it took me falling in love with someone else for her to be pulled back to me. How did she know? How did she know, Anna? Why do things always seem to happen this way? The timing. Why is timing always so fucked up?

I don't know what I'm going to do. There's this woman here, finally here where I've wished her to be all of this time, and she's going to be here in my home where I'd been wishing her to be, and now I don't know if I want it anymore. All I have to do is say yes and I'm back in this relationship that used to be the most important thing in my life.

But now there's you. But you're far away. And you were with someone else, but now you're not, but you could still get back together. We could still get back together. Nothing and everything could happen. Everything's so fucking complicated.

-K

P.S. I realize I just told you that I'm in love with you. It wasn't a mistake.

000074.

My Head
(Get Out!!!)

23 MARCH

These are the thoughts I'd like out of my head, in no particular order:

The nagging guilt over needing an oil change . . . the sinking feeling about the boy with the big decision . . . the craving for McDonald's French fries . . . the deep, pitiful shame over still needing to do my laundry . . . the torture of the theme song to "Punky Brewster" currently playing in my right brain on repeat . . . the sinking feeling that the boy with the big decision just might make it and never tell me and I'll just have to figure it out . . . the worry that tonight I'll make a complete ass out of myself at the bachelorette party and will attempt to take home a stripper, male or female . . . the sweating over the dream I had last night where all the pages of this site were gone and replaced with naked pictures of me . . . the fact that everyone stopped reading my website once they saw me without clothes . . . the concern that since I've never traveled out of this country it makes me less of a person intellectually . . . the fear over the girl with the veil who will murder me tomorrow if I screw up.

Love until later,

Anna K

000075.

My bridesmaid dress was as itchy as my blond wig, and I could feel my panty hose twisting around my ass, squeezing my thighs like tiny pythons. I excused myself to the bathroom to fix them. It was down the hall from the bridal preparation room and was so small only one of us could go in at a time. I opened the door and almost tripped on Becca. She was on the floor with her head over the toilet and her dress hitched up around her hips.

"Oh, my God!" I said.

"Shut the door. Don't tell anyone I'm here," she hissed. "My mom thinks I'm fixing my hair."

"Are you okay?"

She answered by vomiting into the toilet. I grabbed her veil and tied it in a knot on top of her head.

"Shit," she muttered through a wracked sob.

"We shouldn't have had those last tequila shots," I said. My stomach was still queasy from last night, when I tried driving all thoughts of Kurt out of my head by consuming numerous shots at her bachelorette party. Becca had matched me shot for shot, and before I knew it, five women were having a contest to see who could outdrink the other. Each girl became more passionate than the next about how much she needed a drink and how much she could drink before she was unable to stand upright. It was a bad idea to have a bachelorette party the night before the wedding, but I seemed to be the only one having a hard time bouncing back. The other women swooped into the dressing room early in the morning, showered and beautiful, excited for Becca's big day. I had shown up half an hour late, still not in makeup, growling at anyone who tried to have a conversation with me before I finished my third cup of coffee.

"I'm not hung over," Becca said. "I'm terrified."

She leaned back against the wall and took a few deep breaths, wiping her mouth so hard with toilet paper that pieces of it stuck to the corners of her mouth. She carefully dabbed at her eyes, but her mascara had already run.

"Why did I want a wedding? Why? Every single person out there is here because they want to be at a wedding. It's not about Mark and me. It's about free booze and dancing and bridesmaid sex. I paid for all of these people to get drunk and in return they bought us knives and sheets. It's a strange bartering system. It's not about love."

I wet a piece of toilet paper in the sink and fixed her makeup. She leaned her head back against the wall. I tried to breathe away from her face as I wished for a mint.

"Everybody is here because they love you, Becca. The wedding is just a way that we all get to be a part of the day you and Mark become a married couple. It's a ritual. It's a celebration."

"It's a sham. I cheated on Mark and he doesn't know it and I can't walk down that aisle."

I wanted to find a time machine and go back to when my worst problem was crotch pythons. I took a few breaths and waited for the right words to find me.

"Do you love him?"

"I do, Anna. I love him so much. I don't want to hurt him. But I can't marry him without telling him the truth. Aren't relationships supposed to be built on honesty and trust?"

"Not all of them," I found myself saying.

Becca blew her nose into another piece of toilet paper and tossed it into the toilet with the others.

"Pretend I'm Mark and tell me," I said. "Do it quickly and then you'll feel better and then you can go out there and marry him."

Becca rolled her eyes. "That's so stupid."

"You are getting married today, okay? You're just scared and you're using this thing as an excuse. You've wanted this for a long time. You are getting married today." I said it again, hoping the words would penetrate her.

"But what if it doesn't fix everything?" her eyes were brimming with fresh tears. "What if after we get married I still feel like something is missing?"

I didn't know what to say. But I wasn't about to break up her wedding, as it was minutes away.

"Becca, everybody feels like something is missing. We all feel that way all the time. That's what keeps us moving forward. When we're happy with our love lives, we hate our careers. If we have lots of money, we feel like we're unloved. You got lots of wedding presents from your guests, so you think that nobody's really your friend. You're about to get married, so you think that you're not good enough to love."

She snuffed loud and hard. She moaned, "Yeah."

"Telling Mark you cheated isn't going to solve anything. If you really need to tell him, you will when the time is right. I can't think of a worse time."

"Do you think kissing is cheating?" she asked.

"What?"

She slid her body up along the wall. "When Mark asked me to marry him I got really scared. That night I drove to my ex-boyfriend's house. We had dated for four years. He's an idiot, by the way, and I hate that I did this. But I wanted to see if I could still feel something for someone else. I was about to hang it all up and be with Mark forever, and I didn't know if I was making the right choice. Scott opened the door and I pushed myself into him and kissed him."

I untied the knot in the veil on top of her head. "What happened?"

"His wife threatened to call the cops. And I felt really good. Like this was the right decision."

"Then you didn't cheat on Mark," I concluded.

Her face relaxed. Her breath caught in her throat and I thought she was going to vomit again. Instead she said, "You're such a good friend." She held my arm, her perfectly manicured fingers pressing into my skin. "I'm so glad you're here. I'm sorry Ian almost ruined this."

Once back in the dressing room, the group of ladies more qualified to address her bridal issues tended to her every need. When she stood at the doorway, bouquet in her trembling hands, she looked beautiful and confident. She gave me a warm smile.

That moment when the music swells and everyone in the church turns to see the bride—that's what the entire day is about. For just a second everyone in the room is marrying the bride, and this is the first glance at her. She couldn't possibly be any more perfect.

The entire wedding melted away as I looked at her face beaming from beneath her veil as she marched in step closer to us. I could see her eyes wet with tears. She whispered something in her father's ear and he laughed. People stood abruptly to take photographs, quickly ducking back down and out of the way—a Whack-a-Mole of wedding guests all capturing a moment in time.

Will that ever be me up there?

As everyone sat down, my eye caught Ian's. He was standing across from me, a groomsman, and thankfully Becca and Mark hadn't made him my escort. I was standing across from my ex-boyfriend for as long as it took to unite two souls in holy matrimony. Ian and I held each other's stares for a moment, and then both looked away.

He always did look incredible in a tux. It did something to his shoulders, and he looked like he was about to pick you up and carry you off into a sunset. I thought about the weddings we had gone to together during our relationship. The one where I ended up getting lost and chased by a goose. The one where we had sex in the basement of the reception hall. The one where he caught the garter and it sat between us on the ride home, bringing up the subject that both of us actively ignored.

We must not have wanted it. Not badly enough. I wondered why I could be so hurt by him when I knew he wasn't what I wanted forever. I wanted him to be the one who was hurt by all of this. There was sadness in two people breaking up, sure, but what destroyed me was the notion that I wasn't necessary to someone anymore. I was disposable. I wanted to be the one who walked away. Then I knew I was worth something.

I saw Ian smile out toward the crowd. He gave a quick nod of his head. I followed his glance to a redhead sitting on the groom's side. That must be her. His new girlfriend. The one who knew him because of me.

I was the reason they were together. They weren't even grateful. Not only had I gotten them together, I made him the person she loves. I only told the good stories about us. Stupid me—I should have been more honest. I should have talked about his bad habits or the fights we got into over nothing. It was all my doing. I couldn't stop spilling stories. She loved him because I was never anything but complimentary. She loved him because of how much I loved him.

He owed me, big-time.

I followed her gaze and saw Ian watching her. He was smiling. She waved. He blushed and looked at his shoes. I watched them flirt, listening to the priest explain love and commitment.

I decided to name Ian's new girlfriend Mitzi. I made her a shoe salesgirl.

Then it was my turn to speak, and I read a poem written by Becca's father that discussed devotion, honesty, and purity. I wanted to leave. I didn't want to stand there comparing myself to this girl who had what I no longer wanted. And if I no longer wanted it, why did it kill me to not have it? Why couldn't I make real progress away from Ian?

After exchanging "I do's" with Mark and before walking back through the church, Becca ran to me and kissed my cheek. "Thank you," she whispered. As much as I didn't want to be standing across from Ian at that moment, I knew that it was a good thing I was.

I started drinking the second we hit the reception. Everyone was dancing and laughing, dental work sparkling in the chandelier light. Children ran around circular tables, threatening to take down tablecloths with each careless step.

I played with the stem of my glass and let my feet slip out of my shoes. They hurt like a bitch.

Ian sat down beside me in a rush of air.

"Hi," I said quickly.

"I don't want to talk long," he said. "But I'd like to know what makes you think you're entitled to every single relationship of mine?"

I sat up defensively. "Ian, I already apologized."

"Why didn't you tell me about Stephanie? She called me last night panicked because she thought I was getting married. She said you were going to a wedding and some guy was going to make a big decision without you. I told you to take that site down."

People took away whatever they wanted from my entries.

"She just made an assumption. I never said you were getting married. She only e-mailed me once, and she asked me not to tell you."

"Then she tells me that reading your journal made her feel like she was never very special to me. Seeing how I treated you the same way I treated her made her feel like just some girl."

I didn't know what I was about to say, but I knew it wasn't going to start with an apology. "We do feel less special, Ian. We all do. I wouldn't have known this before, but you treat us all exactly the same way. We mommy you, and then when you leave we feel like complete failures and furious that you left a better person because of us. Then you keep us hanging on for months, hinting that you might come back, keeping us wondering what we're supposed to do to get all of your attention."

"Well, we fucking love ourselves these days, don't we?" He spat it at me, then drained his champagne glass. It didn't faze me, as it's impossible to look tough drinking out of a champagne glass. "You call up all of my exes and tell them that bullshit?" he asked.

"I didn't tell Stephanie any of that. I didn't tell her anything. She figured it out on her own. That's another thing you do, Ian. You date smart girls. Smart girls that wise up eventually."

He tossed a napkin on the table and stood up. "So when are *you* going to wise up, Anna?" He leaned down and put his face close to mine. I could smell his breath, still sweet with champagne, but with a sharp twinge of cigarettes. It made me wince as he spoke. "We're over. We've been over. Quit looking like a pathetic puppy."

I watched Ian grab Mitzi and lead her to the dance floor. And as I watched her drape herself over Ian, I suddenly felt calm. I wasn't jealous of Mitzi. I didn't yearn for what she had. She idolized me so much that she decided to get my boyfriend. She had read my love letters and then went for the boy. She read the Ian manual and then acted accordingly. She was in the same room as the inspiration for her relationship, but she had no idea. The reality was she wanted to be me. She wanted what I had. Ian was just a prize.

I imagined kidnapping her, taking her somewhere dark and scary, and then telling her off. "I hope you're happy living in my shadow," I'd say. "I hope you enjoy living in my past."

Dale plopped down beside me.

"You look scary," he said to me.

"I'm imagining telling off Ian's new girlfriend."

"The one you set him up with?"

"Yes." I plopped my head into my hands.

"Careful!" he shouted. "That wig's not going to last much longer if you keep flinging yourself around."

"Everyone in my life got exactly what they wanted from me and then left. But the bitch of it is—I think I wanted it that way. I pushed them just far enough away that they could leave without a shred of guilt."

"The martyr look doesn't become you, Anna. This is such bullshit."

"I must have wanted to be alone."

He turned my face so I looked at him. "Answer me three questions," he said.

I exhaled. "Okay."

"One. Do you miss Ian?"

Easy enough. "No."

Dale nodded. "Right. Because you don't love him anymore. You haven't for a while. You've been angry with him. And that's fine. Being angry is normal. You got your heart broken a while ago and it makes people angry. That doesn't mean you want to still be with him."

I looked up and saw Ian dancing with Mitzi. He dipped her and kissed her under her chin. I felt nothing.

"Okay, question two. Do you love Kurt?"

That wasn't as easy to answer. I didn't know what I felt about him. "It doesn't matter anymore."

I told him about Heather. When I finished, Dale said, "He's practically begging you to stop him from getting back together with her."

"Maybe. But I don't think he really knows me," I said.

"Yes, he does. You like to think that you and Anna K are these gigantically different people. You're not. You're just not used to seeing yourself the way Kurt sees you," Dale said. "You've never had someone love you like that."

"Like what?" I asked.

"With romance and love notes and all that icky yearning stuff he's doing."

"You like him."

"I don't know him. But you do, and I like the way you talk about him. Are you going to forget him?"

"Is this one of the questions?" I asked.

"No. It's a side question."

The music stopped as if the entire room was waiting for my answer. "I think I should just wait for a sign."

The DJ changed songs and "All Out of Love" started up. Dale clapped his hands and cheered. The crowd, thinking Dale was shouting for the DJ, cheered back. "Isn't that your song?" He bounced in his seat.

I felt the grin rise from deep inside of me. "Yes," I said, blushing. "It's the song I picked for us."

"Well, that settles it," Dale said, sitting back in his seat. He ran his hands through his brown hair and then raised his fists in celebration. "Anna's got a new man!"

"Wasn't there a third question?" I asked, blushing.

"Oh, right," Dale said. He leaned forward and touched the ends of my wig. "Do you enjoy looking like Carol Channing?"

000076.

My body was aching when I got home. The champagne pounded in my head and my heart felt like it had gone through a decathlon. An envelope sat on my front steps. Ian's keys were inside. I kicked it into the house with each step. I didn't even want to touch it.

I picked up the phone and called Kurt. A woman's voice answered the phone. I hung up.

I sat at my computer and checked my e-mail.

Subject: HI!!

Hi, Anna K!

My name is Morgan. I'm nineteen years old and I just found
your Web site. One of my friends told me about it. I think
you're so funny and cool. When did you decide to start keeping
a journal? I'm thinking of starting one myself, but I'm a little
worried about my family finding it. I can't tell them everything!

Anyway, I was hoping you would write back because I think
we could be really good friends. We have lots in common and
if we ever met you would see just how alike we really are.

Any tips for starting up a Web journal? I don't think I'll be as
cool as you right away, but it never hurts to try, right?

Thanks so much!!!!!!!!!

Morgan

The last thing I needed in my life right now was Tess 2.0.
Why did so many people, especially girls, glamorize this journal
life? What made Tess decide to use me for my journal, to gain
popularity through people she'd never meet, who read a webpage
on the Internet? It was all so absurd. All of this confusion and
heartbreak was because of binary code. I hadn't done anything
spectacular. I wasn't even a real writer. I was just some girl in
Texas making up a few stories, wondering what would happen if
I pretended to be someone better than I was. Did this happen to
people who write newspaper columns or books? Did real writers
get letters of advice, telling them whom to date? Everything I did
seemed to bring drama with it. I just wanted some quiet.

I opened the software program I used to post my entries. I looked over the directory listing. I saw the hundreds of stories I'd told over the year—the words I had written that made people interested in who I was, the words that made Kurt think he loved me.

Flipping through my entries—stories about my childhood, concerns about love, my feelings for Ian, the way I didn't think about my father until it was too late—too much of me was up on that webpage, plastered like a billboard. The good, the bad, and even the lies were all a part of who I was, just as Dale had said. Tess might think it was just a game to me, but those words had become my reality. It was my life even when I pretended it wasn't. I had become Anna K, and now anybody could wander in and absorb me in one shot without giving anything in return. He or she could just sit down, click a few links, and decide in ten minutes if I'm the kind of person he or she would like to meet. He could fall in love with me and I'd never know. She could think I'm a selfish bitch and I'd never get the chance to defend myself. She could decide to steal my boyfriend. He could find out where I lived. I was blindfolded, up for auction.

I pushed a button, deleting one folder. September. The entire month of September was gone. Just like that. It was still on my hard drive, but no longer online. Nobody could find out what I did in September. They'd never hear those stories. They'd have to ask me in person. Meet me in the flesh. They'd have to earn my stories. Share their own. Talk to me.

I deleted October next. It was so easy, just clicking a button and becoming free. I felt lighter. I was gaining myself back. I was reclaiming parts of me. Taking it away from the world. I wasn't going to stand exposed any longer.

November and December. No longer could people send e-mail telling me how to live my life. No more judging. No more stalking. No more surprises from people in my life who had been reading all along.

January. No more fan mail. No more gifts sent to my house or young girls telling me I'm their idol. No more published stories. No more claiming I'm a writer. No more possibilities of meeting someone like Kurt. No more escape from my daily life. That feeling I had of accomplishing something, that feeling of power when I sat and wrote, that feeling I got when someone sent a compliment on my writing—it was all going to be over.

I stopped deleting.

I went to bed.

000077.

I was buying a cup of coffee three days later when the girl behind the counter asked, "Are you Anna K?"

She was pointing at my driver's license. My wallet was hanging open as I searched to hand her a five-dollar bill. I must have looked shocked because she said, "I'm sorry I was snooping. I could see it from here and I had to ask."

"Yes, I'm Anna K," I answered.

"I read you all the time," she said. "I love your website."

"Thank you," I said.

She went back to grab my coffee and the older man behind me in line leaned forward. I could smell his cologne, fresh from a recent application, swirling between us. His hair was still wet and he was filled with the early morning scent of a businessman. With my hair gone, I was aware of the people near me more than I used to be. I could sense the kinds of people they were. This man had an air of friendliness around him as he said, "Can I ask why you're famous?"

"Oh," I laughed. "I'm not really famous. I just have this website that some people read."

My coffee was free.

I was happy to have the compliment as I was on my way to the gynecologist's office for my annual. I would need something for my thoughts to focus on while I was flat on my back in the stirrups. I've always wondered if I could bring a book or a magazine in there, if the doctor would think it was rude if I read my horoscope instead of paying attention to the little tugs and twists going on inside of my body for five minutes.

I was seeing a new gynecologist. My last one got married and moved to Iowa. She had referred me to Dr. Sanji, whom she knew in med school and said she thinks the world of. I'm not one to get attached to doctors, but when your gynecologist is leaving, you want someone you don't have to worry about. In college I once had a gynecologist with a lazy eye. She'd hunker between my legs and call out like she was looking for cattle, "C'mon, cervix! Miss Cervix! Lemme see ya!"

Since then I've been slightly pickier when searching for that special doctor I see once a year for Paps and pills.

Dr. Sanji's office was small but had the right collection of magazines. I checked in and settled down with a *Bust* until the nurse called me into the office. She weighed me, took my blood pressure, and handed me a crisp, tightly folded paper outfit. She left the room and I took off my clothes, piling them on a chair near the examination table. I pushed myself up onto the table and draped my paper skirt over my legs. It cracked and crinkled as I opened the folds. I tried smoothing the pink corners out over my legs. It felt like I was gift-wrapping myself. I slid the green paper vest on, pulling the open sides over my breasts, wishing for a fastener. The paper hung there limply, allowing all of the drafts in the room to tickle at my thighs, the small of my back, and the curves of my breasts. I sat in silence and waited for what seemed to be forever. I wished I had brought the magazine in with me from the waiting room. I wished I still had my coffee from earlier. Mostly I wished I didn't have to be there at all.

I was going to have to answer questions. It was my first visit, so I was going to have to tell her about myself, about my sexual history, and about my family. She was going to ask what diseases I was likely to die from. She was going to ask what had killed my father. I took a few breaths to prepare myself.

Dr. Sanji walked in and apologized for my wait. She was tiny, with sleek black hair piled on top of her head. It was fastened with a pearl clip. Her eyes were lined in jet-black coal, and they were a beautiful warm brown. Her lipstick was almost the same shade of brown, and she lined her lips with a color slightly darker. She walked over to my chart, resting on the counter, and took a seat on the stool placed in front of me.

"Okay, Anna. I'm going to ask a few questions, and then we'll get started." Her voice was soft and low, like a purr.

"Okay." My voice sounded as thin as my paper vest.

"Are you allergic to any medicines?"

"No."

"Do you have any sexually transmitted diseases?"

"No."

"Do you smoke?"

I paused. I hadn't had a cigarette since the night before. Today, so far, I wasn't a smoker. Could I get away with that? I decided I couldn't.

"Yes, I smoke."

"That's very bad." She stood and handed me some pamphlets. "You should stop smoking."

"I know."

"I'm sure you do." She was standing closer to me now, and I could see how smooth and perfect her skin was. She smiled warmly. "I'm trying to quit drinking so much coffee, so I know how hard it is to give up something that you love."

She patted my naked knee as she sat back down on her stool. It creaked underneath her.

"Any history of heart disease?"

Here it was. I'd never had to say this to a perfect stranger before. I'd never had to speak these words out loud. "My father died of heart disease. A leak from a murmur, I think." I reminded myself to have Mom tell me more specifically what had happened to Dad. I sounded like a distant child, like I didn't give a shit about my father enough to know what killed him.

"You don't know?" Dr. Sanji asked.

"No, I know. I just don't . . . it happened pretty recently. At Thanksgiving."

Dr. Sanji's entire face changed its position, her forehead raised until her eyebrows almost met her hairline. "Oh, I'm so sorry," she said. "Just this past Thanksgiving?"

My throat felt tight. I couldn't speak. I nodded my head.

"Awful," she said, and clicked her teeth a few times. She put her hand on my naked knee again. "You poor girl. It's so sad when we lose our daddies."

It was the kindness in her voice, the sympathy in her eyes that did it. It felt like Dr. Sanji was already inside of me, ripping things apart. My stomach doubled up as tears welled in my eyes. She saw what was happening to me, and she moved in closer. She pulled my head to her shoulder as I began to pant. She patted my back, the paper vest the only sound in the room until the sobs took over my body. Her hands ran to the prickly hairs on the back of my neck, and she cradled my head like a newborn baby. I felt my breasts press against her doctor coat. The coarse cotton fibers rubbed against my nipples. Dr. Sanji rocked me back and forth as I cried, naked in paper, this tiny woman trying to pull all of the sadness out of me.

I missed my father. I missed him so much.

It had been months since he'd died, but nobody had wanted to talk about it. I hadn't spoken to anyone about how sad it was to not have a father anymore. It was more than just a part of me was missing. It felt like my future had been erased. Any thoughts I might have had, any notions I'd entertained about what would happen to me were now negated. It couldn't happen that way any-more because my father wasn't going to be around to see it happen.

Dr. Sanji smelled like curry powder and sandalwood. She pulled my head back and wiped my face with a tissue. "Okay, now," she said. "You lean back."

"I'm sorry," I said, my voice catching in my breath.

"No saying sorry. It's sad when our daddies die. Makes us one less person inside."

Nobody had talked to me about Dad like this, with this quiet sympathy and warm embrace. I wanted to keep doing it. I was on my back, so I couldn't see Dr. Sanji anymore as she went to work. I wiped my face with a balled-up tissue and tried to breathe normally again.

I wanted to call Dad and make small talk for fifteen minutes. I missed having that in my life. I missed having him ask me questions that no longer pertained to my life. I missed him checking on the status of my car. How will I remember to get an oil change now? Who will sit and discuss the changing of the sea-sons with me? Who can I call when I want to ask a question about a Roth IRA?

He always kept a distance from me, but it was a safe distance. He was the person I tried to please. I wanted Dad's silent approval. Who will give that to me now? Without Dad around, will I still date boys just like him? Boys like Ian? I had celebrated any sign of love from Ian as if it was directly from God. I dated men who kept themselves cut off from me emotionally, except for my overly emotional gay male friend. Dale was never going to be a relationship option, and ironically he was the closest man in my life. He was my best friend even when I had a boyfriend.

I was dealing with Dad's death the same way I'd dealt with Ian. I just didn't think about it, wouldn't admit it for months and months until someone made me come right out and say what went wrong. I was pretending I was still at a time in my life where this sadness hadn't happened yet. I wanted a future with my father just like I wanted a future with Ian. I just wanted the knowledge that everybody was going to be okay.

But everyone was very much not okay.

I waited too long to fully mourn my breakup with Ian. It kept my life on hold, my heart trapped inside. I was shaking with fear that someone else would hurt me like they did, like Ian not wanting me anymore and Dad leaving before we got to have a real relationship. I wanted Ian to stay since my father couldn't. But I couldn't keep anyone near me. There were no promises.

So I put off dealing with it. I never wanted to feel like it was over, that they weren't going to be a part of my life anymore. And now, having to admit to this tiny Indian woman that my father was no longer alive, I felt it all crash in front of me. It was over. The desire to reach out for attention from anyone because I didn't get enough from the people who loved me—that was baby stuff. It was childish to demand constant male attention. My father was dead; my youth was over. You couldn't be a girl if you didn't have a daddy.

With Kurt, I wasn't searching for approval. He approached me, already fascinated with me. He approved of everything I said and did, encouraging me to share even more. Was this why I didn't trust him? Was I so used to unavailability that the slightest showing of emotion convinced me it couldn't possibly be for real?

My head felt heavy against the paper-coated pillow. I was sad for myself, sad for my father, and sad that it took so long for my brain to connect all of the dots.

"We're done here," Dr. Sanji said. "All done."

It was the fastest Pap smear ever. I had felt nothing.

In the hallway Dr. Sanji handed me another pamphlet. "This is a support group that I went to when my father passed away two years ago. They're good people."

I wanted Dr. Sanji to take me home with her and make me a bowl of curry and let me talk to her on her couch all night long.

I wanted my head in her lap. I wanted to tell her how my heart was aching, that I was tired of dealing with it all the time. I wanted her to diagnose my pain and kiss my forehead until I felt better. I needed Dr. Sanji to make me feel better. She had done such a good job in the five minutes we'd known each other that I wasn't ready to leave her yet.

She hugged me again out in the hallway. "We'll make sure you stay healthy." She looked me in the eyes and said, "You just work on quitting smoking."

I couldn't stop crying the rest of the day. I tried to go to the grocery store, but I ended up crying into one of the freezer windows. I wished I could wear a sign that read I'm in Mourning, so that nobody would give me those strange looks.

Back at home I held Taylor in my lap and cried into his fur. He knew when I was sad and would suddenly become a very patient cat.

My phone rang. The caller ID said it was Meredith.

"Hi," I answered, unable to hide the emotion in my voice.

"Are you okay, Anna?"

"Mere, I miss Dad."

I could hear her tears start up as she said, "I miss him too, Annie."

We talked and cried for the next three hours. We shared stories and told each other things we didn't know about Dad. Mere had the unique position of being Dad's favorite, and he'd tell her things that he never told us.

"You know, he read your webpage."

"He knew about my webpage? *You* knew about my webpage?"

"Shannon told me. I told Dad and he asked me to print out your stories. He really liked some of them. The ones where you weren't being dirty. You know the one where you wrote about your old car and Dad driving backwards? I took him to the drugstore once and he pulled that story out of his back pocket to show his pharmacist. He called you his 'writer' daughter."

"Which one were you?"

"I was the 'Good Daughter.' "

"And Shannon?"

"The Baby, of course."

Meredith told me she hadn't wanted to bring up my webpage first. She figured if she was supposed to be reading it, I'd tell her about it. She was hurt that I wouldn't tell her about something I'd been doing for almost a year. She had hoped that I'd want to share that with her. Shannon had told her how she'd found it and then filled her in on my fan mail and my trip to Pittsburgh. Meredith seemed to know everything about my life over the past year when I hadn't told her anything. I didn't know she was so interested in me.

"Can I ask you something?" she said as I made myself a third cup of coffee. "Why do you put all of those stories up there? Don't you feel overexposed?"

"I didn't use to," I answered, cradling the phone on my shoulder. "But lately it's felt like someone ripped the Band-Aid off a cut too soon. I'm embarrassed by some of those stories."

I told her about Ian and his new girlfriend, and how she was a fan. I told Meredith about Tess, and how she tried to bust me with Ian when I saw someone in Pittsburgh.

"And finally you mention the new boy," she said.

I plopped down on my couch and flung my body over a pillow. "He's not a new boy. He's nothing."

"He doesn't sound like nothing. Shannon says you really like him."

"He lives in Pittsburgh. And by now he's probably with his ex-girlfriend again."

"That sounds like you don't know if he is. And Pittsburgh's only far away if you want it to be."

We made plans to see each other the next month. I'd come out to Hartford and we'd hang out at her place for a change.

"Let's play Dad for each other," I suggested.

"What are you talking about?" she asked.

"Well, you stay minimally interested in my life, only for me to find out that you actually are engaged in my life by talking to Shannon, and I'll treat you like you're my favorite."

"That sounds complicated," she laughed.

"I'm willing to do it."

"Me too."

"I love you," she said.

"I love you, too. But you're supposed to tell someone else that you love me and have that person tell me later when you're not around."

When we hung up I sat down at my laptop. I pulled up my webpage directories again. I couldn't believe my father had walked around with pages of this website in his pockets. Nobody had seemed to notice the missing entries yet. I'd left off at January. Random months were still there, the past and the recent past. I wondered what would happen if I deleted it all. I highlighted the directories and hit delete.

Gone.

The webpage was gone. Faster than my impulse, even. It was on my computer, but it wasn't out there for anyone else to see. It was my own private journal again. I had taken myself back. I decided who got to meet me now.

I called Kurt. He answered this time.

I told him everything. I told him the truth.

It was quiet for a while.

"I don't know what you want me to say here, Anna," he finally said.

"I'm trying to apologize," I said.

"I understand that. How much of you isn't really you?"

"I used to think that you didn't know me. But recently I realized I was more myself with you than with anyone else."

"I see."

"But you're probably back with Heather now anyway, and this is stupid."

"I didn't say I was back with Heather."

"Oh."

"I mean, I might be."

"I figured."

"I just haven't said yet." It sounded like the phone was away from his face. He was quiet. Calm. I couldn't tell if he was teasing.

"I don't want to waste your time," I said.

"Or have your time wasted," he countered.

"I didn't say that."

"But you want to know if I'm back with Heather."

"Well, yeah."

"Don't you think I should be the one asking questions?" he asked, his voice cracking in midsentence.

"I'm sorry."

His voice was stronger again, his mouth closer to the phone. "You tell a girl that you love her and she ignores you. Then she tells you that the girl you know isn't the girl you fell in love with. Or she *is*, but she isn't really when she writes. How am I supposed to feel, Anna?"

I rubbed my forehead. "I know. I'm sorry. I'm trying to tell you."

"I told a woman who loves me that I didn't want to get involved with her again. I had to tell her I was waiting for a woman who lives on the other side of the country. Then I had to tell her that I've only met this woman once and currently we aren't on speaking terms."

"How did she take it?"

"Bad. She took it bad. How the fuck else would she take it? Do you know how stupid that sounds? How stupid I feel?" His voice was raising in both pitch and volume.

But he hadn't hung up on me.

"I'm so sorry, Kurt," I said. "This all got away from me and I tried to tell you that last night I was there, but you kept telling me to stop talking and . . ."

"None of this is my fault," he said.

But he kept listening to my apologies. He still hadn't hung up.

"I know. I know. I just meant . . . I didn't want to risk losing you. I didn't know when would be the right time to explain."

"Maybe I've been lying to you," he said. "I might have been lying about lots of things. You don't know."

But he hadn't gotten back with Heather. He was waiting. He was interested.

"Were you?" I asked.

"Maybe. I mean, yes. I was. Heather and I . . ."

"Oh," I interrupted.

"You don't know what I was going to say."

"I just figured."

"You don't know. I was going to say that Heather and I never lied to each other about anything. I was going to say that it was nice having that kind of honesty in a relationship."

"Oh."

"That was me making a little dig at you."

"I see."

He might really love me the way I hoped he did. I could finally find out what honest love feels like.

"I'm not perfect, Anna. Once you get to know me, you'll realize that I'm a very flawed man. You don't get to be this old and this single without some serious relationship issues."

"How old are you?" I asked.

"I think it's time for me to have a few secrets."

"Fair enough."

I knew he wasn't perfect. I knew that I was taking a risk by getting involved with him. But the change I'd been craving felt right with him. I wanted to see where this would take me. Even if he wasn't the right person for me. Even if he wasn't going to be my last stop, he would almost certainly be a move in the right direction. I wanted to know what it could be like.

"I want to see you," he said.

"When?"

"Now."

I could hear his breath. I realized I'd been holding my own. "I know," I said. "Me too."

"When can you be here?"

"I have no job. I can't afford to go there right now."

"You quit your job?"

"No." I couldn't believe there was something about my life he didn't know. It was an absurd thought, considering how much he thought he knew about me that was untrue, but he had been so much a part of my daily life that having him not know such a crucial piece of information felt wrong. I realized how much I'd missed him.

"Well, you can tell me all about it when I get there. It's my turn to visit you anyway."

"You'll come here?"

"I'm not moving in or anything, but yeah."

"So, you're just trying it out?"

"I'm trying it out. I might move there even if we don't work out. I hear nice things about your town."

"If you move here, you have to date me."

"I thought you wanted to leave Austin."

"I don't know anymore."

"If I come visit, you have to tell me everything that wasn't true."

My stomach flipped as I said, "How I feel about you was never a lie."

"And how do you feel about me?" he asked.

I hadn't been able to choose a word before, but the right one came to me just then as I said, "Excited."

He was quiet. I heard him give a quick laugh. "I'm exciting?" he asked, trying the word on for size.

"Very. And I'm hopeful about you. I'm . . . I can't seem to get you out of my head at any point."

It was quiet until I added, "And I have a third nipple."

I heard him exhale. "I need to be there very soon."

"You're not mad?" I asked.

"You'll find out," he said.

My body felt warm as my nose scrunched with anticipation.

"I don't really have a third nipple."

"I know. I've seen both of your nipples."

"Oh, right."

"You'll have to work on that lying thing you do," he said. I could hear his smile in his voice.

"The webpage is gone," I said.

"Yes, I was reading it when you pulled everything. I was just about to call you when you called."

"Are we for real?" I asked him.

"It feels like it," he said.

"This will be hard."

"Or it will be very easy."

Subject: just a question

Hello, Anna K

Like so many people, I was sad to see the pages of your website go away. I hope that nothing terrible happened that caused you to end your website, and that you were ready for a change.

That brings me to my point. I'm an editor at *Central Texas Daily,* and I was wondering if you'd like to bring your website to our paper. I'm offering you a weekly column where you'd basically do the same thing you did on your website. The pieces would be shorter, of course, but we'd be honored to have your voice included on our staff. Promise me you'll think about it?

Heidi Truman
Editor, Life and Arts
Central Texas Daily

000078.

So now you're all caught up. We're back where I started. That's the story of Anna K, posted online for the very last time.

Being Anna K allowed me to figure out what kind of person I wanted to be. It helped me decide to be a writer. I love entertaining people. Closing down this webpage is hard, because I really appreciate those of you who supported me along the way. Even with all of its drawbacks, the rewards of this site greatly outweighed the negative aspects. But I don't want to pretend to be anybody else any longer. I'm going to be me for a change, this new me that I've become. She's more independent. She's stronger. Focused. It took time to step back from behind the Anna K curtain and know the girl standing there was just as good. In fact, I'm better. I'm real.

I've become the woman I admired.

One door closes, a new one opens. But this door's got a lock. And a security system. This one won't be open to public scrutiny. Thanks for reading all this time. I wanted to give you a formal good-bye, so here it is. I'm erasing the webpage for good tomorrow. If you miss me, you can visit at my column "Why Girls Are Weird" every Saturday in *Central Texas Daily*. But don't expect to know everything. Some stories will stay all mine.

Love until later,
Anna

acknowledgments

It's very true that this book wouldn't have been possible without this giant paragraph of people. Kim Witherspoon and Alexis Hurley believed in this material so much I was blushing. They also found it a very good home in Amanda Ayers, who is just scared enough about this whole online journal business to understand it. Jennifer Heddle is the reason I ever convinced myself to do this. Without the keen eye and talented mind of Christopher Huff, I never would have made it through all those drafts. He also let me know when I was getting cheesy, as he's known in most parts as the Meat of Cheese. And if Allison Lowe-Huff wasn't around, where would he be? Where would *I* be? Dan Blau, who always knows the words I'm going to say as I'm saying them, helped shape the early versions of this novel and then pep-talked me through the last of them. I miss you, Dan. Jessica Kaman loved this novel so much I had to do something with it so she didn't cry, and Anna Beth Chao told me it was, "Good, Baby." Brently, Liz, Katey, Garnet, and Kyle were my first LA cheerleaders. I owe so much to Tara Ariano, Dave Cole, and Sarah Bunting that I should be recapping for free. But, no. The rest I owe to Omar Gallaga. Erin Searcy, Kim Reed, Jami Anderson, Kevin Smokler, Carrie Weiner, and Martinique Duchene-Phillips were big parts in getting this off the ground. Ray Prewitt put up with my crap. A lot of it. Weldon, Chuy, Cathy, Michelle, Trejo, Becca, Matt, and the Monks let me publicly write about their lives, and sometimes let me steal their punchlines. Thank you and I'm sorry. It's good to have many moms, and both Charlotte Peterson and Michelle's Mom (no first name necessary) always make me feel like I won first place. I love Jeff Long. John Scalzi, it's your turn. Chris Kelman is funnier than I am. Very special thanks to Eric Peterson, who always treated this with patience, understanding, and just enough ego to truly enjoy it. This novel is because of the Squishites, TWoPpers, and pamie.com fans everywhere. This is also because of my mother, father, and sister. But everything, everything, everything is always because of stee.

up close and personal
with the author

1) Is it true that you kept an online journal?

I started Squishy (*pamie.com*) in the summer of 1998 as a writing exercise for my comedy troupe. I was introduced to journaling by a friend who kept a journal and followed her links until I realized there was an entire community of writers online. So I decided to give it a try.

Also, I've always loved zines and created a few underground newspaper-type things in high school that I'm not proud of and won't share with you because they're too embarrassing at this point in my life.

2) So how much of Anna's character is autobiographical?

It's mostly fiction. Even the entries have been reworked a bit so they're now fiction as well. But I tried to keep everyone's "favorites" in there. When I was writing the book I asked my readers which entries they loved the most. I didn't get to keep them all in there, but at least "Tiny Wooden Hand" survived. Otherwise there might have been a riot.

The "Tiny Wooden Hand" was such a big deal that people started sending Tiny Wooden Hands to my house. One reader tried to acquire Tiny Woolen Mittens for the Tiny Wooden Hands so that I could take pictures of the hands having a Tiny Wooden Snowball Fight in my freezer. When the mittens fell through, she sent over an enormous box of candy and homemade cookies. The expensive candy, too! That was when my friends started to realize how big the website was becoming. They also renamed the cookies "Poison Stalker Cookies."

The most autobiographical part of this book for me is Anna's struggle to figure out who she is at this point in her life. I had quite the crisis when I turned twenty-five, realizing I wasn't anything like the person I'd always assumed I'd be when I got there. I wasn't the only one having a mid-twenties crisis either. I have a friend who's eight days younger than I, and when he called on his birthday sobbing, "I hate being twenty-five! Why didn't you tell me it sucks so hard!" I cried back, "I didn't want to scare you! I hate it, too!"

It was a rough year. I didn't know where I was headed or what I wanted. I didn't know who I wanted to be or what kind of relationship I wanted. Once I turned twenty-five, every facet of my life changed. The journal was a big part of that. It helped me find friends, jobs, and some of the most important people in my life. It's really quite amazing, when I step back and look at it.

3) Like Anna, were you concerned about how much of your personal life was exposed on your journal?

I wasn't for a while. I didn't realize how many people were reading, I guess. It was when other people became concerned for my safety, or felt that they were getting exposed in the process, that I started to pull back a little. With any kind of one-on-one relationship there becomes a sense of entitlement. No matter how big my audience, they're all reading one at a time, and that can be a very intimate experience for a reader; it's like getting private e-mail. That's when people can begin to think that we're close friends. I'm telling them stories about my life. It's easy to forget that it's one-sided.

There have been times when I felt someone was pushing into my life because he or she had identified with my writing and felt we should be "best friends." But it's never been often enough or strong enough that I wished I'd never kept a journal. I don't share anything I wouldn't tell a good friend anyway.

4) Why did you take the journal offline in 2001?

Closing *pamie.com* meant I'd lost my job. I was a failed dot com. I had to move forward. It wasn't something I did out of spite.

I had lost my funding from ChickClick. Running *pamie.com* was a full-time job by then and I knew I was spending too much time working on the forum, a place of temporary exchanges that were mostly the writings of other people. I had to shut the site down, but I never imagined the response I'd get as a result!

There were e-mails, bulletin board discussions, letters begging me not to do it. One girl told me that she mentioned the site closing to her therapist, and how that bummed her out. Her therapist asked her, "Is this girl named Pam? Because you're my third patient this week to mention this site closing." Can you imagine? I love that story.

Another girl wrote (and I'll never forget this): "You taught me how to wear a bra, put in a tampon, and to wipe from front to back. For this, I thank you. You've also taught me to follow my dreams." I'm Big Bird for Young Adults!

5) Is that why you returned to online journaling in 2002?

Yeah, I missed it. I missed my readers. And I felt that I'd learned from my mistakes.

6) Did you find writing the book more or less satisfying than maintaining the journal?

It's very satisfying to write a book—don't get me wrong—but compared to the thousands of words I'd written for the journal, it was a much smaller achievement, volume-wise. I'm excited that the book could potentially reach a bigger audience than the site does. But the best part about writing a journal is the immediate feedback; within mintues I start getting e-mail from readers sharing their stories, commiserating, or debating something I was thinking about. That's infectious, that kind of contact. It makes you feel important. The book felt like the next logical step, and that's the best part about it. I want to see what's going to happen next.

Like what you just read?

IRISH GIRLS ABOUT TOWN
Maeve Binchy, Marian Keyes, Cathy Kelly, et. al.
Get ready to paint the town green....

THE MAN I SHOULD HAVE MARRIED
Pamela Redmond Satran
Love him. Leave him. Lure him back.

GETTING OVER JACK WAGNER
Elise Juska
Love is nothing like an '80s song.

THE SONG READER
Lisa Tucker
Can the lyrics to a song reveal the secrets of the heart?

THE HEAT SEEKERS
Zane
Real love can be measured by degrees....

I DO (BUT I DON'T)
Cara Lockwood
She has everyone's love life under control...except her own.
(Available June 2003)

Great storytelling just got a new address.
Published by Pocket Books

Then don't miss these other great books from Downtown Press!